More praise for the

"Julie Ortolon takes her wonderfully colorful and appealing characters on an unexpected journey of discovery. BE PREPARED TO LAUGH."
—Christina Skye

"Ortolon's protagonists must overcome some tough emotional issues before they can set their sights on the future, but their journey is laced with humor. . . . Earnest and endearing, Ortolon's newest is a heart-warming and at times heartrending read."
—*Publishers Weekly*

"So romantic it will make you melt!"
—Virginia Henley

"This is an author on the rise! An endearing, emotional, romantic tale."
—*Romantic Times*

"As long as Julie Ortolon is writing books like this one, romantic comedy is in good hands."
—All About Romance

ALMOST PERFECT

Julie Ortolon

A SIGNET ECLIPSE BOOK

SIGNET ECLIPSE
Published by New American Library, a division of
Penguin Group (USA) Inc., 375 Hudson Street,
New York, New York 10014, USA
Penguin Group (Canada), 90 Eglinton Avenue East, Suite 700, Toronto,
Ontario M4P 2Y3, Canada (a division of Pearson Penguin Canada Inc.)
Penguin Books Ltd., 80 Strand, London WC2R 0RL, England
Penguin Ireland, 25 St. Stephen's Green, Dublin 2,
Ireland (a division of Penguin Books Ltd.)
Penguin Group (Australia), 250 Camberwell Road, Camberwell, Victoria 3124,
Australia (a division of Pearson Australia Group Pty. Ltd.)
Penguin Books India Pvt. Ltd., 11 Community Centre, Panchsheel Park,
New Delhi - 110 017, India
Penguin Group (NZ), cnr Airborne and Rosedale Roads, Albany,
Auckland 1310, New Zealand (a division of Pearson New Zealand Ltd.)
Penguin Books (South Africa) (Pty.) Ltd., 24 Sturdee Avenue,
Rosebank, Johannesburg 2196, South Africa

Penguin Books Ltd., Registered Offices:
80 Strand, London WC2R 0RL, England

First published by Signet Eclipse, an imprint of New American Library,
a division of Penguin Group (USA) Inc.

First Printing, September 2005
10 9 8 7 6 5 4 3 2 1

To Friends

For filling my days with laughter
For three-hour lunches (when we should be writing)
For enabling my Chico's shopping addiction
For unquestioned support, sympathy,
whining and wining
For champagne celebrations (anytime, any reason)
And for e-mailing in the face of deadlines!

Chapter 1

"How to Have a Perfect Life." Maddy shook her head in wonder as she read the title of the slick hardcover book she held in both hands. *"Ten Steps to Outrageous Happiness,* by Jane Redding."

"I still can't believe Jane, our Jane, is now published. On top of everything else," Christine said, staring at her own copy.

"I can." Amy smiled with pride as they moved away from the autographing table where a line of Jane Redding fans waited for their chance to meet the TV-anchor-turned-motivational-speaker.

"Actually, I can too," Christine admitted as the three of them headed toward the coffee shop in the corner of the bookstore. "Jane was always so disciplined and hardworking back in college. She's the only person I know who studied harder than I did. And considering I was premed, that's saying something."

"You were both driven, which is the only thing you had in common," Maddy said as she and her friends passed a decorative handrail that created the feel of a sidewalk café. She breathed in the rich aroma of coffee. Light jazz mingled with the buzz of conversation and hiss of the cappuccino machine. "In fact, given how different the four of us were, I'm amazed at how well we got along as suitemates."

"Opposites do attract," Christine said as they joined the order line.

"That's certainly true for you and me." Maddy smiled at her friend of fourteen years. Most people saw Christine Ashton as an intimidating combination of Ice Princess and Rocket Scientist, with her elegant height, sleek blond hair, and cool gray eyes, but Maddy knew the wicked sense of humor that lay beneath.

"I think the key for us," Christine went on, "was having you and me in one half of the dorm suite and Amy and Jane in the other. Can you imagine if Jane and I had been paired together?"

Maddy laughed. "Amy and I would have been taking bets on which one of you would commit murder first. Perfect Jane the Neatnik or Pristine Christine who is secretly a slob?"

"No, *you* would have been taking bets," Christine corrected. "Amy's too sweet to profit from a friend's demise."

"True." Maddy gave Amy a one-armed hug. "Mother Amy would have been wringing her hands and begging you children to behave."

"Actually Jane was a lot of fun." Amy frowned at them. "And for the record, I always hated my nickname."

"Yeah, me too." Christine gave Maddy one of her aloof looks. "So watch the name-calling, Gypsy Girl."

"Hey, if the nickname fits . . ." Maddy twisted her hips to make the tiny bells along the hem of her skirt jingle. Colorful beads and shiny charms adorned each wrist and a scarf circled her head from nape to crown, holding back a bonfire of red hair.

Four roommates couldn't have been more different, or fit their nicknames better. Amy Baker was an intriguing blend of wisdom and whimsy with a need to nurture. Men, unfortunately, never seemed to look past her plumpness and notice her sensual side. Of course, the fact that Amy wore glasses that obscured her big green eyes, dressed in baggy jumpers that made her look frumpy, and kept her glorious, waist-length brown hair confined in a tight braid didn't help.

And then there was Jane. Glancing back at the signing table, Maddy realized the petite brunette hadn't changed much in the ten years since graduation. She was still immaculately put together and still glowed with an inner light of intelligence and determination. She sat behind the table piled with her books, wearing a stylish purple suit, her shoulder-length bob swinging slightly as she laughed. Her brown eyes smiled up at one of her fans, who stood with a book clutched to her chest, gushing with praise.

Envy snuck up and gave Maddy a painful bite. "God," she sighed. "Jane really did make it, just like she always wanted. But it's not just the fame and fortune. She looks so dang confident!"

"And she's still so beautiful," Amy added with genuine admiration in her voice.

"She looks happy," Christine said with no inflection. "Really happy. Can I kill her?"

"Christine!" Amy gasped. "What a thing to say."

"Aw, c'mon, Mom, can I?" Christine clasped her hands together. "Please, please, please?"

Amy laughed in spite of herself. "You are so bad."

"Which is why we love her," Maddy insisted, since a part of her felt the same way. She was thrilled for Jane's success, but it made her feel like a failure for never achieving her own dream of becoming a professional artist. She'd met and married Nigel, a sweet but admittedly geeky accountant, right out of college. Nigel had loved her art, believed in her wholeheartedly, and insisted she stay home and pursue her art career full time.

Unfortunately, two years into the marriage, he'd been diagnosed with cancer and she'd spent the next six years taking care of him while helping him keep his accounting firm open. If not for the moral support of Christine and Amy, she wasn't sure how she would have made it through those years.

Jane had long since moved to New York, and they'd rarely heard from her. Although they'd certainly heard a lot *about* her lately, with her marriage to a sports announcer, her "lake house" in Austin on the cover of *Homes and Living,* and now her best-selling self-help book.

When Maddy compared her own lack of accomplishments to all that, she couldn't help but feel inadequate.

"Next!" called the tall, skinny kid behind the counter and Maddy realized she'd reached the front of the line.

"Oh." She looked up at the coffee menu hanging overhead. "Hold on. Give me a second."

"Come on, Mad, you can do this," Christine whispered encouragingly. "Make a decision."

"The pressure, the pressure." She touched her fingertips to her brow, like a fortune-teller communing with the other world. "Okay, I got it. I'll have a Mocha Madness. With extra whipped cream. And caramel swirled on top, please."

The kid called out the order to the harried woman manning the industrial-size machine.

After Maddy had paid, Christine stepped up without even looking at the board. "Coffee. The gargantuan size. No fluff and stuff. Just give me caffeine and an IV tube."

Maddy frowned at her. "I thought you were going to cut back on caffeine."

"Damn! You would remember that." Christine made a face. "Okay, make that decaf."

The kid relayed the change in her order and started to ring it up.

"No, wait." Christine reached out and grabbed his arm, desperation lighting her eyes. "Make that decaf with a depth charge of espresso." She made a face at Maddy. "I'll cut back more seriously when my residency is over."

Obviously used to dealing with coffee addicts, the kid rang it up without batting an eye.

Amy came next, chewing her lip and eyeing the pastries. The light from the case shone off her glasses. "I'll have a sugar-free vanilla cappuccino."

"Did you want a pastry?" the kid asked.

She hesitated, but held firm. "No. Just the cappuccino. Skinny, please."

Maddy started to tell Amy to go for a pastry, but reminded herself not to sabotage her friend's diet. Personally, she thought Amy looked just fine and should stop starving herself. Sexy came in many shapes and sizes. Maddy was no Skinny Minnie, but she'd learned to celebrate, rather than hide, her abundant curves. Nigel had certainly enjoyed them in the early days, before he'd become too weak to enjoy much of anything in life.

"So," Christine said after they picked up their orders, "shall we grab a table and look at this book?"

"Sounds like a plan." Maddy headed for an empty table near a colorful display of coffee mugs and gift items. "I'm dying to know the ten steps to outrageous happiness."

"Me too." Christine opened her copy of the book as soon as they were seated. "After the last few years of all work and no play, I could use some happiness, outrageous or otherwise."

"But you're making it." Amy smiled at her. "A few more months and you'll be a doctor. Surely that makes you happy."

"If I live that long," Christine said as she read the contents page. "Let's see. Step one, *Know What You Want.*"

"That's easy." Maddy sipped her sweet coffee, then licked whipped cream from her lip. "A winning lottery ticket that makes all the bills go away forever."

Christine frowned at her. "I thought you were doing okay financially, what with the life insurance and selling the accounting firm."

"I am, but you know I hate balancing a checkbook, or anything else related to numbers. Plus, I wouldn't mind having some money to travel."

Christine squeezed her forearm. "I think traveling would be a good idea. It doesn't have to be an expensive trip, just something that would get you out of that empty house."

"You're probably right." Maddy thought about the letter lurking in the bottom of her purse. The job it described would certainly get her out of the house. *Waaay* out of the house. If she had the guts to apply for it. "What's step two?"

Christine looked down. "Oh, this sounds cheery. *Face Your Inner Fear.*"

Maddy snorted. "Well, hey, I've got that step down at least, since I've just gone through years of facing fear on a daily basis."

"True. Let's see what she has to say on the subject." Christine flipped forward to that chapter. The minute she started skimming the page, her eyes widened. "The bitch!"

"What?" Maddy straightened in surprise.

"She used us in her book."

"You're kidding! She mentioned us by name?" Maddy craned her neck to read the page.

"No, but still, she says, 'I had three friends in college who are excellent examples of how women frequently let fear hold them back from pursuing their dreams.' "

"Does she go into detail?" Amy chewed her thumbnail.

Christine ran her finger down the page. "Let's see, 'I had an artist friend'—gee, I wonder who that could be—'who let her fear of rejection stop her from going after an art career with any real dedication or enthusiasm.' "

"That's ridiculous!" Maddy set her coffee down with a thud. "I didn't pursue an art career because I had a dying husband to care for." Even as she said the words, she knew they didn't explain why she wasn't pursuing an art career now. "What else does she say?"

"Oh, get this." Christine read further. "Apparently my fear is that of parental disapproval. 'My med-student friend spent so much time trying to win her father's approval, she frequently sacrificed her own happiness.' " Christine looked up, her blue eyes blazing. "How dare she print her interpretation of things I told her in confidence? Besides, what is wrong with me trying to please my father? Yes, it's hard to live up to his standards and I've complained a time or two, but he's a great man, a leader in the medical community, and a brilliant surgeon. Just because Jane's mother was an alcoholic and her father skipped out what right does she have to criticize me? In print!"

"At least she didn't use your name," Maddy said.

"She might as well have! Anyone who knows me knows I roomed with her at UT. What if my dad reads this?"

"A self-help book for women?" Maddy raised a skeptical brow.

"Well, someone else could read it and show it to him."

"What does she say about me?" Amy asked in a small voice.

Christine resumed reading. "Apparently your fear is that of taking a risk. According to Miss Perfect, 'My other friend was so afraid of trying anything new and failing, she'd rather stay in her safe routine than take a risk that might bring her a more satisfying life.' "

"That's such bull!" Maddy contemplated marching

over to the autographing table and giving Jane a piece of her mind.

"Actually, it's true," Amy said quietly.

"But you own your own business," Maddy argued. "That took risk."

"Not much." Amy sighed. "Traveling Nannies is a franchise, so it was fairly safe. And since I'm the owner, no one can fire me. It's about as low risk as you can get."

"Well, that doesn't mean you're an unhappy coward," Christine insisted.

"I guess not." Amy dropped her gaze to the table.

"Amy?" Maddy ducked her head to see her friend's face. "You are happy, aren't you?"

"Mostly."

"But . . . ?" Christine made a beckoning gesture with one hand. "I definitely hear a but in there."

Amy hesitated. "I just wish, sometimes, that I was one of the nannies I place with the rich and famous who are traveling on vacation. They go to some really exciting places, stay at fabulous hotels, eat at fancy restaurants, and meet interesting people. I've never been outside of the Austin area."

"Is that really so bad?" Maddy asked. "Considering you have no sense of direction—as in absolutely zip—it's only natural that strange places terrify you. But it's nothing to be ashamed of."

"It is if I let it rule my life." Amy raised her chin, determination on every round curve of her face. "Look at Christine. She's afraid of heights, but every Christmas back in college she went to Colorado with her family and got on a lift so she could ski."

"Actually . . ." Christine looked back and forth between them. "I didn't."

"What do you mean, you didn't?" Maddy frowned at her. "You brought back pictures of those ski trips, so we know you went."

"Okay, truth." She sat forward. "When I was growing up, I was so determined to outdo my brother at something, I forced myself to ride the chairlift even though I nearly fainted every time. As soon as I started college, though, I figured out some inventive ways to spend those family vacations in the ski lodge. Hence pictures, but no actual skiing."

"Inventive ways like what?" Amy leaned forward, clearly intrigued.

"A couple of years I faked altitude sickness. The problem there was I did such a good job, Dad wanted to check me into the hospital. So the next year I showed up at the airport wearing one of those big black boots, claiming I had a stress fracture. But Dad kept wanting to examine my foot. After that, I just insisted I was too busy and didn't even go."

"You're kidding." Amy looked as stunned as Maddy felt. "But I thought you liked to ski."

"I do!" Christine exhaled in a burst of self-disgust. "It's getting to the top of the mountain that I don't like. Although, in my defense, those lifts are nothing more than a bench dangling about a mile off the ground, and they take approximately three years to get from the bottom to the top. The real bitch, though, is I'm a good skier. Damned good. I think I really could best Robby in that one thing if I weren't afraid of the dang chairlift."

"Wow." Maddy stared at her. "I had no idea your phobia was that bad."

"Well, now you know." With a touch of drama, Christine dropped her head onto her arm on the table. "I'm a total wimp."

"No, you're not." Maddy laughed. "Look at all you've accomplished. You save lives, for heaven's sake. Who cares if you're afraid of heights?"

"I care." Christine lifted her head. "Amy's right. It's okay to be afraid, but it's not okay to let fear keep you from something you want to do."

"Exactly." Amy nodded eagerly. "Which is why I think you should go skiing again and figure out a way to conquer the chairlift."

Christine laughed. "I'll make a deal with you, Amy. I'll go skiing again if you take one of those nanny assignments."

"Oh, no." Amy shook her head, her eyes round behind her glasses. "I couldn't possibly leave the office to someone else that long. Could I?"

"I don't know." Christine raised a brow. "But talk's cheap."

"Yes, but . . ." Amy chewed her lip as she considered the idea.

"I will if you will." Christine smiled.

Maddy looked from one to the other. "You know, I think y'all should do it. In fact, make it a bet with a time limit. Agree that one year from today whoever hasn't met their challenge has to treat the other to a fab lunch somewhere fun."

"You really think we should?" Excitement lit up Amy's face.

"Absolutely," Maddy said. "The bet gives you incentive. Amy, when you get scared about heading off to someplace you've never been before, just think about Christine and how your bravery is nudging her to do something she really wants to do. The same for you, Christine. When you balk at getting on the lift, just think of Amy and how you're encouraging her to see someplace new."

"You know"—Christine nodded—"I think that might actually help. I'd crawl over hot coals for either one of you, so why not face my fear of heights? What about you, Amy? Are you game?"

"Oh, goodness." Amy patted her heart. "You're serious, aren't you?"

"I really think I am." Christine smiled. "Yeah. Let's do it."

Resolve spread over Amy's face, followed by delight. "I can't believe I'm saying this, but okay!"

"All right, then." Christine held out her hand. "Deal!" After they shook, Christine turned to Maddy. "So what about you? What will you do?"

"Me?" Maddy froze.

"Yes, you." Christine snorted. "If we have to do something scary, so do you. What's it going to be?"

"I know." Amy held up a hand at shoulder height. "You have to get your artwork into a gallery."

"Within the next year?" Maddy scoffed. "I'm not nearly ready for that. Although . . . there is one thing I've been thinking about—"

"Oh?"

Maddy hesitated, wondering if she had the nerve to even tell them about the letter, much less act on it.

"Let me put it this way." Christine gave her a sweet smile. "Either you join the challenge or it's off. I'll never downhill, Amy will never travel, and it will all be your fault."

"Oh gee, thanks." Maddy smirked at her. "I appreciate the lack of pressure."

"Hey, what are friends for?" Christine batted her lashes.

"Okay." Maddy took a deep breath. "I got a job offer in the mail a few days ago." Retrieving her macramé purse, she dug out the letter. Her hands shook as she laid it on the table. "Do y'all remember me talking about Mama Fraser?"

Christine and Amy exchanged a look and shook their heads no.

"You know, the Frasers?" Maddy prompted. "The foster parents who adopted Joe when he was sixteen?"

"Joe?" Christine's eyebrows went up. "As in your high school sweetheart, Joe? The sexy bad boy who rocked your world, then asked you to marry him? That Joe?"

Maddy nodded, her heart racing. "That's the one. Even though Mama Fraser was really mad at me for breaking Joe's heart, she's kept in touch. After Colonel Fraser died, she moved back to New Mexico, and now she runs a summer camp for girls near Santa Fe. And she's . . . well, she's asked me to come work for her."

Both friends stared at her with wide eyes.

"Aren't you a little old to be a camp counselor?" Christine asked.

"I'd be one of the coordinators," Maddy explained. "I'd have my own living quarters and I'd supervise the arts and crafts activities. It's only for the summer, but it sounds like fun."

"Not to mention that Santa Fe is one of the art

capitals of the world," Christine pointed out. "Maybe you could get your work into one of the galleries out there."

"In Santa Fe? I doubt it!" Maddy laughed nervously. "My portfolio of current work isn't nearly strong enough, but Mama Fraser says I'd have plenty of free time to paint in the evenings."

"It sounds perfect," Amy said. "You should do it."

Maddy grimaced. "There's only one problem."

"What's that?" Christine asked.

"Joe," Maddy said as if it should be obvious. "I don't know how I feel about seeing him again."

"Didn't you tell us he's career Army? In the Rangers or something?" Christine asked. "With everything going on in the world, I doubt he's even in the country."

"Actually . . ." Maddy smoothed the envelope. "He was wounded two years ago and had to leave the Rangers. He works for his mom now as the camp director. So . . . if I take the job, I'll be, you know, working for him. Seeing him. Every day."

"Would that be hard?" Concern lined Amy's face.

Maddy huffed out a breath. "We didn't exactly part on friendly terms. For all I know, he still hates my guts and never wants to see me again."

Amy's frown deepened. "If that were true, why would he have his mother offer you a job?"

"You know . . ." Christine sipped more coffee. "That bothers me. I mean, how dorky is it to get your mom to fix you up with an ex-girlfriend?"

"Joe doesn't know. Mama Fraser says she didn't want to tell him until after she had my answer, in

case I turned her down. Which suggests to me he's
still angry over my rejection."

"Or that his mother knows he wants to see you,"
Amy said, "and she doesn't want him to be disappointed if you say no."

"The important thing here," Christine said, "is
do *you* want to see *him*?"

"I don't know." Maddy rubbed her forehead.
"I'd really like to take the job. It would be a nice
bridge between the last ten years and whatever it
is I'm going to do with the rest of my life. And it
would help Mama Fraser, who sounds a little desperate to fill the position."

"Plus"—Christine wiggled her brows—"you'd
get to spend the summer with an old flame. From
what you've said, things were pretty hot between
you two."

"Christine . . ." Maddy laughed nervously. "I'm
not going to Santa Fe so I can have wild sex all
summer with Joe Fraser in front of a camp full of
young girls and his mother."

"Why not?" Christine sat back with her cup of
coffee. "Sounds good to me. Well, the wild sex
part, not the camp full of girls and the mother. I
know how ill Nigel was those last years, so I can
imagine how long it's been since you had any sex,
much less wild sex."

"Forever." Maddy felt her body heat at the mere
thought of sex with Joe. Saying he rocked her
world was putting it mildly. He'd set it on fire. "But
that is totally beside the point. I just want Joe and
me to get along. Who knows, maybe this is a
chance for us to put the past to rest."

"Either that or rekindle it." Christine grinned.

"You just want a vicarious thrill since you aren't getting any either," Maddy said.

"Only because I made you two promise not to let me date anyone who didn't meet your approval," Christine grumbled.

"With good reason, considering your track record with men." Flustered, Maddy turned to Amy. "What do you think I should do?"

Amy folded her hands on the table. "I think you should do it, for yourself, not as part of this challenge. As you said, it would get you out of the house. As an added benefit, maybe you can make peace with Joe so you can be friends.

"If you do it, though"—Amy took hold of Maddy's hand—"you have to promise to show your work to some of the galleries while you're in Santa Fe. And keep at it until you get one of them to take you on."

"Gee." Maddy tried to laugh. "Facing an old boyfriend who probably hates me isn't enough?"

Amy's eyes narrowed behind her glasses. "Not if I have to risk getting lost in some strange place and Christine has to conquer the ski lift."

Panic crawled up Maddy's throat. "I think the challenges are a tad uneven here."

"Like hell!" Christine set her coffee down. "You just have to get one gallery to take on your work, and considering how good you are, that should be a piece of cake. I'm committing to spending Christmas with my whole family in Colorado."

"Who said anything about the family?" Maddy frowned at her. "You could go on your own."

"No, if I'm going to do it, I'll kill two birds with one stone. Conquer the lift . . . and annihilate my brother on the slopes. Preferably in front of my father."

"A noble cause." Maddy laughed.

"You, on the other hand, are going to go to Santa Fe, have hot sex with your old flame, and jump-start your art career. Agreed?"

Maddy laughed. "Are you making sex part of the bet?"

"No . . ."—Christine grinned—"But we expect a full report. And photographic proof that Joe is as hot-looking as you claim."

Amy snorted into her cappuccino, then had to wipe froth from her nose.

Maddy mulled it over. "I just have to get one gallery to take on a piece of my work, correct?"

"Correct," Christine said.

"Can it be on consignment?"

Christine looked to Amy, who nodded. "Okay, on consignment. Is it a deal?"

Maddy took a deep breath. "I know I'm going to regret this—"

"I'll take that as a yes." Christine held up her coffee. "So here's to us, and facing down fear. May this be the start of a perfect life for all of us."

Maddy's stomach did a somersault as their three cups clinked. "For all of us."

Chapter 2

Never let your past limit your future.
                    —*How to Have a Perfect Life*

Maddy wondered about Jane's advice as she tossed the book into her suitcase and headed for Santa Fe. Was it possible to leave the past behind? With every mile that flew by, she felt more and more as if she were seventeen again and racing off to meet the boy her overbearing, police officer father had forbidden her to see. Her body tingled every time she remembered how Joe used to sweep her into his arms and kiss her as if his life depended on getting her naked as quickly as possible.

They'd been crazy-mad in love in that way teenagers often were, without a practical thought in their heads about the future.

Until Joe had been arrested along with some friends for stealing a car. Then the future had crashed down on both of them.

Colonel Fraser had used every contact he had to get the charges against Joe dismissed—since he'd been an unwitting participant—and have Joe accepted into the Army. To everyone's surprise, and the Frasers' immense relief, Joe really took to the Army and informed Maddy he didn't want a short stint. The day he proposed, he proudly announced he'd been accepted into Ranger School and planned to make the Army his career. He thought she would share his enthusiasm, but her dreams of becoming an independent woman and a world-famous artist did not include getting married right out of high school the way her mother had, then putting aside all sense of self to be the perfect little homemaker. Of course, at the time, she hadn't known that the words "wife" and "slave" were not synonymous.

Memories of how it all had ended made her grimace many times during the drive from Austin to Santa Fe. The scene had been bitter and ugly, and Joe had looked at her with such shock, it was clear he'd felt completely betrayed.

But that had been a lifetime ago. Surely he was over it by now. As a mature adult, he had to see in retrospect that she'd made the right choice. For both of them. She'd been entirely too immature and would have made a terrible wife for anyone. Especially a soldier who would have to deploy at a moment's notice for covert operations that could last for months.

Yes, she'd made the right choice.

And Joe would be long over the rejection by now.

Maddy repeated that reassurance like a mantra as she passed a sign that told her Camp Enchantment was just ahead. She glanced through the trees on her left. The road had been following a river through several miles of untamed countryside, as she climbed from the desert into the mountains, but now there was a collection of buildings on the opposite bank.

Her stomach fluttered with the realization that she'd be seeing Joe face-to-face in just a few minutes. As camp director, he'd be on hand to greet her and the other coordinators who were arriving as an advance guard to get the camp ready for the counselors and campers. Weeks had passed since she'd built up the courage to call Mama Fraser and accept the job. If Joe had any objection to seeing her again, he'd had plenty of time to tell her not to come.

She tried for the thousandth time to imagine how their first meeting would go . . .

He would greet her with a smile and ask how she'd been as each of them surreptitiously took stock of how the other had changed. He'd been a tall, wiry teenager when she'd seen him last, with dark good looks that spoke of some portion of Native American blood. What portion was anyone's guess, since he barely remembered his birth mother and hadn't known his father at all.

She tried to picture him slightly heavier, with the muscles he'd no doubt acquired in the Rangers going soft now that he was out and his jet-black hair beginning to recede. They would laugh—a little awkwardly perhaps—as they remembered how greedy they'd once been for each other. He would politely tell her she looked good, even though she'd gained a few pounds and collected her first faint wrinkles around the eyes. Personally, she didn't mind the weight or the wrinkles. Aging was just part of living, and it beat the heck out of the alternative: dying young, as Nigel had.

A wave of grief threatened to engulf her, so she

straightened her shoulders to shake it off. A part of her would cherish Nigel forever, but the time had come for her to move forward with her life.

Up ahead, a little red sports car turned onto the drive for the camp. One of the other coordinators, she supposed, as she followed the car over a rustic wooden bridge. On the opposite side of the river, an elderly man stepped out of a guardhouse. After peeking through the windshield, he waved the sports car through the open gate, then motioned for Maddy to stop. Rolling down her window, she gave him her name.

A broad smile broke over his craggy face. "Ah yes, the new A and C lady. Mrs. Fraser told me to expect you. You just follow Sandy on up to the office. I'll tell Mama you're here."

Leaving the window down so the breeze ruffled her hair, Maddy followed the other car along the drive until it pulled into a gravel parking lot before a long, one-story adobe building. Two college-age girls were standing in the lot chatting, one a tall black girl, the other a plucky-looking brunette. They let out a squeal when a perky blonde stepped out of the sports car.

Maddy watched, amused, as the girls raced over to greet the newcomer with arms wide. Just before they all collided, they bent forward at the hips for a hug that allowed no part of their bodies to touch below the shoulders. It was a ritual that surely dated back to the dawn of time. If cavegirls had gone to summer camp, Maddy was certain they would have greeted each other with exactly the same squeal, run, hug.

When the girls headed inside, Maddy stepped out of her own car and inhaled a breath of pine-scented air so dry it stole the moisture from her lungs. The brilliant sunlight stung her eyes as she stared at the office.

Joe was in there. She was sure of it.

Eagerness and fear warred in her stomach, making it ache. She bolstered her courage with thoughts of Amy and Christine and headed for the open doorway. Just before she reached it, she heard Joe's voice—and stopped dead.

"Welcome, ladies. I see you've returned for another summer at Camp Enchantment."

"You say that like you're surprised," one of the girls said.

"Not in the least." Joe laughed, a deep, rich sound that sent Maddy tumbling back in time. God, how she'd loved his laugh. Her secret challenge had been to coax a laugh or two out of him whenever they were alone. "Sandy, I have no doubt you'll die of old age right here leading a fireside sing-along."

"One can only hope," the girl responded in a light, flirtatious voice.

Maddy stepped closer to the building and peeked around the doorframe into the shadowy interior. The viga ceiling, terra-cotta tile floor, and beige adobe walls gave the room a rustic feel. Joe stood next to a mission-style desk, clipboard in hand, smiling at the three college girls.

The smile caught Maddy so off guard, for a moment that was all she noticed. He looked happy and relaxed, completely unlike the intense, moody rebel he'd been.

Then she took in the rest of him, and oh dear God! He didn't match her mental image of a starting-to-go-soft man in his thirties at all. He was gorgeous! With a hard body that had her pulse pounding with something more than nervousness.

He stood in profile, wearing a green polo shirt that stretched over big shoulders, bulging biceps, and a chest so well defined she could make out a hint of his pecs through the knit fabric. His khaki shorts hugged narrow hips and showed off rock-solid legs.

He laughed again at something the girls were saying, then turned and bent forward to set the clipboard on the desk. Maddy's mouth fell open as she gazed at the sexiest male butt she'd ever had the privilege to see.

"If you girls will just sign these release forms," he said, "you can get settled. Carol is already here and waiting for you in the Chief's Lodge."

Maddy tore her gaze away from Joe's backside to find the college girls checking him out as well. All three of them smiled and blushed as they took the pen he handed them and signed the forms. No wonder these girls had returned for another year. They all had the hots for the camp director!

Returning her gaze to Joe, Maddy remembered Christine's suggestion that she spend the summer having wild sex with her old flame. The idea aroused her and horrified her at the same time. She couldn't let a man that physically perfect see her naked. It was one thing to be blasé about wide hips and wrinkles when she was around normal people who were aging too. But get naked with a man who looked better now than he had as a teenager? Not in this lifetime!

Although why would a man who looked like that even want to get naked with her when he had a whole camp full of nubile twenty-somethings to pick from?

A thought popped into her head, full blown. Was this why he hadn't objected to her coming? He wanted her to see what she'd turned down all those years ago? Show her that other women—younger, prettier women—lusted after him in droves? Maybe lead her on, make her want him again—then turn her down flat? That would certainly be a nice revenge for him, now wouldn't it?

"All right," Joe said, picking up the clipboard. "You three go settle in. We'll rendezvous on the patio at four o'clock for our first staff meeting."

Maddy jerked away from the door as the three girls headed out an opposite doorway that led to a covered patio and the camp beyond. She stood there, fighting the urge to jump in her car and race all the way back to Texas.

Okay, slow down, she told herself, trying not to hyperventilate. *Think this through.*

The revenge theory was just that: a theory. The Joe she'd known would never be that petty. Although people change. Lord knows she had; she liked to think it was for the better. She'd matured into a responsible, self-reliant adult. Definitely not the sort of woman who would take a job, then not show up. If she left before Joe saw her, that was what he and Mama Fraser would think—that she was an inconsiderate ditz who hadn't bothered to tell them she wasn't coming so they could hire someone else.

Except she'd talked to the guard, so Lord only knew what they'd think.

Plus she'd made that bet with Christine and Amy. If she hightailed it back to Texas without getting at least one piece of her work into a gallery, they'd blow off their own challenges. Damn! Why had she agreed to that dare? Well, she had agreed, and she couldn't get out of it now.

Besides, if she was totally off base on her revenge theory, then maybe Joe was equally eager to put their past to rest. Maybe he'd even be happy to see her. The only way she would know was if she went in there and faced him. And now would be a good time, since he was alone. They'd have privacy, at least, for this first meeting.

Just do it, she ordered herself.

Taking a deep breath, she forced herself to take a step. Then another. Before she knew it, she was standing in the doorway. He'd taken a seat at the desk and was working at a computer. The sound of the keyboard covered up her approach until she was almost to the desk. He looked up—and froze.

Her lips trembled as she smiled. "Hello, Joe. It's been a long time."

"Maddy?" He stared at her, his expression blank. He looked unbearably handsome with his tan skin and dark-chocolate eyes.

She felt her cheeks flush. "It's, um, it's good to see you."

He shot to his feet so fast his chair toppled backward, landing with a clatter against the tile floor. Anger blazed from his eyes in hot waves. "What the hell are you doing here?"

The blood drained from her face.

He hadn't expected her.

And he definitely was not happy to see her.

Chapter 3

Adrenaline pumped through Joe's body as he stared at the woman before him. His senses on full alert, he took in everything in a flash: wild red hair, heart-shaped face, green eyes, lush mouth, and an hourglass figure that had forever set his personal standard for how a woman should look. Beneath a yellow tank top and a long, rust-colored skirt, with a wide leather belt riding her hips, she looked as curvaceous as ever.

"I-I'm sorry," she stuttered. "I thought—"

His gaze snapped back to her face, and he saw her skin had gone white, making her hair and eyes even more vivid. Was this as big a shock for her as it was for him?

"What are you doing here?" he repeated, barely able to think over the sound of blood rushing in his ears.

"I'm going to work here. As the arts and crafts coordinator."

"You're going to *what*?" he barked in his battle voice. But this wasn't a battle. He wasn't shouting to be heard over gunfire, and his body wasn't in immediate danger of getting shot. He was standing in one of the safest places on Earth—the office of his mother's summer camp. The scent of pine and sage drifted through the open windows and doors. Outside, a bird was singing.

And Maddy was standing right in front of him.

Maddy Howard. Not Madeline Mills, the name of the woman his mother had hired. The answer hit him like a blow straight to the chest. His mother had done this. Deliberately! "I'm going to kill her!"

"I'm sorry." Maddy had the grace to blush. "I thought you knew."

"Did she tell you I run the camp for her? Did she mention that you'd be working for me?"

"Of course. I assumed . . . you wanted . . ." She took a step backward toward the door to the parking lot as if ready to bolt. "This was obviously a mistake. Maybe I should just—"

She was leaving.

His heart kicked back into high gear. He'd wanted to never see Maddy again, but now that she was here, more dazzling than ever, like some torturous fantasy brought to life, he didn't want her to just walk away. Jesus, how twisted was that? And how embarrassing to realize he still wanted her. Fifteen years after she'd cut him off at the knees, he still wanted her.

"This was definitely a mistake." He made his voice as flat as possible. "And yes, I think it would be best if you did 'just.' " He motioned toward the door, telling himself to leave it at that. She was already turning, already moving away with her head bent. A few more steps and she'd be gone from his life again. An invisible fist squeezed his chest. "Christ, Maddy, you never were good at thinking things through, but this takes the cake, even for you." Why the hell was he still talking? *Shut up, idiot, and let her go.* "What made you think you could breeze in here and spend the summer working for me as if nothing ever happened between us?"

That stopped her. Her head came up and her eyes flared as she turned back to him. "Maybe the fact that it happened *years* ago and I thought you'd be mature enough to be over it by now."

"Of course I'm over it," he snapped, and started to take a seat to prove how unaffected he was by her presence. Except his chair wasn't there and he nearly fell on his ass before he caught his balance. Wouldn't that have been great? He jerked the chair off the floor and slammed it in place. Dropping to the seat, he blindly shuffled papers. "Just because I'm over you doesn't mean I want you working for me. As I remember, you weren't exactly the most responsible person I've ever met."

"Not responsible!" She nearly choked. "Joe, I was barely more than—than a *child* back then."

"A child?" He raked her lush body with a pointed look. "That's not how I remember it." And he did remember. He remembered how she looked naked, how her skin smelled, how she used to laugh even while they were making out . . . even when his eager teenage body was driving hard inside of her. He remembered clearly how that felt.

Christ. Now he had a hard-on.

He ran a hand over his face. "I don't want you here."

"Your mother hired me."

"And I'm firing you."

"Because of things that happened when we were stupid teenagers?"

"No." He gritted his teeth, refusing to look at her. "Because you're not right for the job."

"Of arts and crafts coordinator?" Her voice went up an octave. "I have a fine arts degree. How am I not qualified to teach craft classes at a summer camp?"

"I know you, Maddy." He shuffled more papers, making a mess of his orderly piles. "You had three jobs in high school and you were fired from every one of them."

"Because you were always talking me into ditching work so we could go to the lake." When he still wouldn't look at her, she marched over and planted her hands on the desk. "Has it occurred to you that I might be a very different person now than I was then? People change, you know."

He looked up, straight into green eyes so beautiful his chest ached. "Not that much they don't."

"Apparently not." Temper added color to her cheeks. "You're still as pigheaded and-and . . . *selfish* as you were at eighteen. God, what did I ever see in you?"

"I think we both know the answer to that." He longed to say something crude that would slice her to the bone, but the words stuck in his throat. "You can't work here. End of discussion."

"You can't fire me!" she shouted back. How like Maddy. Tell her she can't do something, and suddenly it's the one thing she's hell-bent to do no matter what. "It's not your camp. It's your mother's."

"Yeah, but I run it for her." He came out of the chair with his hands on the desk, bringing them nose to nose. "And I say—"

Her scent hit him like a punch to the gut, a wild, sweet fragrance that went straight to his brain and triggered a barrage of memories. The taste of her lips. The feel of her nimble fingers on his body. The expression on her face as she straddled his lap. The sound of her voice saying, "I love you."

That memory cut the deepest.

His gaze dropped to her lips. All he'd have to do to taste that sweet, generous mouth again was lean forward a few inches. She gasped softly, as if reading his mind.

"Madeline?" His mother's voice came from the parking lot.

Joe jerked upright a heartbeat before she came hobbling through the door as fast as she could move with her cane. With frail bones and cotton white hair, she might look every one of her eighty-plus years, but her blue eyes were as bright as ever.

A smile lit up her wrinkled face. "There you are! Harold at the gate told me you were here." She extended her free arm. "It's so good to see you!"

Joe stood in rigid silence as the two women hugged, although he wanted to pick his mother up, carry her outside, and demand to know what she'd been thinking to hire Maddy and not warn him. She wasn't stupid or insensitive. How could she do this?

"It's good to see you too." Maddy closed her eyes as if to savor the embrace. "I've missed you so much."

"Which is your own fault," Mama scolded.

"Please, don't start," Maddy whispered barely loud enough for Joe to hear.

Mama leaned back at arm's length. "And look at you. More beautiful than ever." She glanced at Joe. "Don't you think she's more beautiful than ever?"

Maddy blushed and looked at the floor.

"Mom," he said as calmly as possible. To the rest of the world she might be Mama Fraser, but since the day the adoption became final, to him she'd been Mom. "Could I have a word with you?"

"Certainly." She smiled at him and waited.

"Outside."

"What's wrong with right here?" she asked so innocently he thought his head might explode.

Maddy lifted her eyes to glare at him. "He wants to tell you to fire me."

"Now why would I do that when you just got here?" Mama squeezed one of Maddy's hands. "I'm looking forward to having you around, dear."

"Well, I'm *not* looking forward to it," Joe said. "And frankly, I'd like to know how Maddy even heard about the job in the first place."

"Because I wrote to her, of course," his mother announced, as if it should have been obvious. "We needed a new A and C coordinator, and I knew she'd be ideal. Besides, with her being newly widowed, I thought the job would be good for her. One of the reasons I bought the camp after I lost the Colonel was because nothing soothes a grieving heart better than being around young people."

"Widowed?" Joe stared at Maddy. She was a widow? He hadn't even known she'd married. The few times his mother had mentioned her name, he'd either changed the subject or left the room. Although—*duh!*—that explained the different last name. What was wrong with his brain?

"That's right, dear." Sorrow clouded his mother's eyes. "I know having her here might be a bit uncomfortable at first, but you're both grown-ups now, and I know you're man enough to handle it. Besides, it'll be nice for me to have Maddy around. All the other girls are so young, I'm lonesome for a woman to talk to, one who knows how it feels to lose a husband."

Joe knew right then that he was sunk. What could he possibly say? "No, I'm not man enough to handle this"? Or, "I realize you saved me from a life headed straight for the streets or prison, but no, you can't have a companion to help you grieve"? He couldn't even say, "Come on, Mom, the Colonel died years ago," since he also still missed the man every single day.

Mama smiled at him, her blue eyes twinkling. "You don't really mind, do you?"

He smiled back tightly. "Of course not."

"Fine, then." She patted Maddy's arm. "Maddy, honey, I have my golf cart out front. Why don't you follow me in your car to the Craft Shack so I can show you where you'll be living?"

"I . . ." Maddy hesitated and her gaze darted in his direction.

Had she suddenly changed her mind? Again? *Too late now, baby,* he wanted to tell her. *You're just as trapped as I am.*

Maddy sagged in defeat. "That'll be fine."

When the women had gone, Joe dropped to his chair and rubbed his face with both hands. *Crap!* He'd thought last summer was long, after he'd learned his knee was toast and he would never return to active duty. This, however, had the makings of the longest summer of his life.

Long and painful.

Frankly, he'd rather take another bullet than face Maddy every day for the next twelve weeks.

Maddy wanted to kick herself as she followed Mama Fraser's golf cart up a rough dirt road that wound between hardy cedar trees and mammoth boulders. Coming here really had been a mistake. She should have left the minute she realized that. Actually, she had offered to leave—until Joe had made her mad.

She rubbed her forehead in a vain effort to stave off a headache. She hadn't lost her temper in years. Yet two minutes with Joe and words were flying out of her mouth before they even registered in her brain.

Why in heaven's name hadn't Mama Fraser told him to expect her? If the woman was trying to play Cupid, her aim was way off.

And how foolish Maddy suddenly felt for her own thoughts of reconciliation. She cringed just thinking of all her silly dreams about spending a friendly summer with Joe. This could easily turn into a nightmare!

The road reached a level area on the side of a mountain. Mama pulled to a stop before a two-story adobe building nestled against a stand of aspens. Stepping out of the car, Maddy took a moment to survey the valley.

The view literally stole her breath. Far below her, the river reflected the blue sky as it meandered past tall cottonwood trees. The camp complemented the landscape with a scattering of rustic buildings, while mountains lined the horizon. All the shapes and contrasts called to her artist's soul, making her fingers itch for a paintbrush.

"What do you think?" Mama asked, using her cane to cross the hard-packed earth.

The woman's frailness provided a startling reminder of how many years had passed. Mama had been in her mid-sixties the last time she'd seen her. The Colonel had still been alive. And Maddy hadn't even met Nigel, or Christine and Amy. A lot of years, and a lot of living. What would the next decade or two bring?

She turned back to look at the valley. "I'd say it's beautiful, but that hardly seems adequate."

"There are some things words alone can't express. Which is why God gave us artists. And why so many artists are drawn to the Land of Enchantment. I'll be eager to see what it brings out in you."

If I stay. A weight settled over Maddy's heart.

Joe's mother moved toward the car, peeking through the window to the backseat. "Looks like you brought a bit more than the standard camp trunk."

"I never learned the art of packing light."

"Well, let's get it all up to your apartment."

"Mama . . ." Maddy stopped her when she reached for the door handle. "I'm not sure this is wise—"

"Now, Madeline, you're not thinking of running scared, are you? The girl I knew had more spunk than that."

"The girl you knew has learned a lot in the last few years. Like, it's not always wise to rush straight ahead, ignoring all the warning signs. Reckless actions can lead to head-on collisions."

"Is that how you see what happened between you and Joe? A car wreck?"

"What would you call it?"

"Fate." She nodded and opened the door. "Now come on, let's get your things."

"I got it." Afraid the woman would try to carry the suitcases herself, Maddy wrestled the biggest one out of the backseat. She could always carry it back down, she assured herself as she followed Mama up a staircase along the outside of the building. "You know," she said, grunting as she heaved the luggage up another step, "fate isn't always a good thing."

"It isn't always a bad thing either." Mama pulled herself along, using the handrail. "Oh, I admit, at the time I was plenty miffed at you for breaking my boy's heart, but I think it happened the way God intended. You two may have been perfect for each other, but you both had some growing up to do. So God yanked you apart for a bit. Now he's brought you back together." Reaching a small landing, Mama stopped to take a set of keys from the pocket of her leisure pants.

"Actually, *you* brought us back together." Maddy worked to catch her breath, feeling lightheaded from the altitude. "You realize Joe is extremely angry with you right now."

"He'll get over it." Mama opened the door and stepped inside.

"From what I just witnessed, he's not a man who forgives and forgets too easily." Maddy dragged her suitcase over the threshold, ready to argue further, but the apartment distracted her. The dim light from a single-bulb fixture revealed a tiny, one-room efficiency with a partial wall dividing the kitchen and dining area from the sleeping area. The stale scent of disuse hung in the air.

She nearly laughed, thinking she'd certainly come a long way from her upscale house in the hills of West Austin. But the simple truth was that after growing up in a barely middle-class neighborhood, she'd been a little uncomfortable in Nigel's circle. Not that he'd been mega wealthy, just several rungs up the ladder from a family living on a cop's salary.

Here, though—here was a nice small space she could make her own. A place to escape, paint, and start life anew.

Mama sighed. "Our last A and C coordinator had the place decorated up so cute. It looks downright spartan now."

"It's fine," Maddy assured her as she pictured the possibilities. A pretty tablecloth to cover the wooden spool that sat between two folding chairs. A comforter and sham for the single mattress on the metal frame. And for the tired old armchair sitting in the dark, dusty corner, a slipcover and a reading lamp.

"The good news is"—Mama moved toward a wall of curtains—"around here, we do most of our living outside." With the pull of a cord, she opened the drapes to reveal a wide sliding glass door. Sunlight poured in, transforming the cramped space into something bright and wonderful.

Maddy abandoned her suitcase and followed Mama out onto a huge balcony with a full set of grapevine furniture. An array of clay pots held the remnants of plants that hadn't survived the winter, but Maddy could easily picture this outdoor living room teeming with greenery and cheerful flowers.

She moved to the short wall and gaped at the view, which was even more spectacular from this vantage. Then her gaze fell to the office, and her enthusiasm plunged. "Mama, why didn't you tell him I was coming?"

"Because he would have insisted I take back the job offer. Now you're here and it's too late."

"And you laid a great big guilt trip on him to make him let me stay."

"Yes, I thought that was nicely done." Her eyes twinkled.

Normally, Maddy would have shared Mama's humor. Now she could only sigh with regret. "Maybe it would be best if I did leave."

"Is that what you want to do? Leave without a fight?"

"To be honest, my mind is going in so many directions, I don't know what I want."

"Then I'd say you have some thinking to do. At least stick around until you know what you want."

Know what you want. The words from Jane's book echoed in Maddy's head, stirring all the old longings that had once been so much a part of her. Longings she'd lost along the way. To be an artist. Not just the competent one she was now, creating pleasant oil paintings, but to somehow find the key to unlock the potential she knew was inside her.

Facing the view, she yearned to unpack her paints and set up her easel right here, with a hundred images waiting to be captured in every direction.

"Well, I'll leave you to get settled," Mama said,

moving back toward the sliding glass door. "You're free until the staff meeting."

"Staff meeting?" Maddy pulled herself out of her thoughts as she remembered what Joe had told the other coordinators. "Oh. Yes. Four o'clock." Biting her lip, she looked down at the office.

"Now don't look so worried. Joe has all afternoon to calm down and he's hardly going to make a scene in front of the girls."

"I wouldn't count on that," she called to Mama's retreating back. When the woman's laugh drifted back to her, she felt another old longing well inside—why couldn't she have a mother like Mama? Someone with grit?

When she was alone, she glanced at her watch. She had three hours until the meeting. Plenty of time to check in with Amy and Christine to let them know she'd arrived safely.

Back inside, she wrestled her suitcase onto the mattress, snarled at her copy of *How to Have a Perfect Life*, rummaged past several pairs of sandals, and dug out her sturdy little laptop. Seconds later, she was plugged into the phone jack next to the big ugly chair.

Opening her e-mail, she scanned new messages from her friends. Over the years they'd kept their e-mail conversations going until it was now as much a part of their daily lives as waking up in the morning. This time of day during the week, Amy would be sitting at her desk and generally responded within seconds. Christine wouldn't respond until she woke up to get ready for the graveyard shift at the ER.

When she finished reading, Maddy started a new thread.

Subject: *Well, I made it.*

Message: *And can I just say, I want to shoot Jane Redding for writing that book? "Leave your past behind." What a crock!*

Amy: *Uh-oh. I take it your first meeting with Joe didn't go well.*

Maddy: *You might say that. Which proves Jane was wrong. The past never goes away. It's like the clothing mistakes in the back of your closet. You can forget about them for long stretches, but the minute you dig past your current clothes, there they are, right where you left them, some of them even uglier than you remembered. They haven't magically vanished, or gotten pretty while you weren't looking.*

Amy: *I don't think Jane meant we should or could forget it. I think she meant we have to accept it and move on, without letting where you've been control where you're going.*

Maddy: *Ugh! Christine, why aren't you online? I need a bitching buddy, not maturity. Although, Amy, you're right. I'm sure when I'm feeling calmer, I'll agree. Right now, though, I'd rather shoot Jane. Or Joe. Yeah, actually, I could really get into shooting Joe.*

Chapter 4

Maddy looked up from the notes she'd been reviewing for the staff meeting and realized it was two minutes past four o'clock. Yikes! Where had the time gone? After her e-mail exchange with Amy, she'd jumped into airing out the apartment and unpacking her clothes. Once she'd made some headway into stamping the place as her own, she'd pulled out all the material Mama had sent her when she'd agreed to take the job. In her determination to be well prepared, she'd lost all track of time.

Arriving late was not the way to show Joe what a mature, responsible adult she was.

Stuffing her notes into her big purse, she raced out the door and toward the wooded trail she assumed led to the main part of the camp. Her flat sandals slipped on the damp earth, making her wish she'd taken an extra minute to put on sensible footwear. Especially since she'd gone on a shopping spree before leaving Austin to buy some shoes that could actually be termed "sensible."

The trail gave way to a sun-drenched field, with

the office to her far left. She increased her pace to a light run, forgetting about the thin mountain air. By the time she passed a log cabin with a sign proclaiming it the CHIEF'S LODGE, her head was spinning.

She made out several people gathered on the covered area behind the office and prayed Joe wasn't among them yet. With a last spurt of energy, she leapt onto the patio. "Sorry I'm late." She sucked in a breath. "I got . . . caught up . . . unpacking."

Several heads turned her way, but with the sunspots in her eyes, all she could make out was silhouettes standing or sitting around a picnic table—all of them too small to be Joe, thank goodness.

"Actually, you're fine." Mama's voice came from one of the seated silhouettes. "We haven't started yet."

"Yeah, we're waiting for God to join us," a younger voice said.

"God?" Maddy's eyes adjusted enough to recognize the three girls she'd seen earlier and two others she hadn't.

"He also answers to *sir*!" The blonde who'd driven the sports car snapped a smart salute, making the others laugh.

"They mean Joe," Mama clarified as she rose. "Let me introduce you. Everyone, this is Madeline Mills, our new arts and crafts coordinator."

"Please, call me Maddy." She acknowledged the round of welcomes with a wave.

"This is Carol, our assistant director." Mama gestured to a pretty young woman sitting on the table with her legs primly crossed. Like the others, she wore shorts and a polo shirt, making Maddy realize that maybe her shoes weren't the only thing she should have changed. "Carol's been a part of Camp Enchantment for . . . how long?"

"Fourteen years." Carol's smile held genuine welcome. "I've gone from camper to counselor to assistant director."

"Sandy here is our liberal arts coordinator." Mama motioned to the owner of the sports car, then moved on to the statuesque black girl. "And Dana."

"Outdoor sports." Dana gave Maddy's hand a firm shake. "How ya doing?"

"Leah coordinates our nature studies." Mama motioned to a petite Asian girl seated on the far bench, then moved on to the last of the three girls who'd been in the parking lot, the tomboy with cropped brown hair. "And Bobbi is our water recreation coordinator."

"You know, head lifeguard." Bobbi raised the whistle that hung around her neck and blew. The shrill sound nearly drowned out the screams of protest as everyone covered their ears.

"So," Maddy said when the noise died down, "did all of you start out as campers?"

"You bet," Sandy confirmed, and they all launched into singing, " 'We are family, I got all my sisters with me.' "

Maddy was struck by how very young they looked. Logically, she knew the gap was only about a decade, but it suddenly seemed like a millennium. Although the gap wasn't just the age. These were "good girls." She wanted to laugh at the thought of these squeaky-clean kids working for Joe. And herself being dropped among them. Oh well, she decided, if she could become fast friends with Amy and Christine, she could find a way to fit in here.

A tingle of awareness brushed the back of her neck. She turned as Joe appeared in the doorway to the office. For a split second, their gazes collided. She braced herself for a blast of cold anger, or the spark of heat she'd seen in his eyes the instant before his mother walked in.

Instead, his gaze moved on as if he hadn't even seen her. He strode forward with a stack of papers, his years of military discipline showing in every step. "All right," he said, as if rallying the troops for a briefing. "Let's get this meeting under way."

The coordinators scurried into their seats, taking up notepads and pens. Maddy sat next to Mama, while Joe took the seat farthest from her on the opposite bench.

"We have a lot of ground to cover." Joe skimmed a look around the table that somehow skipped over her. "First, though, I'd like to say welcome back to Camp Enchantment."

A cheer went up from the other coordinators.

He glanced at his mother. "Do you have anything to say before we get down to business?"

Affection and pride softened Mama's face. "I thought I'd let you make the announcement."

"Announcement?" Carol asked.

"Nothing major." Joe shrugged. "Only that my stint as camp director has officially been bumped up from temporary to permanent."

Maddy watched him carefully as a second cheer went up. One corner of his sculpted lips lifted in a smile, but no readable emotion showed in his eyes.

"And here I thought you'd all go screaming for

the front gate." His teasing tone was subtle, the same wry wit he'd once used to charm her.

"Not likely." Carol laughed flirtatiously. It wasn't overt, or even sexual, yet Maddy felt a bond between Joe and every female at the table—a genuine affection that clearly excluded her.

The exclusion, though, allowed her to study him and notice how he'd changed. He wore his hair short and neat, not boot-camp short but not as long as when they'd been dating. His face had hardened too, become more sharply defined.

"In making my decision," he said, "I thought a lot about Camp Enchantment, and the children who pass through here. I know personally what a difference a positive environment can make."

Maddy cocked her head, intrigued by the ease with which he spoke, considering the personal nature of his words. He'd certainly matured from the boy who sat in the back of the classroom, slumped in his chair with a practiced look of disinterest.

"Camp Enchantment is more than just a place for kids to come to spend a few weeks in the out-of-doors," he continued. "It's a place steeped in tradition. Since it was founded in the early nineteen hundreds, the Bobcats and the Foxes have been racing canoes and competing on the archery range."

"Go, Bobcats!" Dana punched the air with her fist.

"Go, Foxes!" Sandy answered in kind.

This time Joe's smile made it to his eyes, a rarity that turned Maddy's insides to pure jelly. "Through teamwork and healthy competition we have helped kids gain the confidence to achieve their personal best. The Rangers taught me the importance of teamwork. In this case, the objective isn't to capture a spit of land or defeat an enemy, but to live up to our motto."

" 'Building character and memories to last a lifetime,' " Mama quoted.

"Exactly." Joe nodded. "As we're working together over the next week, preparing for the annual invasion of five hundred campers, I'd like all of us to keep that objective in mind and look for ways to make this summer a positive experience for everyone.

"Knowing all of you, I'm sure you've been thinking about the summer as well, and what projects you'd like to do. So, I'd like to go around the table and have each of you share your goals. Carol, since you're always the queen of organization, we'll start with you."

"Okay." Carol opened a folder and started handing out papers. "I've made a schedule—"

Bobbi burst out laughing.

"What?" Carol frowned.

"Nothing." Joe smoothed the smile from his face. "We all live for your schedules."

"As well you should." Carol nodded smartly and launched into what needed to be done by what day in order to ensure the efficient running of the camp office.

The others followed with their ideas for the summer and the plans they'd been working on. Listening to them, Joe found himself as impressed this year as he had been last with their ideas. Too bad their enthusiasm wasn't enough to distract him from the woman who sat catty-corner from him.

Maddy, he kept thinking, *what are you doing here?*

She looked unbearably appealing, naturally sexy, and completely out of place. He'd watched her dash across the game field with her skirt swirling about her calves and those ridiculously inappropriate shoes. Even with her feet tucked safely out of sight, his mind kept drifting to the bright orange sandals with long laces wrapped about her ankles—and how much he'd like to unwrap those laces.

Then there was the yellow top. Tank tops normally looked better on someone with tanner skin and more muscle definition. On her, though, it worked. God, it worked. The knit fabric cupped her breasts, showed a hint of cleavage, and filled his head with thoughts of running his hands up and down her arms.

Or simply holding her hand.

He'd forgotten the way they used to hold hands everywhere they went. Now the memory returned along with the memory of other little pleasures. It hadn't all been about sex. There had been genuine caring. At least on his end.

"Maddy," Carol said, jolting him with the mere sound of the name, "since this is your first time working at a summer camp, do you need help planning your activities?"

"Not too much, actually."

He felt her hesitate as she flicked a nervous glance his way. Then she straightened, as if coming to the same conclusion he had: that pretending to be strangers was the best way to get through this meeting.

"Mama sent lots of information from previous years, plus I found a bunch of books filled with craft projects. Here's a list of projects I'd like to do." She started her own stack of papers around the table. "I'm open for suggestions, though, since y'all have more experience working with the kids."

Taking one of the sheets, he saw that she was remarkably well prepared for the job. So much for being able to fire her on the grounds of incompetence. That would have been too neat and easy. And life, he'd learned, was rarely neat or easy.

Finally they finished dividing up the work detail for cleaning and prepping the camp.

"Okay," he said, glancing at his watch, ready to wrap things up. "I think that covers enough for now. We have an hour before dinner, which will be a hamburger cookout by the river."

"So we're free to go?" Dana asked.

"You're dismissed," Joe confirmed.

"Woo-hoo!" Dana jumped up and turned to Bobbi. "You know what that means."

"Badminton rematch," Bobbi answered. "Prepare to get trounced."

"In your dreams!" The two took off at a full run.

The other counselors followed at a more sedate pace. Joe had an uneasy moment when Maddy didn't immediately stand. Surely she wasn't going to sit there with nothing but his mother as a buffer between them. Luckily, Carol turned when she reached the edge of the patio. "Maddy, aren't you coming?"

"Oh," She straightened as if surprised they would include her. "Yes, of course." She grabbed her enormous hippie purse and followed. Apparently her fondness for funky, out-of-date clothes hadn't faded.

Now that her back was to him, he watched her openly. The others quickly closed ranks around her, and she laughed at something one of them said. The sound sent him hurtling back to the first time he'd seen her. It was right after he'd moved from Albuquerque to Austin. He was walking down the hall of his new high school with his head down, his hands in his pocket, and a hitch in his step that let everyone know "Yeah, I'm bad." He heard a laugh, not a girly giggle but an all-out laugh.

He looked up and saw Maddy walking toward him with a pack of girls. The sight of her throwing back her head and laughing stopped him in his tracks. He stood there bug-eyed as she continued past him, sucker punched by something that went beyond the normal adolescent-hormones-gone-haywire. One thought rang in his brain: *I want*. The wanting filled him with an intensity he rarely allowed. Couldn't afford to allow. But with Maddy, he'd dared more than want. He'd dared to have.

And he'd relearned one of life's cruelest lessons, that having and keeping are not the same thing.

He turned to his mother, who sat calmly watching him.

"I have one question," he finally said.

"Yes?"

"What is she doing here?"

"Maddy?" His mother blinked her blue eyes as if the question confused her. Which he knew it didn't. Not for a minute. "She's here to work as our new A and C coordinator."

"But why? It's been bugging me all afternoon. Considering the way she dumped me, I have a hard time believing that she came out here hoping to take up where we left off. And if that was what she wanted, why the job? Why not just contact me?"

His mother pursed her lips, considering. "And if she had called, what would you have said?"

"Nothing. I would have hung up." Then promptly had heart failure.

"Exactly. It's a little harder to hang up when she's here in person."

"Conflicting emotions clamped about his chest.

"Are you saying she does want to get back together?"

"I didn't 'say' that."

"Okay—" He ran a hand over his hair and tried to think. "Let's say she does, which blows my mind to even think about. Why the job? Why not come out here on the pretext of visiting you? Why would a thirty-two-year old woman travel hundreds of miles to take a job at a summer camp? It can't be for the money. The job doesn't pay that much. So what is she *doing* here?"

"Why don't you ask her?"

Because that would involve talking to her.

Leaning forward, she patted his hand. "Ask her, Joe. Otherwise you're just going to drive yourself crazy wondering."

He dropped his head forward in defeat. "I hate it when you're right."

"Yes, I know." She rose and kissed the top of his head.

After she left, he sat a long time—driving himself crazy.

Maddy returned to her apartment after a miserably awkward evening and checked her e-mail. Christine had finally chimed in on her earlier exchange with Amy.

Message: *Come on, Mad, how bad can it be? So the man was startled to see you. He'll recover and things will be fine.*

Maddy: *I don't think so. We just spent three hours together at a hamburger cookout where we managed to not exchange one single word.*

Christine, who was apparently online, responded right away: *I take it the man's a brooder.*

Maddy: *Try World-Class Brooder. And he seems to have matured a lot over the years, but apparently that hasn't changed.*

Christine: *So what did you do in the past when he brooded?*

Maddy stared at the screen, remembering so many things. A bittersweet ache settled in her chest as she typed her reply: *I'd find a way to make him laugh. I don't think that's an option anymore. I feel like such an idiot for coming here. How can I make the next twelve weeks bearable for both of us?*

Christine: *Okay, I'll ignore the obvious wisecrack about sex and try my hand at some serious advice. Reread that chapter in Jane's book about getting along with men in the workplace. It pains me to say this (since I'm still pissed about her using us), but I actually agree with her there. And remember that's ALL you have to do—get along with this guy. He's not the main reason you're there. Patching things up and having wild sex were just a potential side benefit. Your real goal is to get your work in a gallery. Don't lose sight of that. And don't forget that Amy and I think you're wonderful, no matter what some brooding male thinks.*

Maddy: *Thanks, C.*

Christine: *You're welcome. Now you go get some sleep. I'm off to save lives.*

Closing the laptop, Maddy glanced at the glossy self-help book sitting on the end table next to her. She picked it up with a sigh. If nothing else, maybe reading would help her sleep.

Chapter 5

If you want to succeed in the business world, learn to leave your emotions at home.

—*How to Have a Perfect Life*

After a restless night, Maddy rose early enough the following morning to watch the sunrise. She stood on her balcony sipping coffee as the light show played before her, starting with a blush and building to a blaze, like a symphony of color. Dawn had always been her favorite time of day, which was something she and Amy had in common.

More than once they'd watched the sunrise together. For Maddy, the start of a new day held infinite promise and excitement. For Amy, it was a time when yesterday's troubles still lay sleeping.

She remembered one morning when Amy confided in a hushed voice that when she was a child, she believed that if she was very quiet and still, the bad things of the world would forget to wake up. The theory had intrigued Maddy. Too bad she could never be quiet or still long enough to test it. Who could, though, when the world held so many wonderful things to do and see and experience?

This morning was a perfect example. How could

she hold back the thrill of watching a new day begin? The mountain air felt crisp as the smell of coffee rose from the warm cup cradled in her hands. The sun climbed higher, gilding the tops of the peaks while the valley remained cloaked in blue shadow.

The sight brought the never-ending urge to capture it with color on canvas.

If she was quiet and still, maybe the tension with Joe would forget to wake up, but then, maybe the opportunities that lay before her would do the same. Christine had been right about taking Jane's advice. She was here to go after something she'd always wanted. If that meant living with Joe's brooding animosity, she would do so calmly, professionally, and unemotionally.

With that in mind, she started to go back inside, but a movement along the road caught her eye. She peered into the long blue shadows that lay across the road and saw Joe running up the hill, charging toward her at a fast, steady clip. Her heart skipped a beat.

Was something wrong?

Her mind bounced from one possibility to the next: Mama was having a heart attack, one of the girls was hurt, there was a forest fire heading over the mountain and they needed to evacuate. Or some new anger had set Joe off and he wanted to yell at her.

She braced herself, preparing to dash for her robe before he made it up the stairs to pound on her door. Yet when he reached level ground, he veered toward the head of the trail back down the mountain, which would have him jogging right past her balcony. Jogging! She nearly smacked her forehead. He wasn't coming to see her. He was out for a morning jog.

And gifting her with an inspiring sight.

Her chilled skin heated as she watched the fluid grace of his powerful body. He wore a gray sweatshirt with the sleeves ripped off, showing off the sculpted muscles in his arms. She squinted at the armbands circling his big biceps. Were those tattoos? Her gaze drifted lower, past the shorts to his legs. The rhythm and strength behind each step made her heart pound in time.

Then she noticed the brace on his left knee, and how he moved with a slight limp. Was that where he'd been shot? In the knee? Thoughts of him in pain, of what he must have gone through, made her ache—until he moved past her and she blinked at the spectacular view he presented from behind.

The shorts fit just tight enough across his backside to let her see the flex of his gluts. She leaned forward for a better look.

Stop that! she scolded herself. *You're ogling the man's butt.*

Yes, but look at it! she argued back, bending out over the low wall. *It's gorgeous! He's gorgeous!*

He reached the top of the trail and started down, forcing her to bend farther out and over. She craned her neck, tipping her head.

A loud clanging exploded in the air. Crows flew up from the aspens on a rush of black wings. She jumped so hard she bobbled her coffee mug, then nearly tumbled off the balcony catching it. With her heart racing like a scared rabbit, she scurried back from the edge.

What the heck was that? She pressed the now-empty cup to her chest. Her gaze dropped to the camp in time to see Carol stepping away from the big bell mounted on a pole in the center of camp. Maddy let out an embarrassed laugh. Reveille. *Rise and shine, campers. Time to greet the day.*

Deciding to skip another stilted encounter with Joe, Maddy opted for a granola bar she'd unearthed from the depths of her purse. After polishing it off, she headed downstairs for her first good look at the arts and crafts room below her apartment. The door opened with a creak of hinges. Inside, fingers of sunlight strained past the solid wooden shutters that had been battened down through the winter. A flip of a switch next to the door brought a few bare bulbs to life overhead. Not a vast improvement for light, but enough to reveal several dust-covered folding tables and a stack of metal chairs in one corner.

She tried not to think of spiders and other crawly things.

Then her gaze fell on the floor-to-ceiling cabinets that filled the wall to her right. With her nose wrinkling at the grandmother's-attic scent, she headed in that direction and opened two of the doors with another squeak of hinges.

Her breath caught with wonder at the treasure trove that lay within. To someone else the contents might have looked like a jumbled mass of discarded, half-used craft supplies one step away from going in the trash, but to her . . . it was Aladdin's Cave.

She eagerly pushed up the sleeves of the paint-splattered men's shirt she'd tied at the waist over jeans so tattered they'd split at the knees. The shirt had been pilfered from Nigel's "pre-Maddy" wardrobe, since button-down whites had quickly been deemed too boring even for an accountant. They did, however, make perfect painting shirts, and reminded her of the early days of their marriage when he'd been healthy enough to have shoulders broader than her own.

An hour later, craft supplies lay strewn across the closest table like battle-scarred survivors of past summer camps. With a cleaning cloth in hand, she bumped her hips back and forth and belted out a rock song—not that she could carry a tune in a bucket, but she never minded torturing her own ears.

"Wow, you don't waste much time," Sandy said.

Maddy whirled with a gasp to find Sandy and Carol standing in the open doorway. She laughed in embarrassment to be caught singing and doing the cha-cha with a dust rag. "Sorry. You startled me."

"We missed you at breakfast," Carol said, moving forward.

Maddy shrugged. "I was eager to get going."

"Well, you keep on with organizing the supplies. We'll start on cobweb eradication," Carol directed. "First, though, we need more light."

Maddy returned to her task as the other two went outside to prop open all the shutters, which were hinged at the top. By the time they came back inside, sunlight and fresh air filled the room.

"Is it my imagination," Sandy said as she took up a broom, "or was Joe acting a little weird at breakfast?"

"A *little* weird?" Carol replied. Maddy went still at their words, her ears alert. At the sink, Carol filled a bucket with soapy water. "If you ask me, he's been acting a lot weird since the cookout last night. And this morning he was downright surly."

"Exactly. Last year he was a bit of a hardnose, but in a fun way. When we teased him about it, he teased us right back. This year . . ." Sandy shook her head. "It's like he's pissed about something but trying not to show it."

"All I can think is that last year he thought working here was a temporary thing while he was out on medical leave." Carol attacked the tables with a soapy rag. "Maybe he's depressed about leaving the Rangers."

"Well, he doesn't have to act like working here is a life sentence." Sandy swept dirt out the door.

"We should think of something to cheer him up."

"I know," Sandy said with a grin. "Tag football. Tonight after dinner. Maddy, are you in?"

"Me and sports?" She laughed, looking for a graceful way out of their plans. Asking Joe to play tag football with her would definitely not improve his mood. "I'm, um, afraid that's a really bad idea."

"C'mon," Sandy wheedled. "How bad can you be?"

"There aren't enough words in the English language to express how badly I stink at sports."

"Really?" Sandy lit up. "Cool. We'll put you on Joe's team. You can be his handicap."

"No, wait." Carol wrung out her rag. "Let's make it a real challenge. Joe likes a challenge, right?"

"What do you have in mind?" Sandy asked as she resumed sweeping.

"Joe and the geriatrics against the rest of us."

"The geriatrics?" Sandy laughed.

"You know." Carol moved to the second table. "Harold, Mama, and the kitchen staff."

"What about Maddy?"

"She goes on Joe's team. Not," Carol added quickly, "that you're a geriatric."

"No." Maddy tried to smile. "I'm just his handicap."

"We'll trounce 'em!" Sandy grinned.

"Which will at least make him laugh," Carol said.

Maddy started to protest, but their enthusiasm rolled right over her words. By the time the lunch bell clanged, she was torn between panic and depression.

Sandy and Carol headed for the door, still making plans. When Maddy just stood there, Carol turned back. "Aren't you coming?"

"Actually, I have a lot to do. Could you bring me something back?"

"Sure," Carol agreed, and the two started down the trail.

Maddy pinched her forehead. What was she going to do?

Chapter 6

The gift of good intentions is often a burden to the receiver.

—*How to Have a Perfect Life*

"Gee, that went over well," Sandy grumbled as the screen door to the dining hall snapped shut behind Joe's retreating back. Through the large screen windows along the side walls, he remained in plain view as he went down the wooden stairs and toward the riverbank.

Maddy struggled with guilt as she watched him go. Ignoring Joe's silent treatment for her own benefit was difficult enough, but how did she ignore the fact that her presence clearly upset him? She couldn't skip every meal. Yet, all through dinner he'd sat quietly eating while the coordinators and Mama Fraser made plans for the following day. They'd gathered at the long table closest to the massive rock fireplace, amid a sea of other tables that would soon ring with the voices of campers.

Their lively conversation had died, though, when the meal ended and Carol suggested a game of tag football. Joe had simply stood, claimed he had a canoe to fix in the boathouse, and left.

"You're right," Dana said to Carol. "Something's clearly bothering him."

"But what?" Bobbi asked. "I refuse to believe he's depressed at the thought of being the permanent director of Camp Enchantment. How on earth could anyone be depressed about that?" Her gaze took in the lodge-style dining hall with its high log ceiling. Indian designs had been carved into the columns and beams, and years' worth of wood smoke permeated the air. "Living here year-round has to be one of the best jobs ever!"

"To us, yes," Carol agreed with a nervous glance at Joe's mother. "But maybe not to him."

"Actually, Bobbi has a point." Sandy scooted forward, her blond hair in its usual perky ponytail. "It could be something else."

"Maybe it's personal, like trouble with his love life." Bobbi turned to Mama. "Is he dating anyone?"

"Get real." Sandy scoffed before Mama could answer. "Men who look like Joe don't have dating problems."

"You don't know that." Bobbi's face creased into a scowl. "Just because he looks like . . . you know—"

"A total babe?" Leah offered with a sigh.

"Guys, please." Carol blushed. "His mother is sitting right here."

"Don't let me stop you." Mama chuckled. "I'm rather proud that women think my son is sexy. Although Bobbi's right. Being a . . . what did you call him? A baby?"

"No." Leah laughed. "Not baby. A 'babe.' "

Maddy could have argued that after the way he'd acted toward her the last day and a half.

"Well," Mama said. "Being a 'babe' doesn't mean he's never had woman trouble."

"Are you saying that's it?" Sandy frowned. "Some woman messed him over?"

"Give us her name." Bobbi's face turned thunderous. "We'll take care of her."

"Now, girls." Mama held up a hand. "I simply said it was a possibility."

"In which case there's nothing we can do to cheer him up." Carol sighed in defeat.

"Wait. I know," Sandy piped up. "I could date him."

"In your dreams," Dana scoffed. "Face it, Sandy, he's known all of us since we were in training bras, which I think pretty much ruins our chances with him."

"Life is so unfair." Sandy pouted.

Carol looked at his mother. "I don't suppose you have any suggestions?"

"Oh, I never meddle in my son's affairs."

Maddy choked on her iced tea, then gasped for breath.

Dana pounded her between the shoulder blades. "You okay?"

"Fine," Maddy replied, wheezing. "I just . . . swallowed wrong."

"So, Madeline." Mama smiled sweetly. "I don't suppose you have an idea for how to cheer Joe up."

"Not a clue." Actually, she did. She could move back to Austin and get out of Joe's life. Unfortunately, quitting her job a week before camp started would leave him in the lurch—which was not a good way to make up for hurting him in the past.

As the others continued brainstorming about ways to make Joe happy, she took the opportunity to gather her dirty dishes. "If y'all will excuse me, I think I'll head back to the Craft Shack and do a little work."

"Okay." Carol gave her a distracted wave. "We'll see you in the morning."

What a mess, she thought as she slid her tray through the opening to the kitchen. She could hear the kitchen staff, local women from one of the nearby pueblos, talking in their native tongue. It made her feel even more of an outsider. Everyone seemed to belong here but her.

When she left the dining hall, she glanced up to where the Craft Shack sat on the rise waiting for her, then in the direction Joe had gone. Sooner or later, they needed to clear the air between them or they'd both be in for a miserable summer. Unfortunately, she couldn't follow him right then, because everyone would see.

What would the others think if they knew she was the woman behind Joe's dark mood? Visions of them ganging up against her made her cringe. At the first opportunity, she definitely needed to have a very calm, very adult conversation with Joe. Together maybe they could find a mature way to deal with each other.

Rock music blared from the boom box in the corner, warring with the scream of the electric sander in Joe's hand. The sound of wild guitar licks suited him just fine as he sweated over prepping one of the canoes for a fiberglass patch. Finally satisfied that the area was smooth, he flipped off the sander, leaving only the angry beat of the music as he straightened. Removing his protective eye gear, he mopped his forehead with his arm. Fiberglass dust gnawed at his skin, making him contemplate a dive into the river to rinse off. Maybe the exertion of a late-night swim would help him work off the temper simmering in his gut.

For now, he settled for pulling off his shirt and using the sink to wash up. He was drying his arms and chest with paper towels when his sixth sense raised the hair on the back of his neck. He whirled to find Maddy standing in the doorway against a backdrop of moon-washed night.

For an instant, neither of them moved. She stared at him with the wide-eyed shock of a virgin seeing a bare-chested man for the first time. Which might have made him laugh under different circumstances. Maddy was hardly a virgin, and he knew for a fact she'd seen a man's bare chest. His in particular.

Even so, her gaze traveled over his upper body, taking in the tattooed armbands circling both his biceps—which were new to her—then across his pecs and down his abs to the waistband of his shorts. His muscles bunched and fluttered as if she'd brushed him with her fingertips.

Swallowing a curse, he reached over and turned off the boom box, plunging the boathouse into silence. "You wanted something?"

Her gaze snapped back to his face and color flooded her cheeks. "I, um, I . . . saw the light on. From my balcony."

"And . . . ?"

"And, I thought maybe this would be a good time for us to . . ."

"What?" *Screw each other's brains out?* The idea of an angry fuck appealed to him even more than a swim as a way to work off his foul mood. Especially since she had caused both his mental and his physical frustration. The thought made his traitorous groin stir even more. Dammit.

"To talk," she finally managed to get out.

"I'm not sure that's a good idea." He turned his back and tossed the paper towels in the trash. To save himself the embarrassment of standing before her with the beginnings of a hard-on, he reached for his shirt and shook it out with a snap. "In fact, I think you being here right now is a very bad idea."

"Joe."

He sensed her moving toward him and sent her a dark scowl over one shoulder.

She stopped. "We need to work this out."

"No. We don't." He jerked his shirt on, which made his skin itch all over again, but at least it hung down far enough to grant him some privacy. Reaching for a bottle of acetone and a cloth, he crossed back to the boat and started cleaning the area to be patched. "You're only going to be here twelve weeks. I've survived unpleasant situations longer than that."

"So that's it?" Her voice went up in pitch. "We're going to act like the past doesn't exist?"

"That's pretty much the plan, yeah." He concentrated on wiping dust away from the crack in the hull, forcing an outward show of calm when everything inside him wanted to lash out at her with all the things he wished he'd said fifteen years ago. Or pull her into his arms and beg her to take him back. His teeth clenched against the second impulse. He'd actually done that the last time, begged her and humiliated himself. With tears, damn it. He'd literally cried in front of her. The memory made him physically ill.

"Joe . . ." She took another step, sending his nerves on high alert. "I know I hurt you, and I'm sorry for that to the depth of my heart—"

"Stop!" He straightened, but refused to step back even as panic pounded in his chest. She seemed determined to rip open this old wound and watch him bleed all over again. If she stood there much longer, he feared she'd succeed. "Let's skip the big apology scene. What happened between us is ancient history. This may come as a shock to you, Maddy, but I got over you years ago. I've been a little too busy living my life since then for it to even be a factor. So, in case you're worried, let me assure you, I'm perfectly capable of working with you through the summer—at the end of which you'll do me the favor of leaving. Now if you don't mind, I have work to do."

Maddy watched as he bent over the canoe again. As uncomfortable as she felt with his anger pushing her toward the door like a physical force, she couldn't leave. Somehow she had to find a way to get through to him. Unfortunately, with Joe, sometimes prodding his temper was the only way to get him talking. She took a deep breath and braced herself. "Actually, I do mind. Because I don't think you are over it. Otherwise you wouldn't be this upset."

"But then whether I'm upset or not really isn't your business, is it? You made your choice years ago, and it wasn't me." The planes of his face hardened as he went back to work.

She thought for a moment that he'd leave it at that, that she'd never get him to open up, but then he surprised her by straightening.

"Although, for the record," he said, "I never

asked you to choose. I never said you can marry me or you can be an artist but you can't do both."

"Joe . . ." She blinked, dumbfounded. "You asked me to marry you and move onto an Army base halfway across the country knowing I'd just won a full scholarship to UT."

"We could have worked around that, if I'd had some advance warning you even wanted to go to college. But no"—he tossed his rag onto the worktable—"I didn't have time to factor that in before I proposed, because you dropped that bombshell on me out of the blue."

Her own anger rose hot and fast. "Well, you didn't have to freak out about it."

A muscle in his jaw ticked as he spaced his words out. "I did not freak out."

"You panicked, then."

"I was angry." Echoes of the emotion flashed in his dark eyes. "Because you never shared any of that with me. I thought we were moving in one direction, only to learn you were making completely different plans *behind my back*."

"You make it sound like I was cheating on you."

"That's pretty much how it felt!" He took a deep, chest-expanding breath and let it out slowly in a visible effort to control his temper. "Maddy, we'd been dating seriously for nearly two years. Even when I went into the Army, we stayed together. We'd been talking about getting married and having kids for months."

"No, *you* talked about getting married and having kids. I just sat there trying not to freak."

"What are you saying?" Her words seemed to knock the wind out of him. "That the whole time we were together, you were never serious? Christ,

Maddy, what were you doing? Using me for sex?"
He laughed harshly. "I can't believe I said that.
But it's true, isn't it? Shit!"

"No—"

"You were getting off screwing the school troublemaker, running with the bad crowd, pretending to be
one of us and all the while you were top of the class."

"I wasn't 'top of the class.'"

"Damn near." He shook his head in disgust.
"Oh, the media had a field day with you. Daughter
of an underpaid cop, with a stay-at-home mother
and four siblings, has little chance of paying for
college until lo and behold, she wins a full scholarship from the Lone Star Arts League, has her work
displayed in the capitol, gets her picture taken with
the flippin' governor. And if all that isn't enough,
gee whiz, folks, she's not just pretty and talented,
she's running neck and neck on her GPA with the
saluta-fucking-torian!"

Maddy cringed, seeing in retrospect the shock he
must have felt at Airhead Maddy making good
grades.

"You never even told me you'd entered that
competition."

"Because . . . what if I hadn't won?"

"Do you think I would have cared?" Hurt replaced the anger in his eyes. "I was in love with
you. We were practically engaged. Don't you think
I had a right to know you were working your ass
off, trying to make something of your life? Don't
you think I would have been proud of you? Do you
know how insulting it was that you didn't share
your dreams with me?"

"You're right." Guilt swamped her. "I should
have told you. I was just . . . I was afraid."

"Afraid of what?"

"That you'd make fun of me." Tears prickled her eyes. "That you'd think I was putting on airs. Shooting too high. Too full of myself."

" 'Putting on airs'?" He frowned at her. "Jesus, that sounds like something your father would say."

"It is what he said. My whole life, every time I did something good, he . . . insulted me." She bit her lip as the memories swelled into her throat. "Do you know what he said when he found out I'd won a scholarship? I promise you it wasn't 'congratulations' or 'I'm proud' or even 'nice work.' He said, 'Well, la-di-da, look who thinks she's something special.' " The tears tumbled down her cheeks. She swiped at them angrily, hating that her father could still make her cry. "I wanted out of that house, and out of that crummy neighborhood so bad, I could feel it in my bones. And I was going to do it, no matter what it cost or what it took."

"Marrying me would have gotten you out of there pretty damn fast."

"That's not a good reason to make a lifetime commitment."

"You're right." He sighed. "You know, Maddy, a part of me understands. Your father was an insecure asshole who only felt good about himself when he was cutting other people down."

"He's still that way."

"But I'm not him," Joe said quietly. "How could you think I'd be anything but proud of what you were doing?"

"But that's just it. At the time, to my ears, you were starting to sound exactly like him."

"How?" He looked taken aback.

"Being all gung ho military." She held up her

hand when he started to interrupt. "Until I grew up and got out on my own, I honestly thought most cops, and therefore most men in uniform, were like my father. I've since learned that's not true. A good many of them are like the Colonel. They have conviction, integrity, and most of all, compassion. I should have seen that then. You weren't turning into my dad. You were turning into yours. And I can't think of a better man to emulate."

She took a step toward him, aching for him to understand. "Unfortunately, I didn't see that. I was too young. Joe, I was seventeen when you asked me to marry you."

"I know." Embarrassment flickered in his eyes before he looked away. "I actually didn't mean to ask you for at least another year. But then you told me you were going to UT and the thought of you running around campus with all those college boys . . ."

"Made you panic."

"If you call going out and buying the biggest engagement ring I could afford panicking, then yeah, I guess I did." His mouth tightened. "I knew we couldn't marry right away, but I wanted to be sure every guy who saw you saw that rock on your finger and knew you were taken."

She actually smiled a bit at that. It was so like Joe to stake out his territory. As a foster child, he'd learned to travel light, but what was his, he held on to with both hands, and he would battle any kid who touched it. The word "mine" was used sparingly, but when he said it he meant it.

He heaved a sigh. "I admit, I didn't like the idea of you going to UT, but I wasn't trying to hold you back. I was afraid of losing you to some frat boy.

But"—his gaze bored into her—"I never would have stood in the way of your dreams, if you'd only shared them with me."

"The problem is . . . I wouldn't have believed you. I wouldn't have been able to. Not with you standing there wearing a uniform, with your hair buzzed short, spouting macho military jargon." She took another step, laid her hand on the canoe that stood between them. "When you proposed, my whole life flashed before my eyes. Only it wasn't my life. It was my mother's. I didn't want to wind up like her, bowing to a man's wishes, cooking, cleaning, raising kids with little or no help, while all my dreams were trampled over. I didn't know marriage could be a partnership, not a life sentence where the woman's identity is ripped away the first day."

"Fire-breathing Maddy trampled over?" He shook his head. "I can't imagine you ever winding up like that."

"Looking back, I can't either. In fact, the opposite would have happened, and that wouldn't have been fair to you. Back then, I was *too* adamant about my independence, to the point of selfishness. The past eight years have taught me that sometimes you have to set yourself aside and put your own dreams on hold. But at least I did it for love, not lack of a backbone like my mom."

"The last eight years?" Confusion creased his brow.

She hesitated, not sure how he'd react to this topic. "My husband died of cancer after a long illness."

"I'm sorry." The honest sorrow in his eyes added weight to the words.

"I am too." Sympathy always brought the grief welling back to the surface. This time when the tears came, she let them. "I loved him very much, and I miss him every day."

"Oh God, Maddy—" He looked ready to step around the canoe and come to her.

"I'm fine. Really." She raised a hand, knowing she would lose all composure if he touched her now. "It's been hard, but it's time for me to get on with my life, get back to the dreams I set aside. Which is why I came here."

His frown deepened. "To work at a summer camp?"

"No, to Santa Fe. For my artwork." She smiled sadly. "You know what the big irony of my life is? I married a man who was the polar opposite of my father. Intelligent, successful, self-assured, and one of the kindest, sweetest men I have ever met."

"He sounds like a geek."

"He was!" She laughed. "The poor guy actually wore pocket protectors when we first started dating. He was also color blind and had no taste in art, which is how we met. His office manager kept badgering him to decorate. So Nigel—"

"Nigel?" Joe's brows shot up. "You married a man named Nigel?"

"I did." She felt her smile spread across her whole face. "He was a tall, lanky stereotype of an accountant, and the day he walked into the gallery where I worked, desperate for art and hilariously clueless, I took one look at him and thought 'Oh, honey, you so need me. For a lot more than picking out your art.' "

Sadness and envy filled Joe's eyes. "You must have made his life."

"I—" His words touched her so deep she didn't know what to say. "Thank you. I like to think I did. We were very happy together. The irony, though, is I married him thinking here was a man who will never ask me to ignore my needs to take care of him. And then he got cancer and that's exactly what I had to do."

"You're saying you stopped painting?"

"I didn't have the energy or the heart to paint. Not often, anyway."

"You must have resented him for that."

"Not at all. No."

"No?" he demanded. "What do you mean, no?"

She frowned in confusion at his outraged expression. "There were lots of days when I resented life, but never Nigel. I went through the full range of anger and grief, of railing at God, and finally coming to terms with the unfairness of life and injustice of death."

"Yeah, I know all about those last two."

"After serving in the Middle East, I imagine you do."

He studied her. "So you're telling me you gave up your chance to become an artist for this man and you have no regrets?"

"Regrets? Now those I have plenty, but marrying Nigel isn't one of them. I think we were meant to have that time together. Nigel helped me grow up, and I think I brought a lot of joy into his short life." She cocked her head, studying the man before her, this grown-up version of the boy she'd loved. "What about you? Regrets?"

"None I care to dwell on."

"There's a difference between dwelling on and dealing with. So, the question is"—she took a deep breath—"where do we go from here? Can you and I put the past behind us and be friends?"

"Maddy . . ." A humorless laugh escaped. "A five-minute conversation doesn't make fifteen years of anger go away. Especially after learning that you weren't willing to give up a single thing for me, but you gave up years of your life and the thing I thought mattered to you most for another man."

Her back stiffened. "I'd like you to remember, I was seventeen when I broke up with you—and twenty-four and married when my husband was diagnosed with cancer. What was I going to do? Divorce him?"

"No." Anger glinted in his eyes. "But it still pisses me off."

"I'm sorry you feel that way. I can't change the past. What concerns me now is the present. Can we or can we not work together without this bitterness constantly between us?"

"You're asking a lot."

"I know that." She wanted to shake him, since she was doing this as much for his sake as her own.

He finally sighed. "The most I can promise is to continue being civil."

"You call that civil?" She gestured toward the camp. "You're treating me like a total stranger whose presence you can barely tolerate."

"You are a total stranger! The Maddy I knew would never have put her art aside for anyone. I still can't believe you did that."

She shook her head. Reasoning with Joe was like reasoning with a rock. "If it helps, that's why I'm here. To find out once and for all if I'm good enough to make it as an artist."

"What do you mean 'if you're good enough'?"

His temper built again, but oddly, it seemed to be on her behalf. "You were good enough back in high school to win that scholarship."

"That doesn't mean I'm good enough to get a gallery to represent me."

"What kind of bullshit is this? Of course you're good enough." He paced away, confusing her with his agitation. Her art was the reason she'd tossed out for rejecting him. Why would he defend it? Turning, he came back. Planting both hands on the canoe, he leaned toward her. "You want to reach a truce with me? Fine! Here's my conditions. If you're going to put me through a whole summer of hell, you damn well better make it pay off."

"What are you saying?"

"I want you to do what you said you were going to do. Become a professional artist. That's why you jilted me, right? Well, if you want me to stop being pissed, you damn well better do it."

"Joe . . ." She blinked in surprise. "It's not that easy—"

"I assume you brought a portfolio or something."

"I did, but—"

"Good." He straightened. "I have to go into town tomorrow to pick up paint for this canoe. You're going with me so I can take you to some galleries."

"Joe, I have work to do tomorrow." And riding around with him was the last thing she wanted to do. "I'm supposed to help Sandy clean out the prop room."

"Tough. She'll have to manage without you, and you'll work twice as hard the next day to make it up to her."

"But—"

"I'm not kidding." He leaned forward again. "If you're staying, you are not going to play around at this. You're going to do it."

"I see." Her own jaw tightened. "Is this where I snap to attention and say 'Yes, sir!' "

"Damn straight. I'll pick you up at the Craft Shack at oh eight hundred."

Chapter 7

Sometimes in life, we all need a little nudge to get us moving in the right direction. If we ignore it, we're likely to get a shove.

—How to Have a Perfect Life

Joe felt a little shell-shocked the following morning as he drove his truck toward the Craft Shack. How had the conversation gone from Maddy telling him about her perfect late husband, the Geek, to him offering to take her into town? Offering? Hell, he'd *told* her he was taking her, which was nuts in the first place and even crazier because he'd gotten away with it. The Maddy he knew hated being ordered around.

Instead of getting her back up, though, she'd agreed.

Or maybe she'd been too tired to argue anymore. He'd watched her run the full gamut of emotions last night, which, admittedly had weakened his defenses. When he got to the Craft Shack, she would probably march out to the truck and tell him what he could do with his offer to help.

That would be for the best, he assured himself. Far wiser than spending the day with her, having her near enough to touch, close enough to smell. Listening to her talk about her husband, the Geek. Joe tightened his grip on the steering wheel as he pulled to a stop. The thought of her giving all that joy and life to another man for years when he could have had her for himself made him want to punch something.

He settled for hitting the horn hard enough to produce a satisfying blast of noise. A flock of crows flew up from the trees, their black bodies in sharp contrast to the vivid blue sky. The day promised to be sunny, with only a few white clouds peeking over the tops of the mountains—although weather in the mountains could change in a heartbeat.

As he settled in to wait, he accepted that what drove him crazier than learning she'd given her heart and her body to another man was finding out she'd set her art aside to do it. The emotion that flared inside him at that wasn't jealousy but outrage.

How dare she set her art aside for anyone?

He might not have spent the last fifteen years with Maddy in the forefront of his mind, pining for her like some pathetic sap, but there had been times when the image of her had sprung full blown into his thoughts: when he'd been deployed in the Middle East and he'd been dirty, tired, and frustrated, when a member of his battalion was blown to bits, when locals hurled insults along with bullets. At times like those, he'd wondered why the hell he was doing it. Why was he risking his life? During those moments, most men thought of family, of their wives and children, their sweethearts or their parents—someone they loved more than they feared death.

For Joe it was Maddy—not her the person, but

what she represented in his mind. A free spirit with enough heart and passion to claw her way out of a mediocre existence to achieve her fullest potential. Wasn't that the American dream? The very essence of what men and women were giving their lives to protect?

Maddy's decision to choose an art career over him may have ripped him apart, but he'd never doubted that she would make it. So when he'd needed something to cling to, he'd pictured her in his mind, drinking champagne at some gallery show with patrons raving over her work. The frustration and bone-numbing fatigue of an operation would fade, leaving room for conviction to return. *That* became the reason he risked his life. Not just for the lofty concepts of freedom, democracy, and justice—although those were powerful ideals when a man was surrounded by oppression and fear— but that image of Maddy the successful artist became his personal talisman, something to conjure up when he needed to draw on his last ounce of strength.

He'd risked his life, sweated blood on foreign soil, so people like Maddy could live free and go after their dreams.

And last night she tells him she didn't do it?

That was not acceptable.

By God, if she came down those stairs and refused to let him help her, she'd have a fight on her hands. She was going to get her art career if he personally had to take her work around to every gallery in Santa Fe.

Just then, she appeared on the landing—and Maddy the ideal vanished in the face of Maddy the flesh-and-blood woman.

Good God, she dazzled him every time he looked at her.

Get over it, Joe, he ordered himself. *Don't be a sap. Ancient history, remember?*

As she skipped down the stairs, he forced himself to look away, with a stern reminder that he was on a mission that had nothing to do with getting close to Maddy on a personal level. Where this woman was concerned he needed a T-shirt that said BEEN THERE, DONE THAT, HAVE THE SCARS TO PROVE IT.

Today was about setting the world back on its proper axis. Period. And if that meant ceasing hostilities, he'd do it. He'd be downright pleasant, if he had to.

He heard the truck door open. "Okay," she said, sounding breathless. "How do I look?"

Even though he braced for it, a bolt of need punched through his defenses when he turned and saw her. She stood back a few paces so he could see all of her.

"Is this all right? I was going for artsy but professional." Holding a leather portfolio out to one side, her purse to the other, she twirled about, showing off an outfit that was pure Maddy: a crocheted sweater that was more air than yarn, belted at the hips over a sage-colored tank dress that fell to her ankles.

His body tightened as his gaze ran the full length of her. "I think the boots might be a bit much for summer."

"Oh, no, they're just ankle boots." Hitching up the skirt, she plopped her foot on the floorboard so he could see the 1890s brown-leather boots, an inch of frilly sock, and a lot of creamy bare leg.

"I see." He cleared his throat.

"They're fine?"

"More than."

"What about the hair?" She cocked her head back and forth. With Maddy, the hair was always the crowning touch, but today it was more glorious than ever, a full mane of wild red hair around her heart-shaped face. "Too much? Too big? Too messy?"

"I don't think anyone will doubt you're from Texas, if that's what you're asking."

"I knew it. Too big. I should pull it back. I have a scarf in here somewhere." She started digging through her massive purse.

"Maddy, no, it's fine."

"Really?"

"Really."

"Okay, then." She released a huff of air. "I'm a little nervous."

"I never would have guessed." As he waited for her to get settled, he wondered which made her more nervous, the thought of showing her portfolio, or of spending the next half hour trapped alone with him in his truck. Personally, he wasn't too thrilled with the second idea either. They'd both just have to make the best of it. "Seat belt."

"Oh. Yeah. Right." She fastened the belt, then shifted toward him as he put the truck in gear and drove down the mountain. "Okay, last question, so be honest. Did I manage to hide the circles under my eyes? Or can you tell I got zero sleep last night?"

"You didn't sleep well?" He felt a surprising stab of concern, remembering how emotionally wrung out she'd looked after their discussion.

"It's a little hard to sleep when your head doesn't

even hit the pillow until four a.m." She gave a breathy laugh. "My mind's been busting with images the past few days, but I haven't had a chance to set up an easel and break out the paints. That's the problem with oils. You can't just pick them up and set them down on a lark. Then yesterday, when I was cleaning out the supply cabinets in the craft room, I ran across a bunch of oil pastels. How perfect is that?"

"I wouldn't know." He gave her a questioning look, which was all she needed to launch into one of the chatty monologues that had always amused him. This one was about the history of oil pastels, and how artists like Monet and Renoir had used them as a means to make color sketches while hanging out in Paris cafés.

The neutral topic also provided a safe zone for them to operate. He welcomed it with the hope that the day wouldn't be too uncomfortable after all.

"Is that what you were doing last night?" he asked when her monologue ran out. "Preliminary studies?"

"About a dozen of them. Heavens, it was so liberating. I haven't played with oil pastels in years. I'd forgotten how fun they can be. They're so fast, you don't have time to think about the rules. You just let the image spill out of you onto the paper with quick strokes and squiggles. I'll rein all that in when I do the real paintings, but it was a blast to just let it rip."

"Rules?" He raised a brow. "Since when did you care about the rules?"

"You get enough technique hammered into you

by art profs, some of it's bound to stick." She turned toward him. "Okay, here's the deal."

"The deal?"

"About today. I brought photographs of my work, just in case, but today is mostly for me to get a feel for the various galleries If I'm not comfortable talking to any of the owners yet, I'll wait until I'm ready."

"We'll see."

"I'm serious, Joe. I worked in one of Austin's best galleries, so I know how to play this game. You don't blow your chance with a sloppy first impression. Plus I really want to turn some of the sketches from last night into paintings before I make my move. The images are good. They have an energy my work hasn't had in a long time."

"I look forward to seeing them," he said as he drove.

"Then we're agreed?"

"Hmm."

"Great." She let out a sigh of relief, then turned to take in the scenery. By the time they arrived in town, they'd established an amiable note for the day, even if it ran only skin deep.

Santa Fe. The artist's Mecca. Fabulous shops, trendy restaurants, historic buildings—and traffic jams! Maddy felt like a kid with her face pressed to the window as Joe maneuvered the black pickup through narrow streets originally designed for men on horseback. Finally, they inched their way onto the famous Canyon Road, where finding a parking place was as much a battle of wills as a game of chicken.

After Joe snagged a spot, Maddy stepped out of the truck and took a deep breath as she looked around. Adobe-houses-turned-art-galleries stood shoulder to shoulder as far as she could see in both directions. Tall spikes of flowers bloomed in tiny rock gardens, adding splashes of color along with turquoise window and door frames, and artwork displayed on porches. Over the tops of the flat roofs, the scalloped edge of mountains gave way to towering white clouds that dwarfed the land beneath them.

Everywhere she looked, her mind gathered images to be stored and painted later. Beyond the visible, though, was a feeling, a mystical call of the land that made her long to capture it with imagery.

Joe joined her on the narrow gravel path beside the line of parked cars. Wearing jeans, a denim shirt, and cowboy boots, he fit right in—and looked sexy as all get-out. "Where would you like to begin?"

"I don't have a clue." She laughed. "Any suggestions?"

"That depends. How would you describe your current work?"

"Impressionistic landscapes, garden scenes, a few still lifes." A steady stream of art lovers moved past them, stepping in and out of open doorways. "I don't suppose you know the galleries well enough to have a favorite."

He chuckled. "I have about ten."

"Really?" That surprised her.

"When Mom moved back to New Mexico, I started collecting Native American crafts, which spilled into art. Around here, it's an easy addiction to slip into."

"I can see that it would be." She nodded. "Sounds like you'll make a perfect guide. So, lead on. I place myself in your hands."

"Very well. Let's start with this place up on the right."

Joining the flow of foot traffic, they made their way up the street and through the first of many doors. By the time they'd gone through the tenth gallery, she was on sensory overload. And more intimidated than ever. The art ranged from pastoral to whimsical to avant-garde, some of it bizarre, but all of it top-notch quality.

"I know the owner here," Joe said as they entered yet another gallery. The place was a maze of rooms with thick white walls, wood floors that creaked, and track lights aimed at several large canvases. Somewhere in the distance she heard drum and flute music playing and a woman talking on a phone. Piñon incense drifted on the air.

Joe studied her. "Would you like me to introduce you?"

"No!" she said too quickly, then released a breath to relax. "No. I just want to look."

"Are you sure?"

"No," she said weakly. "To be honest, I think I've seen all I can absorb for one day. Can we take a break?" She saw an argument spring into his eyes. "Please. My head is spinning, and my feet are killing me."

His jaw worked for a moment before he sighed. "Fine. We'll have lunch, then see how you feel."

"Thank you." She sagged in gratitude.

If there was one thing Joe didn't miss about the Army, it was the food. Living in Santa Fe, with its

Mexican food and haute cuisine, was a welcome
break from MREs, Meals Ready to Eat. Since
Maddy looked in need of a complete change of
scenery, he battled traffic into the heart of Old
Town to take her to the Ore House, one of his
favorite restaurants.

"This is fabulous," she said as they stepped onto
the second-story balcony that overlooked the plaza.

"I thought you'd like it," he replied as the host-
ess laid two menus on a table against the rail.

The server came as soon as they'd settled. "Can
I get you something to drink?"

Joe ordered a locally made pale ale, while Maddy
asked for a glass of white wine. Sitting back, he
watched Maddy scan the menu he knew by heart.
Midday sun slanted in, turning her hair to orange
fire, all the more striking with the row of red chile
ristras hanging behind her. Their truce had been
going surprisingly well. He'd even managed to go
for several minutes at a stretch without old anger
and renewed attraction playing tug-of-war in his
gut.

Although that had been easier to do while wan-
dering the galleries. Sitting on a crowded balcony
with nothing but a very small table between them,
he felt a low hum of awareness start deep in his
belly.

"So," he said when she finally closed her menu,
"what do you think of Santa Fe?"

She laughed, tipping her head so the sun shone
off her eyes. "A part of me thinks I've died and
gone to heaven."

"And the other part?" He shifted sideways, creating more space between her legs and his.

"Is a little overwhelmed." She turned as well, so

they both looked out over the plaza. A child threw a ball for a Jack Russell terrier near the Civil War monument. Vendors from the various pueblos were out in force, selling their jewelry on blankets in front of the Palace of the Governors. The bell at St. Francis Cathedral proclaimed the hour of one o'clock. "I never should have promised Christine and Amy I'd get a piece of my work in a gallery out here. I should have started off at one of the galleries back home and worked my way up to the big time."

"Christine and Amy?"

"My two closest friends in all the world. You'd like them." She wrinkled her nose in a playful manner. "They're as pushy as you about wanting me to put my neck on the chopping block."

"Maddy"—he shook his head—"I refuse to believe you're not good enough. You were fantastic back in high school, and you've had fifteen years to mature in your work."

She sighed, and some of the tension he'd seen earlier returned. "Do you think we could talk about something else over lunch, so that I have some hope of actually eating?"

"All right. What would you like to talk about?"

"You."

He laughed dryly as he toyed with the salt and pepper shakers. "A boring subject, I promise you."

"Then bore me." She shifted back to face him, folding her arms on the table as she leaned forward. "Please! It'll get my mind off my nervous stomach."

He stared at her eager face and felt a tug of need so strong it wiped all thought from his brain.

Fortunately, the server arrived and plopped their

drinks down on the table. "Here you go. Are you ready to order?"

Joe gave himself a mental shake. "I'll have the Hatch green chile cheeseburger."

"And you?" The woman turned to Maddy.

"Oh. Let's see." Straightening, she opened the menu again. "It all sounds so good." Scanning the options, she struggled to make a decision. "Okay, I'll have the soft chicken tacos. Can I have extra cheese? And the jalapeños on the side?"

"Absolutely." The woman snapped her order book closed and moved away.

"Okay, where were we?" Maddy turned back to Joe, determined to keep the pleasant mood going. "Oh yes, talking about you. Tell me about running the camp. Do you enjoy it?"

"Yes and no." His gaze dropped to the finger she was running around the rim of her wineglass before he looked away and took a swallow of ale. "No, because I miss the hell out of being in the Rangers. Yes, because . . ." He hesitated as color climbed up his neck. "This is going to sound hokey."

"What?" She leaned forward, remembering a time when he'd shared things with her that he would never share with others. She realized she missed that. He'd always had so many interesting facets once he opened up. "Come on," she coaxed. "Tell me."

He straightened the linen-wrapped silverware and turned the beer bottle so the label faced him. "I like the kids. They give me hope."

"Hope?"

"For the world. That's hard to hang on to sometimes with so much hatred out there. God, the things I've seen . . ." He shook his head. "I miss being a part of the action. Not just the adrenaline rush of being on a mission, but feeling like I'm making a difference, like I'm doing something to make the world safer." He gazed back out at the plaza, watched the little girl playing fetch with her dog. "What I don't miss is looking into old eyes filled with mistrust in the faces of children. Or worse, the kids who are like children the world over, young, innocent, and happy one minute, maimed bodies the next. Jesus." He scrubbed his hands over his face, shuddered, then rolled his shoulders. "Sorry."

"It's okay." Maddy laid a hand on the table in front of him, wanting to touch, but not sure it would be welcome. "You wouldn't be human if that didn't affect you."

"Yeah." He tried to laugh, but the sound held no humor. "I guess it's taken me a while to decompress. Actually, strike that. I'm not sure a man ever decompresses from that. Or if he should. But when the camp fills up with children, most of who have never been touched by all life's ugliness . . . it feels good. Really good."

He smiled that crooked smile of his. And when his dark eyes met hers, Maddy swore she heard a thud as her heart hit the floor. Just like that, she fell smack-dab in love with Joe Fraser all over again.

Startled, she sat back, her pulse racing. No, it couldn't be love. Love happened slowly, grew over time, and endured. It wasn't like a light switch that you turned on, then off, then back on again. Did that mean she'd never fallen out of love with him? Was this an echo from the past, or something entirely new?

She blinked at him, remembering the intensity of what he'd once felt for her. He'd actually overwhelmed her with it at times. Did a part of him still feel traces of that for the impulsive girl she'd once been?

Fortunately, their lunch arrived, saving her from saying something stupid.

"So . . . then . . ." Her hand trembled slightly as she spooned salsa into the tacos. "You're happy running the camp?"

He shook salt and pepper over a mammoth burger heaped with chopped green chiles. "During the summer, when the kids are there, yeah. The rest of the year it drives me crazy. There just isn't enough to do, and man does not live on skiing alone."

"You couldn't use the camp for other things the rest of the year?" She took a bite of taco and nearly moaned with pleasure at the sharp, spicy flavors.

"Actually, I've been toying with an idea."

"Oh?" She waited while he chewed and thought even that was sexy—all those strong muscles in his face working together.

"Okay." He swallowed. "You can't mention this to my mom."

"Is it something she wouldn't like?"

"The contrary, actually, which is why I want to think about it before I mention it to her. I want to be sure she's physically up to having the camp open year-round. I mean, God, the woman's *old*. Which shocked the heck out of me when I came here to recuperate. When did that happen? I've seen her on a regular basis over the years. How could I not notice?"

"You were busy chasing bad guys?"

"That's no excuse," he insisted. "Do you know she was one step away from having to sell the camp when I agreed to take over as director? She loves that camp. Kids are her life! If I hadn't gotten shot in the knee, she'd have lost everything. The camp, her home, and a good chunk of her heart. After everything she's done for me, I absolutely will not let that happen."

Maddy's heart took another hard bounce on the floor. "So"—she cleared her throat—"what's your idea?"

A smile teased up one corner of his mouth. "A boot camp for civilians."

"A what?"

He popped a tortilla chip into his mouth as the smile reached his eyes. "There's already a few of them up and running. Former special-ops guys giving civilians a taste of the physical training we go through. Some of the camps are geared toward physical fitness for adrenaline junkies. Others offer group programs to corporations for employee team building. That's where the Rangers excel, working as a team. I think the concept of 'no man left behind' is sadly lacking in corporate America."

"I think you're right. And the idea sounds great."

"So far that's all it is, an idea in my head, but I'd like to pitch it to Socrates."

"Who?"

"Corporal Derrick Harrelson, nicknamed Socrates because he's always spouting philosophy."

"Did you have a nickname?"

"We all did."

"So, what was yours?"

"Promise not to laugh?"

"No, but tell me anyway."

"Scout."

She frowned. "Because you're part Indian?"

"No." His cheeks darkened. "After the mess I got into over the stolen car, I went a little overboard for a while, determined that would be the last time I ever disappointed the Colonel. So every time some of the guys tried to stir up trouble off base I served as the voice of reason. Or, in their words, the wet blanket. Finally one of the guys told me to quit being such a damn Eagle Scout, and it stuck."

"Eagle Scout? You?" She snorted with laughter.

"Yeah, that was pretty much my reaction. I did eventually loosen up a bit, but by then it was too late."

"So tell me about Socrates." She dipped a chip in the salsa.

"We served in the same battalion and got pretty tight. Now that I'm out, he's making noises about not reupping. His current hitch is almost over, so I thought maybe the boot camp was something we could do together. I need to think it through, though. Be sure before I ask Mom to put up with a camp full of people year-round."

"It sounds exciting." She found his enthusiasm contagious. "If you decide to do it, let me know. I'd be happy to help design your promotional material."

"What?"

"I took a few graphic art classes at UT. I'm really good at layout and design. I'd be happy to help."

"Ah . . ." He raised a brow but said nothing else.

She felt the instant shift in mood, like a wall had dropped between them, and realized she'd taken their truce one step too far. "I mean . . ."—she back pedaled quickly—"if you want any help."

He polished off the last of his burger. "I'll think about it."

She tried not to show her disappointment, but her lunch had lost some of its flavor. Pushing the plate away, she struggled for a way to get things back on a friendly footing. When the check arrived, she reached for it. "Why don't I get lunch as a thank-you for showing me around?"

"Absolutely not." Joe's hand came down over hers. Heat raced up her arm at the contact. He had large, powerful hands, and his fingers easily circled her wrist. "Here's the deal. I'm getting lunch, but there's a condition. Before we go back to the camp, you will show your portfolio to one gallery."

"I'd prefer to treat you to lunch." She tried to tug the check out from under his hand.

His grip tightened painlessly, just enough to make her aware of the strength he possessed. He leaned close, his gaze intent and his voice smooth as tempered steel. "This is not negotiable."

"Joe . . ." She laughed nervously, her whole body tingling at his nearness. "Come on. Be reasonable. I'll show my work when I'm ready."

"Maybe I don't feel like being reasonable."

"I told you—"

"I know. But I have just the place in mind." He plucked the check out from under their joined hands and reached for his wallet. "It's small, unassuming, and well outside of Old Town. If they reject you, no biggie. At least you will have gotten your feet wet."

"That's all I have to do?" She nearly protested the loss of contact. "Get my feet wet?"

"That's it."

"What if they like my work? I don't want to sign an exclusive if the place is a dump."

"It's not a dump. It's perfectly respectable." He handed some money and the check to the server. "It's just not as highbrow as the galleries on Canyon Road. Besides, you don't have to say yes to the first offer you get, but having one gallery interested will give you more clout with the others."

"True." She took a deep breath. "Okay. You're on."

Chapter 8

The only way to conquer fear is to face it.
        —*How to Have a Perfect Life*

Outside of Old Town, Santa Fe resembled any other growing town across America. The strip centers offered the same hardware stores, discount chains, mega bookstores, and fast-food restaurants. Except that here all the buildings maintained the "Santa Fe look" to meet building codes, and the urban sprawl ranged between pine-covered mountains and sage-dotted desert.

Maddy frowned as Joe turned off one of the main roads into a light industrial area. Even here, the metal buildings had adobe facades. Her frown deepened when he pulled into the parking lot of what looked like a warehouse. "Is this it?"

"Yep," he confirmed, parking in the shade of a tree in the far corner of the crowded lot.

Maddy twisted in her seat to study the place. "I thought you said it was small."

"The gallery only takes up a small portion in the front."

"What's in the back?"

"Hmm . . . frame shop and storage?"

Something in his voice made her study him. He wore a highly suspect look of innocence. "This is a reputable gallery, right?"

"Absolutely."

She looked back at the building. The sign above the covered porch read IMAGES OF THE WEST. That tickled some memory, but she dismissed it. With a name that generic, of course it seemed familiar.

"You ready to go in?" Joe asked.

She pulled the portfolio into her lap but made no move to open the door. "Give me a minute to think of what I'll say."

"What's to think about? We'll go in, I'll introduce you to the owner, then you'll take it from there."

"You're right. I don't know why I'm so nervous." She took a deep breath and let it out slowly. "I've been on the other end of this enough times to know what to do. Artists came into the gallery where I worked all the time. Even though we rejected most of them, we were never mean about it."

"Exactly." He reached for the door handle. "Now, let's go in."

"In a minute."

"Maddy . . ." He sighed impatiently.

"Don't get all exasperated. I know it won't kill me to have them reject my work, but . . ."

"I know. This is important to you. I understand. Now, let's go."

"It's hugely important." She laid her hand on his bare arm before he could open the door, then pulled it back when he turned. "I don't want to mess up my chances by jumping the gun. My portfolio is okay, but if I wait just a bit, it will be even stronger."

"All right, here's my take." He settled back against the seat. "You're projecting too far ahead, not concentrating on the task right in front of you. A solid long-term strategy is made up of steps. Today's step is to get past your first jump."

"First jump?" She frowned.

"As in parachuting. The first jump is the scariest. You scream—if not aloud at least inside your head—the whole way down. After that"— he flashed a devilish grin—"the fear becomes part of the thrill."

"You are so warped." She laughed, which helped to loosen the knot in her stomach. "So, was that the scariest thing you did in training? Parachuting?"

He narrowed his eyes. "Are you stalling?"

"Maybe." She grinned unabashedly. "So was it?"

He relented with a sigh. "No. Jumping out of a plane from twelve thousand feet was nothing compared to jumping off the high diving board into the deep end of a swimming pool."

"Why was that scary? You're a good swimmer."

"Not when I'm wearing combat boots, fifty pounds of gear, and I'm carrying a rifle. Add to that the little fact that I was winded from all the P.T. they'd just put us through and blindfolded so I couldn't tell which way was up or down."

"Oh my God!" Her eyes went wide. "Why on earth would they do that to you? And why would you let them?"

"Because I wanted to be a Ranger badly enough to do damn near anything." Resolve sharpened the planes of his face. "To make it past each cut, we had to prove we were tough enough."

"And that's what they made you do to prove you were physically tough enough?"

"Not just physically, but mentally. The instructors came up with a lot of drills to prove we wouldn't panic under pressure and start acting on our own instincts rather than following orders. For me those tests were the hardest because I've never been real big on trusting other people."

"Nah." She feigned shock. "Surely you jest."

" 'Fraid not," he confessed, straight-faced. "In fact, they actually put that in my psychological evaluation file. 'Has difficulty trusting his teammates.' "

She laughed. "That sounds like something a teacher would send home in a note to your parents. 'Little Joey doesn't play well with the other boys.' "

A corner of his mouth kicked up. "No, I only play well with the girls."

She gave him a look. "Go on with your story. I take it you passed all their diabolical tests, since you made it into the Rangers."

"I did." Pride joined the resolve. "I made it because I learned to suppress fear, to follow orders, and to focus on the task at hand."

She glanced back at the building and made a face. "I suppose the moral of the story is that I should trust you and follow your orders."

"You follow orders?" He put his fingertips to his chest. "Please, let's try to keep our objective obtainable here. Besides, there is no moral to the story. There's only the question: How bad do you want it?"

Determination filled her. "Bad."

"Okay, then." His voice turned tough and ready for action. "Let's go do it!"

"Right." She nodded and climbed out of the

truck, then fell into step beside him as they crossed the parking lot. "What's the owner's name?"

"Sylvia. She knows the art business inside and out, and she has a formidable reputation."

"Gee, thanks for the effort to keep me calm."

"No, she's nice. That's why I picked this place for your first jump."

"Translation: She'll be gentle when she rips out my heart and stomps on it."

"What I meant was if she offers you advice, take it."

"Got it." They stepped onto a covered porch and Maddy reached for the door.

"Wait." Joe closed his hand over her forearm. "I just realized there is a moral to the story about the diving board."

"Oh?"

"The last thing the instructors said before they sent me charging down the board for the big drop was, 'Oh yeah, extend your arms.' "

She gave him a questioning look.

"I was holding a rifle with both hands right in front of my chest. If I hadn't thrust my arms out in front of me, I would have broken my jaw the instant gravity took over. So the moral of the story is, don't hold anything too close. Keep things at arm's length, or you'll get busted in the chops."

An incredulous laugh escaped her. "You mean, want it badly enough to do anything to get it, but don't care enough to be hurt when it doesn't happen?"

"Something like that."

"That's stupid."

"But it works."

"No it doesn't. You macho men just like to pretend it doesn't hurt when you take it on the chin. I, on the other hand, have no problem screaming 'ouch' and bawling my eyes out."

"Whatever works for you." He opened the door for her and a bell jingled from the handle.

Still shaking her head, Maddy passed into a large room that had been partitioned off to create small alcoves with lots of wall space to hang art. The ambience was straightforward, almost businesslike compared to the other places they'd been.

Off to one side, a young woman with long black hair was talking on the phone. The minute she hung up, a smile lit her face. "Joe. We haven't seen you in a while."

"I've been busy getting the camp ready for summer."

"Well, you picked a good day to stop by. We just got in a new shipment from Red Feather and there's one little gem I think you'll fall in love with at first sight."

"No, please." He covered his eyes. "Don't even start. I have no willpower to resist her work, and my walls are covered. Seriously. I don't have an inch of space left."

"Not even for a little painting?"

He started to object again, then lowered his hand. "How little?"

Maddy cocked her head, caught between anxiety and amusement to see this side of Joe. The movement was small, but it brought his attention back to her.

"Oh." He pulled her forward. "Maddy, this is Juanita, a former counselor at Camp Enchantment. Juanita, Maddy, an artist from Texas. We're hoping to see Sylvia. Is she in?"

"She's in the back. I'll buzz her."

"Thanks."

While Juanita made an intercom call, Maddy looked around to get a feel for what sort of art they liked. The galleries on Canyon Road had handled originals almost exclusively. This gallery, however, dealt heavily in limited edition prints by big name artists. That hardly surprised her since prints were the bread and butter of many galleries.

Then she peeked into one of the back alcoves and wrinkled her nose at the mess. More paintings leaned against the walls than hung on them. She started to turn away, but her gaze landed on a large canvas by one of the better-known cowboy artists.

"Wow," she whispered, moving toward it.

"What?" Joe whispered as well, although he sounded more amused than reverent.

Maddy checked to be sure Juanita was out of earshot, then started flipping through the stacks of paintings. "I'll say this, what they lack in ambience, they make up for in quality."

"Oh?" he prompted.

"Definitely." She moved to another stack. The originals were all by established names in the world of Southwestern art, the very same artists whose prints filled the front. Any print gallery or mall poster shop who offered Southwestern art carried these artists' works, but few could get their hands on this many originals. "Your friend Sylvia has some major connections."

"Didn't I just say that?"

"Yes, but . . ." Maddy turned in a slow circle, taking it all in as jitters assailed her stomach. "I am way out of my league here." She rolled her eyes sideways to look at Joe, wondering if he'd stop her if she tried to bolt.

His eyes narrowed in warning.

An image suddenly popped into her head of her running for the door, Joe making a diving tackle, and them landing sprawled on the floor with his arms wrapped about her legs.

Okay, so escape was not an option. She faced one of the few paintings actually hanging on the wall, gathering her courage and ordering herself not to panic.

"May I help you?"

With a start, Maddy turned. The woman stood nearly six feet in height with a rigorously maintained figure, a long fall of silver hair, and a face that took the word "weathered" and turned it into a fashion statement.

"Hello, Sylvia." Joe extended his hand.

"Joe Fraser." The woman smiled. "Always good to see you. Are you looking for anything special today?"

"Actually, I'd like you to meet an artist friend of mine." He placed a hand on Maddy's back, right between her shoulder blades, and exerted enough pressure that she either had to step forward or fall on her face. "This is Maddy Howard—"

"Madeline Mills," she corrected.

"—from Texas. I wanted you to be the first dealer in Santa Fe to have a shot at taking on her work."

"Oh?" The woman turned to Maddy with genuine interest. "What sort of work do you do?"

"Oils mostly." She lifted the portfolio. "I brought photographs if you have time to take a look."

"Always. Bring them over to the framing table where the light's better." Sylvia glided away.

Maddy started to follow, but realized Joe was glued to her side. She stopped and lowered her voice. "I can handle things from here, okay?"

"You sure?"

"Yes." She made a shooing motion with her hand. "Go browse. Please?"

Joe scowled, but stayed where he was, watching as Maddy joined Sylvia at a large table covered in carpeting. Molding samples filled the wall behind them. Maddy laid her portfolio on the table and opened it to the first page. She pointed and talked, apparently telling a bit about each piece. Nodding her head, Sylvia lifted the reading glasses that hung from a chain about her neck and slipped them on.

Remembering Maddy's order to browse, he pretended to study a painting, but his gaze kept darting toward them. What if Maddy was right and she wasn't ready yet? What if a couple of weeks would have given her a better edge? What if he'd pushed her into blowing this chance?

He reminded himself of all the things he'd said in the truck, things he believed. And yet . . . what if Sylvia crushed Maddy's ego with one glancing blow?

He saw Sylvia straighten. She smiled. Politely. Damn. A polite smile was not a good sign. Maddy smiled as well. Stiffly.

They shook hands, and Joe wanted to kick himself.

The instinct to protect made him take a step toward them, but he stopped. His presence might make things worse. He and Maddy weren't close anymore, even if they had spent a remarkably pleasant day together.

Besides, Maddy looked admirably calm.

Until she dropped her portfolio on the floor.

It landed with a splat and photos went everywhere.

Joe mobilized, crossing the room in long strides, scooping up photos as he went.

"I am so sorry," Maddy was saying as she scrambled to recover her pictures and her dignity.

"What are these?" Sylvia bent down to retrieve several pieces of colored art paper.

Maddy looked over and realized what the woman held. The oil pastels. "Oh." She straightened, alarmed at having this woman who had rejected her finished pieces see rough work. "Those are just some preliminary sketches for a new series of oils I want to do."

"Now these I like!" Sylvia announced, laying them out on the table. "Sophisticated yet playful. Vibrant colors. Very distinctive."

Distinctive. There was the word the woman had used at least three times while flipping through the photos. *Yes, it's all very good. You clearly have talent. But your style isn't distinctive enough.* Maddy frowned at the pastels. "You really like these?"

"Definitely." Sylvia held one at arm's length. The image was the aspen trees behind the Craft Shack, done in squiggles and slashes, the shimmer of silver-green leaves against white and black trunks.

"So," Maddy ventured, "when I finish the paintings will you take a look at them?"

"Oh, good heavens, don't do that!" Sylvia gasped as if Maddy had offered to kill someone's pet. "You'll ruin them!"

"What?"

"Your oils are fine. Excellent, in fact. Perfectly conceived and perfectly executed."

"But . . . I thought you didn't like them."

Sylvia looked at her over the top of her glasses. "They also happen to be perfectly bland."

"Oh."

"But these. These!" She held out another image, this one of a gnarled piñon tree growing out of sunbaked boulders. "They're perfect just the way they are."

"You just said perfect was bad."

"There's perfect, then there's *perfect*. Do you have any larger pieces like these?"

"I'm afraid not. But I can do some."

"Excellent." Sylvia removed her glasses. "Here's what I'll do. If you agree to have these framed at your expense, I'll take them on consignment here in the retail showroom as a test. If they go over well, we'll talk about limited-edition prints."

"Prints?" Maddy nearly choked.

"For our next catalog."

"Prints," she repeated. The memory that had tickled her brain out in the truck clicked into place. *Images of the West*. Of course that sounded familiar! They were an art publishing company. One of many, but one of the best. She glanced around again, at the caliber of artists they represented, then looked at Joe.

He turned sheepish. Well, as sheepish as a man with his build and dark good looks can manage. "I, uh, guess I forgot to tell you this isn't a normal gallery."

"Gallery, showroom, whatever." Sylvia waved a hand. "I assume you understand I want an exclusive."

"That's, uh . . ." Maddy's head took a dizzy spin. If this panned out, she wouldn't be in just one gallery. She'd be in galleries across the country! "Not a problem."

"All right, then." Sylvia nodded. "Juanita will help you pick out some framing while I go to the office and get a consignment form."

Maddy managed to control her excitement during the paperwork. It broke free, though, as she and Joe left the gallery.

"Can you believe that?" she asked the minute they stepped outside. "She likes the pastels!"

"I like them too."

"Really? You mean that?"

"I do." He smiled at her as if suppressing laughter at her enthusiasm.

She didn't care if he did laugh. "She took all of them on consignment! And she wants to see more. Oh my God!" She did a little dance as they crossed the parking lot.

Joe did laugh at that. "Congratulations."

"My work is in a gallery. In Santa Fe!" She twirled about, making the skirt of her dress flare, then wrap around her legs. "And not just any gallery, but *Images of the West*. An art publishing house. I can't believe this! I can't wait to tell Christine and Amy. This is so great!"

They'd reached the truck and Joe hit the remote to unlock the doors. Maddy climbed into the passenger seat as he slipped behind the wheel.

"Oh, Joe." She crossed her hands over her heart and sighed. "This means so much to me. I can't even tell you. Why didn't you tell me this was a publishing house?"

"If I had, would you have gone in?"

"No way!" She laughed.

"Exactly. I picked this place because it looks so unassuming, I knew you wouldn't chicken out."

"You didn't expect her to take me on, did you?"

"I knew it was a long shot—but you know what they say: Start at the top. And damn, Maddy, you nailed it."

"I did." Her body sagged as realization hit her. "Holy cow, I really did." She looked at him, overcome, then threw her arms about his neck. "Thank you!"

He returned the hug without thinking. Then the feel of her in his arms slammed into his senses on one blinding wave. He closed his eyes as the impact sucked him under. Desire delivered a second blow, sending him into a roll.

Before he knew how it had happened, his hands were in her hair and his mouth was on hers. The taste of her made joy flood his veins. Her name beat in time with the pounding of his heart. After years of starving for her, he was holding Maddy, kissing Maddy.

He tipped his head and deepened the contact, thrilling to the feel of her kissing him back the way she always had—with an eagerness to match his own. His whole body came alive as their mouths opened and mated. He wanted to lift her over the gearshift and onto his lap, slip his hands under her dress and feel her warm skin. She moaned again, and arched toward him as if wanting the same thing.

Maddy! His heart sang. He was kissing Maddy! *Good God!*

His brain kicked in and his body froze.

He was kissing Maddy!

He jerked back and held her at arm's length, his pulse pounding like surf against rocks. She stared back at him, her eyes wide, her breath coming as hard and fast as his. "What just happened here?"

She blinked as if stunned. "I don't know."

Releasing her as if she'd turned to fire, he plastered his back against the truck door. "We are not doing this."

"I think we just did."

"It was habit." He put his hands on the steering wheel. "A knee-jerk reaction. Put us in a vehicle and *bam,* we're back in high school making out in the front seat of the Colonel's station wagon."

"Actually, it usually progressed to the back of the station wagon." She looked at the bed of his pickup. "I don't think that's a good idea, considering where we're parked. Unless we want to get arrested for public indecency."

"I don't care where we're parked." His hand shook as he inserted the key into the ignition. "This will not happen again."

"Of course not." Maddy clasped her hands in her lap and stared straight ahead. "Not if you don't want it to."

"I don't." Was she saying she did? The thought made him edgy with panic as he drove out of the parking lot. What had he been thinking to kiss her like that? Or had she kissed him? He honestly didn't remember. The only thing he knew was that barely forty-eight hours had passed, and already she was slipping past his defenses. Had he learned nothing from his last go-round with this woman?

The Rangers had taught him how much physical pain his body could endure, but he refused to spend the summer letting Maddy back inside his heart, only to have her walk away come fall. That much pain he couldn't handle.

Chapter 9

The minute Maddy returned to the safety of the camp, she shot an e-mail to Christine and Amy.

Subject: *Help!*

Message: *Something happened today, and I'm totally freaked out. I think I'm falling in love with Joe all over again. Only, this is different than before. Even scarier somehow. I'm not ready for this. Not with anyone. And especially not this fast. How do I stop it?*

Amy: *Whoa, wait, back up. What happened?*

Maddy: *Joe kissed me. Or I kissed him. It's kind of a blur. He took me to some galleries today, and everything was going great. In fact, one of the galleries took some of my work. (Details later, I promise. You're going to be ecstatic.) When we got back to his truck, both of us were excited, and the next thing I know, we're kissing. And it was like WOW! I'm not sure I've ever had a kiss like that. Not even with Joe.*

Then suddenly he got angry—whether at me or himself, I'm not sure—and he made it clear he has no interest in getting involved with me ever again. So now things are even more awkward than they were this time yesterday. Help! What do I do?

Amy: *Okay, first, CONGRATULATIONS on the gallery!!! I can't wait to hear details. Now, back to Joe. When you say he doesn't want to get involved, does that mean you do?*

Maddy sat back as the air left her lungs in a whoosh. She remembered that moment at the Ore House, when he'd let his barriers down enough for her to see the wonderful man he'd become. In some ways he was still the wounded rebel, but he was also strong, compassionate, responsible, and endearingly enthusiastic even when he tried to hide it. But he'd certainly slammed those barriers back down in a hurry.

Her hands shook as she typed out her reply: *I don't know. I'm attracted to him on several levels. Definitely no denying that. If he were a stranger, I'd date him in a heartbeat. Nigel's been gone nearly two years. I need to start dating again sometime, and Joe—this new Joe—is a really great guy. But he's not a stranger, and he wants nothing to do with me. I dread the thought of facing him again at dinner. What a disaster.*

Amy: *Maybe he will have calmed down by then, and the two of you can get back to where you were before the kiss.*

Maddy hoped so. Her nerves remained tangled though, as she waited for dinner.

Unfortunately, she returned from the dining hall that evening more shaken and confused than ever. She found an e-mail from Christine asking for details about the gallery. It ended with: *As for Joe getting bent out of shape over the kiss—which sounds really hot!—maybe it scared him as much as it scared you: hence the anger. It's a known fact that men don't react well to fear. They much prefer getting mad. It's how he acts after he calms down that matters.*

Maddy: *I think we can safely say he's calmed down. Completely. Now he's acting like nothing happened and I'm no different to him than the other coordinators. I don't know whether to be angry or relieved.*

Christine: *Well, I know which I'd be if a man kissed me senseless, then acted like nothing happened. Give it time, though, Maddy. He may not be as calmed down as you think.*

Days passed with no change in Joe's outward demeanor. He was painstakingly polite but distant. On Maddy's seventh morning at the camp, she sat through another breakfast meeting with Joe at the far end of the opposite bench. A week of sharing meals, and somehow they managed to sit as far as they could from each other every time. Even so, she felt herself flash hot and cold simply being in the same room with him. Her bones literally ached with embarrassment, regret, and a longing for things to be different.

That realization made her frown. Maybe she was coming down with the flu. Which meant her sick stomach had nothing to do with him.

Or it could be the slightly runny scrambled eggs they had every morning. Testing the theory, she poked at the eggs, then glanced around the table to see if anyone else was getting sick.

The minute her gaze landed on Joe, the nausea got worse. Lord, she hadn't felt this weird sort of sickness in years. Not since her last teen crush before Joe came along and obliterated all thoughts of any boy but him. It was a horrible pining ache for someone's attention to the point of feeling physically ill.

Damn it, why hadn't doctors invented a cure for this? She'd take the issue up with Christine in her next e-mail, that was for sure.

"I think that covers everything," Joe said calmly as he glanced over the notes he'd brought to breakfast. He certainly didn't seem to be suffering any ill effects from their forced proximity, which added a little dose of resentment to the mix. "Any questions?"

The others all assured him no while she remained silent and seething.

"Well, then." He stood, all six-plus feet of muscular male. "If anyone needs me, I'll be in the office."

She nearly groaned. Did he have to put it that way? Making her mind conjure up a completely different need than what he meant?

Until coming to Camp Enchantment, she would have sworn she wasn't a sex fiend, that she didn't play out intimate acts in her mind any more than the average healthy woman did. Since arriving, though, it seemed as if she thought about sex constantly.

Although, she argued back, maybe that was understandable, considering she hadn't had sex in a *very* long time. Nearly four years. Or wait, had she actually passed the four-year mark? Good Lord, she had. And the years before that had been sporadic at best.

She glanced in the direction Joe had gone, watched his broad back and very nice behind as he walked away. After years of abstinence, suddenly here was Mr. Virile Army Ranger right before her day after day. A male specimen like that would have any female taking notice. So of course her hormones were firing on all thrusters.

That was it! She wasn't in danger of falling in love with him. She was sex-deprived. On a wave of relief, she turned back to her eggs, deciding they weren't so nauseating after all.

"Is he gone?" Carol whispered into the suddenly quiet dining hall.

"Hang on." Dana craned her neck to see out the windows. "Yep, he's gone."

"Okay then." Carol motioned everyone to lean closer. "Let's get down to business. Operation Make Joe Happy is not going well. Clearly, more drastic action is in order."

What? Maddy blinked.

"Agreed." Sandy nodded. "But what? We've tried enthusiasm about the coming summer and working hard to get the camp in shape. He's appreciative enough, but it hasn't lightened his mood."

Maddy put her fork down. "Excuse me. What are you talking about? Joe seems happy enough to me."

"On the surface, maybe," Carol said. "But you don't know him as well as we do. He's definitely upset about something, but he's trying to hide it."

Dana nodded. "There must be some way to make him stop missing the Rangers and feel better about running the camp."

"Actually," Maddy said, "he is happy about running the camp."

"He is?" Carol brightened.

"Are you sure?" Sandy frowned.

"How do you know?" Dana asked.

Maddy hesitated, wishing she'd kept her mouth shut. "He, um, told me."

"That's right," Carol said. "You rode into town with him that day."

"What did he say?" Sandy asked.

Maddy cleared her throat and yearned for escape. "He said that he loves working with the kids and that the camp means a lot to him."

"Really?" Sandy turned hopeful.

"But that doesn't make sense," Dana said. "If he's happy about running the camp, why is he acting so weird?"

"Maybe he's upset about something else," Sandy suggested.

Dana groaned. "Don't tell me we're back to the mysterious woman who broke his heart."

Carol turned back to Maddy. "Did he say anything else?"

"Uh, no," Maddy insisted quickly. "Not really. At least, not anything important."

Dana narrowed her eyes. "Why are you blushing?"

"Blushing?" Maddy pressed a hand to her cheek. "I'm not blushing. It's . . . the coffee. It's really hot." She hid her face in the mug.

"Uh-huh." Dana looked at her disbelievingly.

"All right, Maddy." Carol crossed her arms. "What gives? Is there something going on we don't know about?"

"No!" She tried for a calm smile. "Really."

"Do you want there to be?" Dana asked.

"Why would you think that?" Her cheeks flamed hotter.

"Because now you're acting even weirder than him."

"I'm just tired. And busy." Maddy looked at her watch. "Speaking of, wow, look at the time. I have a ton of stuff to do. Let's not forget the counselors arrive today."

She rose and gathered her tray, moving away from the table as quickly as possible. Silence reigned behind her, but she felt the gazes of the coordinators on her back all the way out the door.

Oh brother, she thought when she stepped outside. The last thing she needed was to spend the summer as the camp pariah. Having Joe want her gone was bad enough.

Fortunately, the rest of the day was total chaos, with counselors arriving in droves, so no one had time to question her further.

Chapter 10

The first day of camp arrived along with busloads of screaming kids. Maddy stood in the middle of the game field, marveling at the energy that bounced around her.

"Hey, Maddy," Carol said, coming up to her with clipboard in hand and a whistle around her neck. "How are you holding up?"

"Great, actually," she said, deciding she preferred the camp this way, filled with bustle and noise. "What do you need me to do?"

"I think we have everything under control." A group of shrieking girls ran past them. "Sort of." Laughing, Carol turned to answer a question from one of the newly arrived counselors.

Maddy looked around, taking it all in. Mama had been right about young people making her feel more alive. Maybe the summer wouldn't be so bad now that the kids were here. As a side benefit, she barely had time to think about Joe, or the way his behavior had shifted subtly the night before. During the welcome cookout for the counselors, he'd started watching her. Perhaps with so many people around, he didn't think she'd notice, but several times she'd turned around and caught him staring at her with an intensity that had her nerves on edge.

Of course, the coordinators saw him watching her and exchanged a few looks of their own, which was not what she needed.

"Here comes another bus," Carol said. The counselor she'd been talking to headed off to greet it as Carol turned back to Maddy. "Hey, will you do me a favor and let Joe know? He was up at High Mesa Lodge last I heard, chasing off a badger."

"A badger?"

"Apparently one decided to take up residence in the bathroom and gave the counselors quite a start when they woke up this morning."

"So that's what that screaming was at sunrise."

"That was it." Carol laughed. The screams had ricocheted up and down the canyon at dawn. "Anyway, find Joe and let him know more campers are here."

Maddy frowned since talking to Joe was on her list of things to avoid. Besides, the big yellow school bus was in full view of the entire camp. "I'm sure he can probably see that."

"Yes, but we, um, might need him to help us unload trunks." With that, Carol hurried off before Maddy could point out that several able-bodied counselors were already unloading trunks.

Well, dang it. She looked around. Maybe she could find someone else to relay the message. All she saw, though, was a thundering herd of little

girls charging straight for her like a band of screaming banshees. She spun around as they rushed
past—and found herself face-to-face with Joe. With
a shriek of her own, she jumped back.

"Sandy said you were looking for me." His sunglasses hid his eyes, guarding his expression, but
his voice didn't sound any warmer than it had for
the last several days.

Deciding she'd had enough, she planted her
hands on her hips. "What, you're actually speaking
to me?"

His brows snapped together over the dark lenses.
"You're the one who asked to see me."

"No, I didn't."

"But Sandy said—"

"I haven't spoken to Sandy since breakfast. Although Carol did ask me to tell you another bus
is here."

He looked over her head. "I see that."

"Apparently she wanted you standing by in case
they needed help unloading."

"Carol asked you to tell me that?"

"Yes."

"And that's the only reason you were looking
for me?"

"Yes," she snapped irritably. "So you can relax."

"Relax?" The line between his brows grew
deeper.

"Look, I just—" She struggled for a way to clear
the air between them. This constant tension was
killing her. Before she could say anything, Carol
blew a whistle, reminding Maddy where she was.
Looking around, she had to laugh to herself.
"Never mind. This isn't the time or place."

"For?" he asked blandly.

She narrowed her eyes, trying to see past the blasted shades. His body remained rigid, nearly standing at attention. She made a helpless gesture with her hands. "Nothing. If you'll excuse me, I have work to do." As she turned to walk away, she muttered under her breath, "To think I was having a good day."

"Maddy," he called after her.

She turned back to him, waiting with no small amount of impatience. "What?"

The muscles in his cheeks moved as if he were chewing on words. Just when she thought she would scream, he nodded and said, "Nice shoes."

"Excuse me?" She scowled in confusion as he turned and marched away. *Nice shoes?* She looked down at the Keds she wore with the khaki shorts and green golf shirt the coordinators were required to wear. They were the shoes she'd bought before leaving Austin for exactly this purpose. At the last minute, though, she couldn't bring herself to put on plain white sneakers. So she'd covered them in fabric paint, creating a whole garden of bright flowers.

Granted, they looked great, but after days of ignoring her, that's the grand total of what he had to say? *Nice shoes?*

She squinted at his retreating back. Okay, so what had he really been about to tell her? "Pack your bags, you're fired"? Or "I'm miserable too, can we please talk?"

Dread and hope played on her nerves the rest of the day. One way or another, this dance they were doing had to end. Perhaps the next time he approached her, she could try not snapping at him. If he approached her. If he didn't . . . she'd just have to build up the courage to approach him.

But approach him to say what? Let's be friends? Let's be lovers? Or, let's simply stop ignoring each other?

Joe was headed for trouble. He knew that with every step he took three days into summer camp as he set off for the Craft Shack to deliver a message to Maddy. He could easily have asked Carol to relay the message, but had he? No. Against all instincts for self-preservation, he was hiking up the trail himself, straight toward the woman he'd tried desperately to get out of his head and away from his heart.

The problem was, a twisted thought had wormed its way into his brain. He was going to suffer no matter what happened. It was like taking that bullet in Kabul. Time had clicked into slow motion. He'd literally seen it coming and he'd known it was going to hurt like hell. But he'd also known there wasn't a damn thing he could do other than grit his teeth and wait for the impact.

Apparently Maddy was another bullet he couldn't dodge.

So, in the last few days, he'd finally decided that, by God, if he was taking a hit, he might as well get some enjoyment out of having her around while he waited for impact. Assuming she was even interested, which was what he'd stupidly started to ask the day the kids had arrived. Thankfully, he'd chickened out at the last minute. They had some air to clear between them before he blurted out that he'd changed his mind, that he did want to get involved with her—with a desperation that left him physically aching for her day and night.

No matter how hard he tried, he couldn't stop wanting her.

As he reached the top of the trail, he heard children laughing. Normally the sound loosened something inside him. Today, however, his stomach remained cramped as he approached the building.

All the shutters had been raised, allowing the mountain breeze to drift through the classroom. He zeroed in on Maddy as she moved about the room. She wore khaki shorts, as required by the camp dress code, but the green shirt with the camp logo she'd been issued had been replaced by a paint-splattered men's dress shirt tied at the waist. So much for her staying in uniform, he thought with a wry smile.

His focus broadened enough to take in one of the cabin counselors and a couple dozen little girls. The kids looked cute as all get-out in their white camp shirts, half of them wearing red shorts for the Foxes, the other half in blue for the Bobcats. Most of them sat or knelt in chairs, diligently gluing noodles and buttons to pieces of colored paper. Two campers he remembered from the previous year chased each other about the room.

"Amanda! Kaylee!" Maddy called, her voice calm in spite of being raised. "No running. If you're done with your pictures, you may play with the toys in the corner."

"Teacher!" a girl he didn't recognize screeched in an octave barely audible to humans. "Rachel tored my picture!"

"Rachel, no, no, honey." Maddy hurried over as two girls began a tug-of-war over a piece of crumpled paper. "You mustn't tear other people's artwork."

"But she scribbled on mine!" Rachel complained.

"All right, all right." Maddy managed to separate them with remarkable skill. Although, stepping closer to the door, he saw her smile looked a bit frazzled. "Here, I'll get you both fresh paper."

Down in the camp the bell clanged, signaling the end of the after-nap activity period. The art room erupted with noise as children either jumped to their feet or worked furiously to finish their pictures.

"Wait," Maddy called over the clamor. "Be sure and sign your picture before you turn it in."

Joe watched as Maddy and the counselor herded the children into a line at the door.

"Hi, Joe!" Amanda waved at him.

Hearing his name, Maddy whirled with a start, and their gazes met. Color sprang to her cheeks, as it did so frequently when she looked at him. The anger from the other day seemed to have faded, which he took as a good sign.

A loud shriek pierced the air and she turned back to the wiggling, giggling line of little girls.

"Okay, shhhh." She held her finger to her lips and was completely ignored. "Quiet, please. Quiet."

"Listen up!" he ordered. Silence fell instantly. "That's better. You girls weren't giving Maddy any trouble, were you?"

"No, sir," they assured him in chorus.

"Good." He nodded curtly.

Maddy sagged a bit as she cast him a grateful look, then addressed the kids. "You were all very good today. I'm proud of you. Now follow Susan down to the game field and get ready for the sack race."

"Yea!" The girls jumped up and down. With Susan in the lead, they filed past Joe, singing, "This old man, he played one, he played knickknack on his thumb . . ."

Kaylee jumped to a halt before him and planted her hands on her hips. Golden curls bounced about her chubby face. "Gueth what?"

"What?" he asked with equal enthusiasm.

"I loth-t a tooth." She pulled her lips back so he could admire the gap where one of her front teeth was missing.

"Yep." He studied it with the gravity due such an auspicious occasion. "You sure did."

Her brow puckered with a frown. "Do you think the Tooth Fairy will find me here?"

"I absolutely guarantee it."

"Thath what Maddy said too."

He lifted his gaze to find Maddy watching him. Her soft expression made his chest even tighter. Looking back at Kaylee, he mussed her hair. "And she's right. Now why don't you and Amanda go win the sack race?"

"Okay!" Kaylee raced off to catch up with the others.

"Kaylee!" Maddy stepped into the doorway, standing so close he could smell the fresh scent of her hair. "Don't run on the trail! You'll trip and fall."

The girl leapt over a small boulder like a relay racer and disappeared around a bend at full speed. With a sigh, Maddy turned and slumped against the doorjamb. She eyed him for a moment, her face guarded now that they were alone. "That child is going to be the death of me."

"Why do you think we needed a new A and C coordinator?"

Maddy tipped her head. "Kaylee and Amanda tied the last one up and used her for target practice?"

"Nah. They only do that to the archery instructors."

She smiled. "Then what happened to the A and C coordinator?"

"We're not sure." He kept his face straight. "We're still looking for the body."

She laughed, giving him hope. What an idiot he'd been these last few days, holding her at bay. The moment stretched out as they both became aware of how close they were standing.

She shifted uneasily. "You're very good with the children. I wish I had your knack."

"You looked like you were holding your own."

"Just barely." Exhaustion sounded in her sigh. "And the day isn't done. I still have to go help Sandy with the sack race as soon as I clean up this mess." She looked a little overwhelmed as she surveyed the room.

"Actually, that's why I'm here."

"Oh?"

"Sandy asked me to tell you she has the races covered. So it appears you're free until dinner."

"You're kidding."

"Nope."

"Thank God." She slumped further down against the doorframe. "Maybe I'll survive after all. And even sneak in some time to finish another pastel."

"Oh? You're getting some work done?"

"Quite a bit, actually. I've done several pieces I'm eager to show Sylvia."

"That's good to hear." This was his opening, he realized. All he had to do was take it. Except no words came to mind.

"Well." She straightened. "I guess I'll get this room clean, then go upstairs and work for a while."

She left him standing in the doorway. He glanced back the way he'd come, knowing he still had the chance to go back down the trail and leave things as they were—stilted but safe.

He took a deep breath, and turned back toward her. "I'd like to see them."

"Hmm?" She looked up from the chairs she was pushing into place.

"The pastels you've done. I'd like to see them."

"Oh." A myriad of emotions moved over her face, from confusion to caution. Was she looking for a way to tell him no? "They're in my room," she finally said. "Would you . . . like to come up?"

"I would," he said slowly as his heart raced. "Let me help you clean up."

"That would be great." A smile blossomed across her face, lighting her eyes, and melting him inside. "Thanks."

Yep, he was definitely headed for trouble.

Chapter 11

Nerves tickled the backs of Maddy's knees as she led the way up the outside stairs. "I can't vouch for how straight the place is. I was up late last night working and just sort of stumbled out of bed this morning."

"I promise not to write you up for slovenly behavior."

"I'm not that bad." Her laugh came out a bit breathy as she stopped at the door. She looked up when he joined her on the landing, trying to gauge his mood. His height blocked the sun, leaving his face in shadow. Why was he here? He didn't seem angry, but he didn't seem eager to be with her either.

"Are we going in?" he asked. One of his black brows lifted above the sunglasses that hid his eyes.

"Of course." She opened the door, peeked in, then rushed ahead of him to toss the bed comforter into place, scoop yesterday's clothes off the floor, and snatch the bright flower-print bra off the arm of the big chair in the corner. At least the kitchen area was clean, she thought as she hurried back to the closet by the front door and threw the clothes inside.

"There." She leaned her back against the door. "Not so bad."

"Not bad at all." He stepped farther into the apartment, filling the small space with his broad-shouldered presence. As he removed the sunglasses, she watched him take in her decor. Since days off were scarce, she'd purchased everything in one mad shopping spree, going with jewel-tone fabrics for the bed, chair cover, tablecloth, and place mats. On the walls, she'd hung a few of the oils she'd hoped to get into a gallery, cheerful garden scenes done in vibrant colors.

"These are good," he said, studying them.

"Those are some of my older pieces."

"So I assumed." He looked around again. "Where are the new pieces?"

"I'll get them." She retrieved a large black portfolio she'd left leaning against the wall, then looked around for a surface large enough to lay it on. Seeing no other choice, she maneuvered past Joe to put it on the bed.

He came up behind her to look over her shoulder. The nervous flutters turned to tingles of awareness at how close he stood. His scent filled her, a healthy, vital blend of soap and the outdoors.

He reached down to turn the drawings like pages in a giant book. "Maddy, these are great." He stopped at one of the bigger pieces, which depicted the view of the canyon from her balcony at sunrise. A fiery sky blazed over the cool greens and blues of the land. "Especially this one."

A glow of pride expanded inside her. "You really think so?"

"Absolutely." He leaned a little closer, his chest brushing her shoulder. With a sideways glance she realized he was peering at her signature. "Just 'Madeline'? No last name?"

She laughed. "During my die-hard feminist days I decided that last names were a stamp of male ownership. Your maiden name is your father's and your married name is your husband's. A woman's first name is the only thing that's really hers. And since my art is mine and no one else's, that's the only name that goes on it."

"Makes sense."

He continued flipping through images of the landscape, close-ups of wildflowers, studies of clouds in various light from bright white to blood-red. "I can see I'll need to find some more wall space after all."

"You don't have to."

"I want to." He said it with such conviction, she grew flustered.

Her gaze drifted to the play of muscles in his forearms, the strength in his large hands. Her thoughts took off on their own—as they did far too often—with fantasies of his hands on her body, being naked beneath him, feeling the weight of him cover her. No doubt about it, she was definitely sex-depraved. Deprived! She meant sex-de*prived*.

She pressed a hand to her forehead and realized she'd actually started to sweat.

"Is something wrong?"

"What?" She snatched her hand away when she found him looking at her instead of at the artwork.

"I asked when you planned to take these by the gallery to show Sylvia."

"Oh." *Think, Maddy, think. Of something other than his body.* "As soon as I can manage a trip into town."

"Tell me when you're ready, and I'll have Mom take over your after-nap activity period. That'll give you half a day off."

"Really? Thanks. That would be great." She told herself to step away but wound up just standing there, staring up into his dark-chocolate eyes, remembering the kiss in the truck and wondering how shocked he'd be if she asked him to kiss her again, just for the hell of it. She could assure him it didn't have to mean anything—since he'd clearly stated he didn't want to get tangled up with her again—she just desperately wanted to feel those lips on hers, feel his arms wrap tightly about her, feel the full length of his body with the full length of her own . . . all the way from shoulders to shins.

Jeez, Maddy, get a grip.

"So . . ." He broke the eye contact and looked around awkwardly. "I suppose I'm in the way here if you want to work." His voice went up at the end, as if asking a question rather than making a statement.

Was he trolling for an invitation to stay? "Actually . . ." she hesitated. What if she was reading him wrong? Although nothing ventured, nothing gained. She took a breath and plunged ahead. "I could use a little break. Between the camp and staying up every night drawing, I haven't had much down time to just relax. Would you . . . care to sit on the balcony a while? I could open a bottle of faux wine."

"Faux wine?" Amusement danced in his eyes.

"Well, it does say in our contract that we aren't allowed to drink any alcohol while camp is in session, but I can only take so much coffee, iced tea, and cola in one day, so I just thought— Never mind. I'm rambling." Embarrassed laughter bubbled out. "And I'm sure you're busy, so—"

"I'd love a glass of wine."

"Oh?" She straightened in surprise. "Well. Okay, then. Why don't you have a seat on the balcony and I'll get it."

"Do you need help?"

"No, no." What she needed was a moment to compose herself. "I'll get it. You go . . ." She waved her hands. "Sit."

"Yes, ma'am." His lips quirked with a smile as he complied.

Plucking at her shirt to cool herself off, she put the portfolio away, then went to the cabinet and wrestled the cork from a bottle. She filled two plastic cups, fanned her cheeks for good measure, and went to join him on the balcony. She found him standing at the wall, looking out over the camp. As if sensing her presence, he turned and smiled at her—one of his slow, melting smiles that turned her to mush.

Flustered, she stepped forward, extending one of the cups. "Here you go."

"Thanks." Their fingers touched as he took it from her, sending a little jolt through her. He looked down at his cup, then back at her. "Well, we've come a long way, from drinking hard liquor when we were underage to froufrou grape juice just so we can follow the rules."

"All part of growing up." She laughed. "But it does seem strange."

"I feel like we should drink to something."

She longed to say: *To new beginnings. To starting over. To second chances.* But the words stuck in her throat. Was he simply aiming for renewing their truce, or something more? Was she ready for more? Casual dating, yes. But nothing about this situation felt casual.

"I know," he finally said. "To your art career."

"Oh no, don't jinx it!"

"What?" He frowned.

"A toast like that without a lot of wood to knock on would be chancy enough. But to make it with fake wine in plastic cups? No."

"Very well." He held his cup out. "To nothing."

"No. To everything." She touched her cup to his.

"Even better." He took a sip, then looked at the wine, startled. "Mmm, this is actually good."

"Surprised me too." She drank, enjoying the subtle blend of smoky, fruity flavors that slid over her tongue.

"See, you should have let me toast your career."

"When I have one, I'll let you." They crossed to the grapevine chairs that sat on either side of a little table. She'd added emerald green cushions to make them more comfortable, and filled the pots with new plants and flowers.

"So," she said, "how'd you get to be so good with children?"

"I've been home on leave enough over the years to learn my way around these little monsters."

She smiled thinking of the opening-night bonfire. She'd sat across from Joe, watching in fascination as the little girls climbed on his back as if he were their personal jungle gym. "They clearly adore you."

"The feeling's mutual"—one side of his mouth turned upward—"most of the time."

"Most of the time?"

"When Mom first bought the camp, I went through culture shock every time I came here." He stretched out his long legs, making the chair creak beneath his weight. "Try going from living with an all-male special-ops team to being dropped into a camp full of females who are constantly chattering, bursting into tears, or screaming. Why do little girls do that, by the way?"

"Do what? Cry?"

"No, scream. Jeez." He stuck a finger in his ear and wiggled it. "I think I'm losing my high-range hearing—which may actually be a blessing."

She laughed. "I have no idea why they do that. I suppose for the same reason little boys hit each other. Too much energy for such tiny bodies to contain, so it has to go somewhere."

"At least hitting is quiet."

"That depends on who's being hit."

He studied her, then looked away. "I, um, take it you never had children?"

"No." Her smile faded.

"Did you want any?"

She hesitated, not sure how much of her life with Nigel she wanted to discuss with Joe. But there didn't seem to be a good reason not to discuss it. "We wanted children very much, and had been trying for more than a year when we went in for testing. That's when they discovered the cancer."

"Oh." The usual curiosity paraded across his

face, all the things people wanted to ask but rarely did for fear of being insensitive.

"It was testicular," she said, answering the unspoken question. "And very advanced. In the rush to get Nigel into treatment, we skimmed over the subject of infertility, never really addressing our options until it was too late."

Joe shifted in his chair. "Would you have, you know . . . gone that route?"

She hid a smile at how awkward some men were when the subject of freezing sperm came up. "I don't know. If Nigel's cancer had ever gone into remission long enough, maybe. While he was ill, I didn't have the emotional energy left to care for a child. It wouldn't have been fair to create a life when I didn't have the time or energy to nurture it."

"No, it wouldn't," he answered simply, but the words carried a wealth of personal experience.

She sipped her wine as she searched for a way to lighten the mood. "So, what about you? I assume you never married. Do you still want children?"

"Actually, the answer is 'almost' to the first and 'definitely' to the second, which is what caused the 'almost.'"

"Okay, there's got to be a story behind that." She ignored the little spurt of jealousy at hearing he'd almost married.

"It was all Fish's fault."

"Fish?"

"Major Thomas Jenkins." He smiled. "My commanding officer. He had a baby."

"Wow." She blinked. "That must have been quite a feat. I know you guys can do some pretty special stuff, but childbirth? And it didn't even make the news?"

"Smart-ass," he teased. "His wife had a baby. A little girl. You should have seen Fish. I'm talking total mush. He carried pictures around everywhere—a few we all could have done without, believe me." He grimaced in a way that let her know they were delivery room pictures.

"Men are such wimps."

"Guilty," he admitted. "But man, he was nuts over that baby. I started remembering how much I'd always wanted one."

Maddy remembered too. As a teenager his sentences had frequently started with the phrase: "When I have a kid . . ." The rest of the sentence could be anything from making sure the child knew it was wanted to the child not getting away with some stunt one of their bonehead friends had just pulled. Her heart ached on behalf of an imaginary child who would have been showered with all the love Joe was dying to give.

"Anyway," he said, "I happened to be involved with a woman at the time, and I started thinking if I'm ever going to have a kid, I need to get married. I found myself looking at Janice and trying to picture her as a mother."

"I take it the picture didn't jell."

"Not even close." He snorted with laughter. "Janice was smart and ambitious and a lot of fun. But she liked to party as hard as she worked, and believe me, she was completely driven in her career."

"What did she do?"

"Fashion buyer for a department store and a total clotheshorse. You'd have liked her."

"Somehow I doubt it," Maddy muttered into her cup.

"Oh yeah, I forgot. You like those used-clothes places."

"Vintage boutiques," she corrected.

"Janice was pretty much straight-line New York chic."

That wasn't why Maddy wanted to rip the woman's hair out, but she let it pass. "So, what happened?"

"I was smart enough to realize she would have been a disaster as a mother and I was determined enough that my children have a good home not to make that mistake. Like you said—hell of a thing to do to kids, bring them into the world, then ignore them. It's too big a responsibility to take lightly."

"Agreed."

Quiet fell between them and stretched out long enough to become awkward.

Joe looked out over the valley. "I really like this view."

"Me too." Maddy turned as well, but all her senses remained tuned to the man beside her, sitting so close she could easily reach out and touch him.

"When I realized I was moving here permanently, I nearly took this place for myself."

"Why didn't you?"

"It seemed more practical for me to move into the rooms behind the office."

"You sleep in the office?"

"You didn't know that?"

"I assumed you'd moved in with your mom."

Which proved how much she'd isolated herself from the rest of the camp.

"No, the owner's house is really small. While I love my mom to death, I like having a little privacy."

A little privacy to do what? All her thoughts from the first day returned, about Joe having a camp full of nubile counselors to pick from. She glanced sideways to find him watching her. "What?"

His lips quirked. "Do you know how easy it is to look at your face and tell what you're thinking?"

"I wasn't thinking anything." Heat rose in her cheeks.

He leaned forward, resting his forearms on his thighs. "Well, the answer to the question you weren't thinking is no. I don't have wild orgies in the office with the camp counselors. They're kids, Maddy." He looked straight into her eyes. "I like my women a little more mature than that."

Her breath turned shallow. Was he saying he wanted to sleep with her? "Some of them are older than you and I were when we were dating."

His brows snapped together. "God, were we really that young? Ever?"

"We were. Which sort of proves my point that I was too immature to get married back then. I panicked and I made a mistake."

"I thought you said you wouldn't trade your years with Nigel for anything." A bitter edge crept into his voice. "But then, oh yeah, you loved him."

"Are you saying I didn't love you?"

He looked away without answering.

She sat, gripping her cup, trying to figure him out. One moment he was practically hitting on her, the next he was back to being angry over their breakup. How could she know how to act or what to say when he gave her such mixed signals?

"I need more wine." She stood and hurried inside. In the kitchen she braced both hands on the counter and dropped her head forward. Fear and confusion and a crazy hope that refused to die left her shaky.

A soft sound told her Joe had followed. Turning, she looked at him, and wanted him more than she ever had in the past. She wanted the wonderful caring, compassionate, yet still wounded man who stood before her. To love him and heal him and be healed in his arms.

"What are we doing here, Joe? What is going on between us? What do you want from me?"

Without a word, he walked to her, set his cup beside hers and took her head in both hands. For a moment, he simply stared down into her eyes, long enough for the barriers to drop away. Long enough for her to see the hunger he'd kept hidden. Then slowly he lowered his head.

A whimper escaped her when he covered her mouth with his. Her world tilted. She gripped the counter at her back and accepted all the pent-up desire he poured into her. Took from her.

He deepened the play of lips and tongue, taking her mouth as if starved for the taste of her, then tightened his fingers in her hair. Lifting his head, he stared at her again. "You want to know what I want, Maddy? I want you. I don't think I've ever stopped wanting you."

A part of her leapt with glee even as another part of her remembered how much her body had changed since the last time they'd made love. "I'm not the same girl I was back then."

"I don't want a girl. I want you." His mouth was on hers again, his lips molding hers, his tongue sweeping deep inside.

As if he'd hit some hidden switch, her reservations vanished and years of buried need ignited inside her. Her mouth went from accepting to ravenous in a flash. He pulled back, startled. She gripped the front of his camp shirt and rose up on her toes to keep the kiss from being broken.

With a groan, he pinned her against the counter, his hips tight against hers. His hands held her still as his mouth grew rougher. His tongue plundered, taking everything she offered and demanding more.

His erection rose against her soft belly, making her head spin with thoughts of having him inside her. Greedy now, she rubbed against him, wanting more, and wanting it right now. In answer, he swept a hand down the back of her leg and lifted it high against his hips. His hardness connected with her aching center and nearly sent her straight over the edge.

Panic jerked her back.

She slapped both her hands flat against his chest as she tore her mouth free. "Okayokayokay!" She struggled not to hyperventilate as spots danced before her eyes. "Ohmygod!" She saw his frown of confusion and laughed, although it sounded slightly insane. "I think I need to warn you . . . it's been a really long time since I did this. I mean a really, *really* long time."

His frown deepened. "Are you telling me to stop?"

"No! Good God, no." Another shaky laugh came out. "I'm just warning you I feel like a whole case of dynamite that's about to . . . go off."

A purely male smile tugged at his lips. "Good thing I'm rated expert in handling explosives."

His mouth descended again. Before she quite knew how, she was perched on the edge of the counter with both her legs wrapped tightly about his hips. His hands were inside the legs of her shorts and under her panties, cupping her bare bottom as he moved against her through layers of clothes. The sheer pleasure of it made her head fall back. Taking advantage, he moved to her neck, teasing her pulse to a faster pace.

Then his hips shifted, struck just the right angle, and pleasure shot through her in a blinding flash. Arching her back, she gasped in shock. Fireworks went off throughout her body, then she drifted slowly and ever so sweetly back to earth.

She opened her eyes to find him staring at her with a look of amused wonder.

"Did you just . . . ?"

"Oh yeah." She laughed and blushed. "Sorry."

"Are you kidding? Do you have any idea how hot that was? I nearly came myself."

"Don't you dare," she ordered, then blushed even more. "I mean—"

"Not until I get inside you, I swear." He shuddered when she licked his neck. "I hope."

"I did try to warn you."

"I may forgive you." He pressed kisses along her hairline. "On one condition. Lose the shirt. I'd rip it off myself but my hands are kind of full." He squeezed her bottom to demonstrate.

She glanced toward the sliding glass door where sunlight poured in. "Do you think we could close the draperies first?"

"Why?" He pulled back. "No one can see in."

"I know. It's just really bright in here."

He wiggled his brows. "I know."

"Joe, I'm not kidding." She crossed her arms over her breasts. "I'm not the same girl you remember. I'm thirty-two years old. I have . . . bulges. And cellulite. As much as I am dying to see you naked, I would prefer you not see me all that clearly."

"You want to see me naked?" The thought clearly flattered him.

" 'See' you naked?" She snorted. "I want to *draw* you naked. Preferably while I have my clothes on."

He considered it a moment. "Okay. Now, open your shirt."

Her heart skipped. "Are you saying you'll let me draw you?"

He arched a dark brow. "Those buttons better start popping open in the next two seconds, or they'll be popping off."

"All right, all right." She untied the shirttail at her waist. "Jeez, you are so demanding."

"Yeah, and I can tell you find it a real turnoff."

He was right, she realized. This alpha male side of him thrilled her on a purely primal level. Her nerves sparked with little thrills as she opened the shirt, then held in her stomach as best she could before spreading it open to hang on either side of her breasts.

His hot gaze fell to the abundant swells of creamy flesh over the bronze-colored bra. Feeling wicked and female, she unsnapped the clasp between the cups and parted the bra slowly. The brush of air puckered her nipples to aching peaks.

His expression went blank as he stared down at her, transfixed. "God, how can you be even more beautiful?"

She wanted to point out that she wasn't. She was bigger, true, but she wasn't as firm.

He didn't seem to care. Almost reverently, he pulled his hands from her shorts and cupped both breasts, stroked them softly. With her hands on the counter, she arched back, offering herself to him. Glorious pleasure filled her at the feel of him lifting the weight of her breasts, at his mouth suckling one nipple and his fingers teasing the other.

Her legs tightened about his waist as pleasure built and built, then burst again, as bright and wondrous as it had been the first time.

He chuckled against her breasts, but she refused to be embarrassed this time. As her senses cleared, she grabbed his shirt and tugged, wanting to get to bare skin.

In one swift move, he had his shirt off and sailing for the far corner. He started to return to feasting on her breasts, but she held him back so she could have her turn touching him. Oh wow. He felt even better than she'd expected, she marveled as she ran her hands over his shoulders and down his arms.

The tattoos were like Celtic armbands, but the designs were Native American. They distracted her only briefly before she moved on to his torso. Her mouth watered as she learned his contours with her eager hands.

His muscles twitched at a touch here, a caress there, but he held himself rigidly still, allowing her to explore. When she leaned forward, though, to lick one flat, male nipple, his control snapped.

"Okay, that's it." He scooped her off the counter. "If I don't get inside you quick, this will all be over."

He strode toward the bed with her arms and legs wrapped about him. They tumbled onto the mattress, pulling at their remaining clothes until they were finally naked and free. And he was kissing her. Kissing her the way he always had. Long and deep, as if he could kiss her forever.

Her whole body sang with joy as he rolled her onto her back. He'd pulled a condom from somewhere and had it on with lightning speed. When he settled between her thighs, bracing himself on his straight arms so he could watch her, she smiled up at him and stroked his hard abs.

Nothing existed but the two of them and this moment. She lifted her hips in invitation. And when he sank slowly, fully, into her, stretching her and filling her, she laughed and came apart again, just like that. Just from the feel of him inside her once again.

"I love the way you laugh," he said in a low rumble, rotating his hips.

She smiled weakly and out of breath as he moved inside her. "I love the way you make me laugh."

She waited for him to take her hard and fast, in a blinding race toward fulfillment, but somewhere along the way, he'd learned restraint—learned that prolonged pleasure burned hotter and sweeter.

Slowly, he drove her mad with long, deep, calculated thrusts. She felt half crazed and on the verge of begging by the time he lowered his body over hers and took her mouth in a fevered kiss.

Yes, she wanted to shout as she moved her hands down his back and cupped the tight backside she'd drooled over since seeing him again. She squeezed the flexing muscles, pulling him to her as she lifted her hips. Finally he gave himself over to that wild rush toward the pinnacle. They reached it together, and hung suspended for a moment, before he collapsed on top of her, boneless and spent.

"Oh God yes." She laughed again as she wrapped her arms about him. "I think I could do that about five more times."

He moaned into the pillow. "I thought you just did. At least five times."

"I said five *more* times."

Groaning, he rolled off of her the best he could on such a narrow bed and draped an arm over his eyes. "Okay, I'm game. Just . . . give me a minute. Or ten. To catch my breath."

She snuggled against him with her head on his shoulder. "And here I thought Rangers were tough."

"Honey . . ." He lifted his arm to look at her. "If I weren't, we never would have made it to the bed."

"I'm not that heavy."

"No, but you are that hot." He kissed her forehead, stroking her hair. "And that beautiful."

Ducking her head, she bit her lip to hold back a rush of words. It was all so much, so fast. Was either one of them ready for where they might be headed?

Chapter 12

"I can't believe you talked me into this," Joe grumbled as his butt grew chilled.

"It wasn't that hard."

"Actually, at the time, it was very hard. That's how you caught me in a weak moment." He felt ridiculous, lying facedown on Maddy's bed, bare-ass naked while she sat in the big armchair across the room drawing him.

"Trust me." She laughed. "You and the word 'weak' do not belong in the same sentence."

With his weight on his elbows, he watched her over his shoulder. She'd closed the drapes and set candles on every conceivable surface "for effect." The play of light over her face and hair provided a nice distraction. An even better distraction was the fact that the red Chinese silk robe she'd put on barely covered the vital regions. With the way she sat, curled up in the chair, he had a good view of thoroughly female thighs. Plus, each time she reached for a different color in the box of pastels, the robe gaped down the front, teasing him with glimpses of her breasts.

"Maddy?"

"Yes?" She reached toward the box.

"You know that ten-minute rest I said I needed?"

"Um-hm?"

"I think we can safely say I'm fully rested."

She went still, then dragged her gaze up his body to his face. "Oh?"

"Ho-yeah." He cocked a brow as he felt himself lengthen and harden against the mattress. "So why don't you put down that sketch pad and come back over here?"

"I'm not done yet." She changed colors again, frustrating him when the robe refused to gape enough to show a nipple. Then she sat back, tipped her head to study him. A grin played across her face as she went back to drawing.

"What is it you keep smiling at? You're not doing a caricature as a joke, are you?"

She laughed and blushed. "Trust me, there is no exaggeration going on here."

"Exaggeration?"

"A caricature is when you exaggerate the subject's natural features. Like if they have a big nose, you make it even bigger."

"So, if I turned over, and you drew my other side—"

"No, don't move! I'm almost done." She made a few more quick strokes, then looked around and fanned herself. "Is it getting hot in here?"

"Maybe you should take off that robe." He gave her a smoldering look.

"Hold that!" She grabbed another color. "That look right there."

"You mean you're drawing more than my ass?"

"Oh, baby, I'm drawing everything." She grinned from ear to ear as she worked.

"Maddy," he said in a low, even voice.

"Yes?" she answered, clearly distracted.

"Remember our agreement. You don't show this to anyone, right?"

She glanced up, blinked, and her silly grin shifted to something much deeper. Much hotter. "I'm definitely not sharing this. With anyone." She uncurled from the chair with seductive grace and headed for him with a sway to her hips that had his blood pumping.

When she reached the bed, she dropped the pad so it landed on the floor. As she moved to the foot of the bed, he looked down to see what she'd drawn. He expected to be embarrassed, but the sensuality of the image hit him at gut level. This was how she saw him: a hard masculine body covered in molten shades of skin glowing in candlelight, surrounded by rumpled sheets and dark shadows.

It was mesmerizing. And arousing.

He felt the mattress dip as she climbed onto the bed, then her hands on the backs of his calves. He dropped his head forward and closed his eyes as her hands slid up the backs of his legs. His body tightened as she cupped his butt, caressing the cheeks, then kissing them.

He went rock hard against the mattress and flexed his hips instinctively, which increased the pressure in that strange pleasure/pain of intense arousal. Straddling him, she explored his whole back, and he could feel the moist heat between her thighs resting at the juncture of his legs.

Need built until he clenched his jaw to keep from turning over and taking her. Her tongue ran up his spine, making him shiver. Then her breath warmed his neck.

Her lips touched the edge of his ear as she whispered, "I want you. Now."

He rolled onto his back and sucked in a breath at the heated look she gave him. Rising up on her knees, she opened her robe, let it drop against his thighs. Candlelight glowed on her round shoulders, her full breasts. He ran his palms over her belly and thighs, enjoying the contrast of her pale softness beneath his strong, dark hands.

Her eyes shone with passion as she smiled down at him, then sank slowly, taking him inside. He savored every sensation, every touch, every sight and scent as she pleasured herself and him.

He knew he'd pay for this eventually—everything in life had a price—but for now there was only pleasure. Only joy. Only Maddy.

"Promise me something."

The lazy rumble of Joe's voice roused Maddy enough for her to open her eyes. They must have drifted to sleep after crawling beneath the covers. Glancing over her shoulder, she didn't see any light seeping around the draperies and guessed that full night had fallen.

Yawning, she settled back against his chest and wondered if anyone had missed them at dinner. "What was that?"

"I don't want there to be any lies this time."

"Lies?" She struggled past the layers of sleep to

make sense of his words. "What are you talking about?"

"People say 'I love you' all the time, but rarely mean it. In fact, I think very few people even know what it means."

Propping up on her elbow, she looked at him, his face mostly shadows in the darkness. "You think I lied before, when we were dating and I told you I loved you?"

"I think you believed it at the time, because it gave you permission in your mind to sleep with me." Faint light glinted in his eyes as he caressed her cheek. "But we're adults now, and we don't need that. What we do in private is nobody's business but ours. The only thing I ask is that you don't say anything you don't truly mean."

The words hit her like a punch. "I can't believe you think I lied about loving you."

"You cared for me, and you liked being with me, but it wasn't love, Maddy." When she started to argue, his thumb moved over her lips. "I know the difference."

She pulled his hand away. "Before I get mad, perhaps you can explain what the difference means to you."

His eyelids lowered, shielding his eyes from her as he spoke. "I was only six when the state took me away from my birth mother, but I can remember her. She used to tell me she loved me all the time—when she wasn't passed out with one of her druggie boyfriends. She even cried and made a big scene when Child Protective Services hauled me away."

. She tightened her hold on his hand and waited, knowing how much he hated to talk about his childhood. There was so much he'd never shared. So much she'd only been able to guess.

"She was pretty wasted that day," he finally said. "So much so that she could barely form a sentence, but I can still hear her wailing about how much she loved me and how she wouldn't let them keep me. Through the whole scene, I remember being terrified, not just for me, but for her. Because who would take care of her if I wasn't there? She promised to get me back. But . . . she never even tried."

"Oh, Joe, I'm so sorry—"

He moved his head, shaking off her words. She fell silent, aching for him but knowing that sometimes sympathy made the pain worse.

"I went from one foster home to another after that. Some of the foster parents weren't too bad. Other couples were only in it for the monthly check. A few, though . . . a few tried to care, which hurt even more. They'd say they loved me and they were going to take good care of me. But eventually even they'd get tired of me causing trouble, so I'd get carted somewhere else and it would start all over.

"By the time I was twelve and landed with the Frasers, you might say I was a little jaded."

"With good reason."

"The last couple who'd had me were pretty vocal about how much trouble I was, going so far as to say I was little more than a wild animal. I overheard the caseworker jokingly say, 'What are you suggesting we do, put him down?' "

"That's awful!" she gasped.

"In their defense, I was pretty bad—and pretty sick of people pretending to give a rat's ass about me when they didn't. By that point, CPS was running out of options on places to put me. So they begged the Frasers to take me on."

He finally looked at her. "The deal with Mama and the Colonel was that once you were in their house, you stayed until you were adopted by another couple, put back with your birth family, or old enough to be on your own. That was their commitment. No matter how much trouble you caused. They never sent one of their boys away."

"They're an incredible couple."

"Yeah." He looked away. "Unfortunately, when CPS asked them to take me, the Colonel was four years away from retirement and wanted to move home to Texas. I was only twelve. Now, I might have been a troublemaker, but I could do the math. I'd be sixteen when they wanted to move across state lines, if I lasted with them that long. Besides, I overheard enough of the conversation to know they were down to only two boys and both of them were about to head off for college, which meant that for the first time in years, the Frasers were going to have their house all to themselves."

"But they agreed."

"Yeah." His short laugh held amazement. "All the way over there I was thinking 'sure they're gonna keep me.' Then we got to their house and the caseworker introduced me to the Colonel right in the front yard. Lord, he was a big man, with that hard, craggy face and that way of putting privates in their place with just a look."

"I know exactly the look you're talking about." She nodded. "He scared the tar out of me the first time I met him."

"Try being twelve and knowing what I did about the foster care system. I assure you, child abuse is

not unheard of. He looked down at me and said in
that deep voice, 'Here's how it works, son. You will
follow the rules of this house. Or you will suffer the
consequences.' I gulped so hard I nearly swallowed
my tongue."

"I don't blame you."

"At that point, I decided maybe the caseworker
hadn't been joking after all. They really were going
to have me put down like a wild animal. Then
Mama came out of the house, put her hands on my
shoulders, looked me straight in the eyes and said,
'You're ours now, and we love you already because
you're ours. And nothing you can do will ever
change that. Ever.' "

An ache of tears filled her throat as she pictured
the scene.

Joe toyed with her hand, looking at it rather than
her. "Of course I didn't believe her. In fact, it made
me mad that she would even say it. Mad enough
that I continued to act up even though I feared the
wrath of the Colonel."

"What would he do when you got in trouble?"
Concern welled inside her.

Joe's smile flashed in the darkness. "He'd give
me one of his looks and say, 'We're disappointed
in your behavior.' And that would be it. At first
I'd just snort in contempt and think 'Big deal. He's
disappointed. Whoa, I'm scared.' But then I noticed
that Shawn and Mark had a lot more privileges
than I did and the Colonel was always smiling at
them and going on and on about how proud he was
of both of them. Now that pissed me off. Couple of
goody-two-shoes wimps."

"I thought you liked Shawn and Mark."

"I do now. That first year, though, I hated their

guts." He looked at her. "Do you know that they and most of the others still keep in touch with Mama?"

"That doesn't surprise me."

"Me either." He went back to toying with her hand. "Anyway, what all of this is leading up to is . . . when I was fourteen, I got caught stealing beer from a convenience store. Fortunately the store manager called the Colonel, not the cops. Actually"—he scowled—"the cops probably would have been easier. I got the usual 'We're disappointed in your behavior' speech, only . . . somewhere along the way it had become a big deal. I felt like shit. Like I was never going to get my life right, and it was just a matter of time before the Frasers sent me packing right when I'd started to believe that maybe I could have stayed this time if I hadn't screwed up."

His hand tightened about hers. "The thought upset me so much that I actually started crying like a stupid baby. Mama heard me and came in my room. She didn't say anything at first, just sat on the bed beside me and put her arms around me. Man . . . I broke down completely, which just added a big dose of embarrassment to everything.

"When I finally got it together enough to talk, I asked her why they didn't just go ahead and send me away and get it over with. And she told me they would never get rid of me, they loved me, and they would always love me, no matter what. When I pointed out that I hadn't done anything to earn it, she said, 'You don't have to earn love. It either is or it isn't. All you have to earn is our respect.' "

Maddy squeezed his hand, struggling against tears.

"It took a long time for that to sink in. I guess I'm a slow learner. Even after they adopted me, which I firmly believe—which I *know*—had to do with more than just being able to move across state lines and take me with them, I kept waiting for the day when I'd finally cross some invisible line and they'd tell me that was it, they didn't want me anymore. But I finally, finally realized that line didn't exist. It was the most liberating thing in the world, to know love wasn't just a word to them. When they said it, they meant it, absolutely.

"So . . . when you told me . . ." His voice grew rough, and he wouldn't look at her. "When you said that you loved me . . . I believed you. I thought you meant it the way they meant it."

"Oh God, Joe. I—" Her throat closed. "I did love you. I think I might—"

"No. Don't." He pulled his hand free to place his fingers against her lips. When his eyes lifted, light gleamed off unshed tears. "I can accept that you believed it at the time. You're right. You were young, and you didn't know the difference between saying it and meaning it. But . . . I knew. I think that's why it hit me so hard when you dumped me. It was the last thing in the world I expected, and it . . . God, Maddy, you blindsided me."

"I'm sorry." Tears welled up hot and fast, filling her eyes. She dropped her forehead against his chest as a sob shook her shoulders. "I'm so sorry."

"I know." He wrapped his arms fiercely about her and held her tightly while she cried. The irony struck her that he was the one comforting her, when she was the one who'd caused the pain. "You would never intentionally hurt anyone. I know that. So, I'm asking that this time we don't say anything we don't mean, okay?"

"Okay."

Chapter 13

Nothing comes without a price, so don't whine when the bill arrives.

—*How to Have a Perfect Life*

The days that followed were filled with glitter. Literally. Maddy marveled at the younger girls' obsession with sprinkling bits of silver, gold, hot pink, and electric blue onto acres of glue, gleefully spilling it onto tables, chairs, and the floor like mad little fairies, then tracking it outside, and down the mountain until the trail to the Craft Shack positively glistened.

But more than the days, it was Maddy's nights that truly sparkled, nights in which Joe waited until taps played over the loudspeaker, then followed that glittering trail up the mountain under cover of dark. Their nights together shone with laughter and passion.

Oh, they were very discreet during the day. They never allowed their gazes to linger. Too long. They didn't exchange silly grins. Too often. And if they had to talk about camp business, she managed not to blush with memories of the night before while he kept thoughts of the night to come from shining in his eyes. Most of the time.

Yet, on the day that Maddy returned to the camp after taking her newest pieces to the gallery, she knew she wouldn't be able to wait until nightfall to see Joe. Happiness bubbled inside her as she parked before the office. She bounded into the front room, hoping to find Joe alone. Instead, she found Carol sitting behind the desk.

"You're back." Carol looked up from the computer screen. "And you're smiling, so I assume things went well."

"What?" Maddy pulled up in surprise.

"Joe mentioned you were taking your artwork to a gallery in town. So, how'd it go?"

"It went great! Fabulous, in fact." She refrained from bursting into giddy laughter as she marked down the time of her return on the sign-out sheet.

"Well?" Carol prompted. "Tell, tell."

Smiling, she shook her head, wanting Joe to be the first to hear her news. "It's too much. I'll give you the details at dinner. So, um, is Joe around? I'd like to let him know I'm back."

"He's in his apartment." Carol pointed her thumb over her shoulder toward the almost closed door. "On the phone . . . like he's been all day."

"Oh." Maddy glanced at the door and felt her cheeks heat knowing he was right on the other side. In his private apartment. Which she'd never seen but felt certain had a bed. Although, with the way things had been between them the last few days, a floor, a wall, or a countertop and ten minutes of privacy would do.

Her cheeks flamed hotter as she searched for an

excuse to get rid of Carol, go through that door, and lock it behind her. Unfortunately, her brain cells were too scrambled lately to function properly.

"Well." Flustered, she motioned toward the door to the parking lot. "I guess I'll . . . see you at dinner."

"No, wait," Carol said. "Why don't you poke your head in the apartment? Tell Joe you're here?"

Maddy laughed, which was a silly response.

"Besides"—Carol rose, straightening papers—"I have some, um, things I need to do. Yes. Things. So I actually need you to tell Joe I'll be gone for a while."

"A while?" Maddy struggled to keep the leap of excitement from showing on her face. "How long a while?"

"An hour?" Carol asked, then quickly dropped her voice to remove the question mark. "I mean, an hour. At least." Blushing, she headed for the back door. "Well, gotta run. You two have fun." With a little snicker, she disappeared.

Have fun? Maddy's mouth dropped open, and then she laughed. Oh man, she and Joe were so busted! And after being so careful. How had Carol figured it out? Did any of the others know? Did Joe's mother know? Okay, Mama would probably be happy, but still, she found it mildly embarrassing and highly amusing that they'd gone to such lengths to be discreet.

Shaking her head, she looked at the door. Joe's voice drifted out, a low, sexy rumble. She moved closer, eased the door open, and peeked inside. She saw a tastefully decorated room done in natural colors, from dark brown to pale beige with a few splashes of earthy red. The louvered shutters were tilted to allow privacy but still let in sunlight. Two big leather chairs sat before the windows, flanked by wooden bookshelves that held his collection of pueblo pottery, kachinas, and art books. As for framed art, he hadn't exaggerated when he told Juanita he had no wall space left. His taste ran toward domestic pueblo scenes, homey, peaceful images.

"Sounds like we're nearly good to go." His voice drew her attention the other direction. Peeking around the door, she found him standing with his back to her, talking on a cordless phone while washing dishes in a kitchenette that was only slightly larger than hers.

Curious, she scanned the room again and found a door directly across from her that stood open enough for her to make out the foot of a sturdy-looking bed. The bedspread echoed the patterns of the Navajo rug that covered the floor.

Excellent taste, she thought.

Joe turned with the phone pressed between his shoulder and ear. He froze when he saw her. Then smiled. "Hey, look, I need to let you go. Call me back when you know for sure." He hung up and faced her fully. "You're back."

"I am." She started to return his smile, but a mischievous imp took hold and she scowled instead. "And I have bad news."

"What?" Concern registered on his face.

"I'm afraid they're on to us. Carol, for sure. Maybe the others." She shook her head gravely. "I think they know we're"—she wiggled her brows—"you know."

"Sneaking around? No!" He feigned shock, then

lowered his voice to a whisper. "Maddy, I'm fairly certain a blind monkey could figure out I've got the hots for you so bad I can barely see straight."

"You don't have to whisper," she whispered back. "We're alone."

"We are?" His face lit up.

"Carol just left to do some 'things,' assuring me she'd be gone 'at least an hour.' "

"Oh really?" The interest deepened as he came toward her, moving with a slow, predatory step. "Remind me to add a big bonus to her paycheck."

"You're not upset?" He didn't look upset. In fact, he looked like a panther spying a nice, juicy steak. She backed up a step, then two, toward the sitting area.

"Why would I be upset?" He closed and locked the door as he passed it.

"I thought you didn't want people to know." She held a hand up, continuing backward. Fantasizing about jumping Joe in his apartment in the middle of the day was one thing—but the reality was a camp full of people just beyond the windows. "You've been so circumspect."

"Well, I'm hardly going to flaunt the fact that we're doing the wild thing in front of the campers and counselors, but no, I don't mind if the coordinators know. All of them are old enough that I think it's a safe bet to say they've discovered sex. Now, come here."

He took her hand and tugged her forward so fast she fell against his chest. Before she could think, she was in his arms and he was kissing her—a slow, deep, sweet kiss that went on and on until her knees were weak.

Then he lifted his head and caressed her cheek. "I missed you today."

A glowing happiness filled her as she smiled up at him. "You saw me just last night."

"That was forever ago." His head started to lower.

Laughing, she rose up to meet him, but pulled back at the last instant. "Oh! I have news."

"It can wait."

"No, I have *news*. Big news!"

"Let me guess." He nibbled her neck. "Sylvia loved your work and wants to do the prints she talked about."

"Yes!"

"Maddy, I hate to tell you, but that is not news. Now, about that hour of privacy we have . . ." Without warning, he bent down and hefted her over his shoulder.

"Joe! What are you doing?" she shrieked as he headed for the bedroom. He tossed her playfully onto the mattress, then climbed on after her. "Wait." She placed a hand against his rock-hard chest to keep him from kissing her again. "It's more than just them wanting to do prints. They have a show scheduled in a couple of weeks to launch their fall catalog."

"And?" He traced her jaw with kisses.

She took his face in both her hands to get his attention. "They want to include me in the show."

"Makes sense." Brushing her hair back, he went for her ear.

The tip of his tongue traced the shell, sending a delicious shiver all the way to her toes. "Mmm, that feels good." What had she been saying? Oh yes. "They, uh, they're even going to include me in the invitation as the"—his lips teased the pulse point in her neck—"as the, mmm, star attraction."

"Really?" He lifted his head, finally looking impressed. Then his attention dropped to the peasant blouse she wore with a colorful skirt. He tugged slowly on the tie. "Star attraction, huh?"

"No, not star." Laughing, she batted his hand away. "With the heavy hitters they have, I'm way down the list. But I'm the . . ." How had Sylvia phrased it? "The hook."

"The what?" He cocked his head, actually listening now.

"I told you it was big news." She smiled up at him. "They haven't ordered the invitations yet, so they're changing them to add me. Only they aren't going to use my name. They're going to say something about unveiling their newest find, an artist whose work has never been shown in Santa Fe."

"Ah, a mystery hook. Great idea. This town has so many art shows, even the die-hard collectors get a little tired of them."

"Do you have any idea how exciting this is?" She wiggled out from under him to sit against the headboard. "And how scary?"

After a resigned sigh, he moved to sit beside her. "Why scary?"

"I don't know. This could be huge for me, but it's happening so fast I feel dizzy. Sylvia is making all these plans for how to 'launch' me after the unveiling. She's talking about ads in *Southwest Art*, and how her sales staff will pitch my work to other galleries."

"That's great. Right?"

"It is! Except what if no one else likes my work? What if—"

"Maddy, stop." He hugged her, laughing. "You're going to do fine. With a power like Sylvia behind you, you're on your way to the big time."

"Oh God." She placed a hand over her heart and found it beating way too fast. "That sounds so weird."

"Why? Isn't this what you've always wanted?"

"It's what every artist wants! But something like this normally takes years."

"You have been working for years. You just haven't been selling for years."

"But that's the point. I haven't struggled, or paid my dues, or been the starving artist."

His brows snapped together. "I'm not sure I see the problem here."

"You don't just walk into a Santa Fe art gallery, open up your portfolio, and have your dreams come true."

"Again, I'm not seeing the problem."

She flung her hand out in frustration. "Every artist out there is going to hate me."

"*Every* artist?"

"Enough."

"So?"

"So . . ," Her stomach churned. "It's like high school all over again."

"Excuse me?" He didn't quite suppress his chuckle.

She took his hand in hers, searching for a way to make him understand. "I had lots of friends. *We* had lots of friends. I was happy. Well, as happy as any teenager with a dysfunctional family can be.

Plus I had you. Then I won that scholarship, and everything changed. Everyone turned against me. They hated me."

"Okay, Maddy, first of all, you're not in high school anymore. Back then, we ran with a crowd of losers, most of whom were doing or dealing drugs. So of course they grew distrustful when they found out you weren't really one of them. You had goals and dreams they couldn't understand, and you were actually going after them."

"It isn't going after your dreams that makes people resent you, it's having your dreams come true without paying a price."

"No, it's pursuing them behind people's back." Anger flared in his voice.

She bit her lip, watching as his face hardened.

Exhaling in a gust, he looked away. "I'm sorry. I didn't mean—" He turned back to her, calm now but intense. "Maddy, you are meant for great things. I think I've always sensed that about you. You have so much talent. So much . . . *life* inside you. I think that's what drew me to you then and now." His hand tightened on hers. "Don't hold yourself back because of what people think. Who cares what people think?"

"I care! I like people. I don't want to hurt them."

"Hurt them?"

"Yes. It's like with Tammy Andersen."

"Tammy who?"

"Andersen. We had several art classes together in high school, and she was really good." He still looked blank, so she smirked. "A lot of the kids called her Tammy the Toad."

"Ah, yes. I remember. The girl who had no neck."

"Of all the friends who turned against me, she was the one who hurt the worst. I didn't know until later that she'd applied for the same scholarship—because I'd told her about it. I'd told her how good she was and encouraged her to show her work. So she applied. And I beat her out. After that, she would never look me in the eye when we talked. She wasn't openly ugly to me, like some of our friends were, but I felt like I'd run over her cat and had no idea how to tell her I was sorry."

"Maddy . . ." He let out a scoffing breath. "Screw sorry. She was jealous. That was her problem."

She pulled back, aghast. "That is so cruel. And you aren't a cruel person. Normally."

"Life is cruel."

"Oh yes, let's be glib. 'Life is cruel.' That may be true, but I don't have to add to it."

"What, by succeeding? By knowing what you want and going after it? And when I said that was her problem, I meant she wasn't your friend if she let that get between you. You cared enough to encourage her, and she got miffed over your success rather than cheering you on? Definitely screw sorry."

"I just . . ."

"What?"

"I want everyone to succeed."

"I know." He caressed her cheek. "That's part of your magic."

"What am I going to do?" She turned fully toward him. "I want to grab on to this, but it's so big, and I don't know if I'm ready. Plus, I've made friends here, and I don't want to alienate them."

"Who, Carol and the others?"

And you, she thought.

He studied her a long moment, then moved off the bed to prowl the room. "I don't understand why your friendship with the staff here should hold you back. This is a summer job for you. Your main objective in coming here was to check out the galleries. The coordinators are barely more than acquaintances to you. Temporary friends. When the summer is over, you'll get on with your real life back in Austin." He turned back to her. "Right?"

What was he saying? Was he asking if she had any interest in staying? Before she could ask, the phone in the other room rang.

He glanced toward the sound, then mumbled something about needing to get the call.

She sat, wondering for the thousandth time what was going on between them. She knew she wanted more, but how much more? And what did he want? Perhaps it was time to build up the courage to ask.

She rose on shaky legs and moved to the doorway. Listening absently at first, then with growing interest as she realized he was talking to Derrick, his Ranger buddy, about starting the boot camp he'd mentioned. By the time he hung up, she was staring at him in disbelief.

"What's wrong?" he asked, frowning.

"You're going ahead with your plans for the boot camp."

"Yeah." He shrugged as if it were no big deal. "I talked it over with Mom, and she insisted she'd be fine with it."

"When?"

"A few days ago?"

"And you didn't think about sharing that with me?"

That internal wall he'd perfected rose up in an instant, blocking her out.

She flung an arm toward the bedroom. "You just chastised me for not sharing my dreams with you fifteen years ago, and now you're pursuing this behind my back?"

"It wasn't 'behind your back.' I told you I was thinking about it."

"But not that you were going through with it."

"This has nothing to do with us." He headed for the refrigerator and pulled out a can of cola.

"I told you I'd help—"

"I don't want you to help!" He whirled to face her, his expression so hard, hurt struck her chest. He turned back to the counter, popped the can open. "You're leaving at the end of summer, remember?" He glanced back at her, but only briefly. "Why waste what time we have together talking about business plans?"

"Because this is your dream. And you weren't going to share it with me . . . even though we're sleeping together."

"One has nothing to do with the other."

"Oh, well, excuse me for confusing sex with intimacy."

"Maddy, don't do this." He sighed heavily. "We're barely feeling our way along as it is. The past doesn't disappear just because we're getting along in the present."

She stared at him. "You said love was something that didn't have to be earned. It either is or it isn't. What about forgiveness? Does that have to be earned? If so, give me a task. Tell me what to do. How do I earn your trust if you're not willing to give me a chance?"

"What exactly are you asking for here? Do you even know what you want out of this thing between us?" Exasperation hardened his face. "Don't jack with me, Maddy! You can't come out here for one flippin' summer and expect me to jump right back into a serious relationship."

"What is it *you* want from this 'thing between us'?"

"Stop—" He took several deep breaths, but when he looked at her, his eyes blazed. "I took a blind leap for you once and fell flat on my face. Don't ask me to do it again. I prefer to take things slower these days."

"Apparently!" Her anger ignited. "You're only willing to jump off the high board when it's something you really want. I guess I don't meet that criteria." She started to storm out, but whirled back. "You want to take things slowly? All right. No problem. In fact, I think we should take things very slowly. As in, I need to be in your life more before I share my body with you again. Because until you're willing to share something of yourself, that's just a little too personal for me." She strode toward the door.

"Maddy . . ."

"Forget it, Joe. I realize you're worried about getting hurt. Well, join the club. We're all worried about getting hurt. That's part of being alive. When and if you decide to share something more than sex, let me know."

Chapter 14

Subject: *Men are such jerks!!!*

Christine: *Whoa, what happened? I thought all was bliss with you and Joe?*

Maddy pounded out an e-mail explaining everything, how Joe was doing to her the very thing he'd never forgiven her for and he didn't seem to see it. To him it was all her fault that he couldn't trust her.

Christine: *You're right. Men are jerks.*

Amy: *Wait a minute. Let's not be too hasty. Maddy, what's Joe's side?*

Christine: *Who cares? We're having a bitchfest. We'll be mature later. For now, Mad, feel free to let it rip. We promise that if things work out for you and the Jerk, we won't hold anything you say now against him.*

Amy: *Well, of course she's free to bitch to us, but I'd still like to know Joe's side.*

Maddy burst into tears as she typed her response: *Have I mentioned lately how much I love you guys?*

I don't suppose there's any way you'd come to the show so I can see you in person.

Christine: *We love you too. And I'd be at the show in a heartbeat, but I'll still be in residency. Amy?*

There was a pause before Amy responded: *I wish I could. Really. But I couldn't possibly train someone to cover the office that quickly. Plus there's my grandmother.*

Maddy knew Amy was making excuses, but let it slide as she typed: *It's okay, Amy. I wasn't thinking.*

Christine diplomatically shifted the subject away from Amy's fear of traveling: *Okay, let's figure out a way to have Joe crawling on his hands and knees when he comes over tonight thinking a simple apology will get him back into your bed.*

Only Joe didn't come that night.

The following day, when Maddy saw him in the dining hall, he marched in, grabbed his tray, stabbed at his food as if trying to kill it, and left.

Naturally, the coordinators noticed and had their heads together in an instant, whispering. Maddy wanted to scream. Confiding to Amy and Christine was one thing. That didn't mean she wanted Carol and the others plotting ways to get her and Joe back together.

As the days passed, however, the likelihood of a reconciliation seemed less and less likely. Weighed down by the thought, Maddy opened her laptop.

Message: *I'm ready to be mature. Any advice on how I fix this? I miss Joe so much, I ache all over. Things were so perfect for a while. I want that back. Oh God, I think I really am in love with him.*

Her hand hovered over the SEND key as her stomach churned. Should she delete that last sentence? Did telling someone make it real? Squinting her eyes, she hit SEND . . . and waited in agony for her friends' responses.

Amy: *Oh, Maddy. I'm so sorry you're hurting. Have you told Joe how you feel?*

Maddy: *Good God, no. Are you kidding? I told y'all some of his background. If I said the L word, he'd just put up more barriers.*

Christine: *You don't know that. Maybe he's just waiting for you to say it first. He could be thinking "By God, I stuck my neck out last time, this time it's her turn."*

Maddy: *There's a terrifying thought. Especially since he's given me NO indication that he wants something serious. I'm not even sure I want something this serious. My home, my family, and both of you are in Austin. What am I doing falling for a guy who lives in a whole different state?*

Christine: *Talk about your lame excuses! Maddy, houses can be sold, your family drives you nuts, and even though we'd miss meeting you for lunch, friends should never stand in the way of love. As for repairing this rift with Joe, I think you need to tell him at least some of how you feel. You don't have to use the big L word, but tell him something.*

Maddy: *How can I when he's not talking to me?*

Christine: *Sheesh. You wait until all the little kiddies are asleep, you knock on his door, and when he answers, you say, "Yo, Joe, let's talk."*

Maddy stared at Christine's post for several long minutes before closing her computer with a snap. Advice was easy for someone who didn't have to take it.

Realizing the sun was setting, she walked out onto her balcony. The sound and scent of the mountains at dusk filled her senses. Down in the camp, she saw a light glowing in Joe's apartment.

Maybe Christine was right. Maybe Joe wanted her to make the first move. She tried to picture it in her mind, what she would say and what his response might be. Fear swelled inside her with staggering swiftness, making her heart pound and her palms sweat. Good heavens, was this how Joe had felt all those years ago when he'd been building up the courage to propose?

And then she'd told him no?

Guilt stabbed at her, making her wince.

Although what if the reverse happened this time? What if she got up the nerve to tell him she loved him, only to have him reject her?

She stared at the light in the office a long time as the shadows lengthened and the air grew chilled. Finally, the campers on flag duty headed for the pole next to the big bell. Mama's voice came over the speakers with the evening prayer as the girls lowered and folded the flag. Then taps began to play, a soft, sleepy version that she usually found soothing.

Tonight it sounded so plaintive her chest ached.

She watched as the campers walked away from the flag pole. Watched Mama leave the office, climb into her golf cart, and head toward the little owner's house on the rise near the gate. And she wished for the sight of Joe stepping out of the office and heading up toward the Craft Shack as he'd done every night for that magical week.

The sky grew darker, the air colder.

She finally turned and went back inside, where she lay awake most of the night. The narrow bed had seemed so crowded with Joe in it, making them laugh more than once.

Now it felt far too empty.

Her friends were right. She needed to make the first move. With sleep evading her, she searched her mind for the right way to take the first step. If only she knew where that step would lead. Why did love have to be so scary and painful?

The following evening, Joe glared at the paperwork in front of him, wishing it would do a better job of distracting him from thoughts of Maddy—and the temptation to go up to the Craft Shack and beg his way back into her bed. Everything had been perfect. Couldn't they just go back to that?

Watching her leave at the end of summer was going to be hard enough. How much more would it hurt if he let her all the way into his life? If he let her be part of making plans for the boot camp, it would serve as one more reminder of her when she was gone. Couldn't she see that?

At the sound of crunching gravel in the parking lot, he looked up and was surprised to see his mother entering the office. He glanced at his watch. "You're a little early for taps, aren't you?"

"I thought I'd come by for a visit. Things have been so busy, we hardly get time to talk."

"Oh?" He tensed. Anytime Mama Fraser wanted to "talk" she definitely had something to say.

"Yes." Smiling, she sat in the chair between his desk and the back door. Outside, evening was settling over the valley. He could hear the campers enjoying their free time between dinner and lights-out with a game of tag out on the playing field. "I was up at the Craft Shack having a nice cup of tea with Madeline. She showed me some of the artwork she's done for the show. What talent that girl has!"

"Yes, I know." His gut twisted at the mere mention of her name.

Mama leaned forward to lay an envelope in front of him. "She asked me to give this to you."

"What is it?" He frowned suspiciously at the envelope. As strained as things had been between them the last few days, it could be anything from a scathing note telling him off to a letter of resignation. The thought of the latter sent panic racing through him. Seeing her every day was killing him by slow degrees, but it was better than not seeing her at all.

"Well?" his mother prompted. "Aren't you going to open it?"

Bracing himself for a "Dear John, screw you" note, he sliced the envelope open with a knife, then stared at the printed card inside. "It's an invitation to Maddy's show."

"So it is."

He felt a surge of hope, followed by frustration. "What? She couldn't be bothered to hand it to me in person?"

"With the way you've been acting lately?" His mother lifted a brow at him. "Maybe she didn't want to get growled at."

His teeth clamped together. "I haven't been growling at her."

"No?" She chuckled, then sighed. "Maybe not, but you have made it clear you don't want her here."

"Did she tell you that?" He fought the need to get up and pace.

"No. But I have eyes. You've been giving her the classic freeze-out for more than a week now." She shook her head sadly. "And just when I thought things were going well between you two."

"They were going well, until she—"

"Until she what?"

"Nothing." He straightened a stack of papers on his desk.

"Joe, do you want Maddy to leave?"

"No!" Alarm kicked up his heart rate. "I want—"

"What?"

Everything! he nearly shouted. *I want her to love me and mean it this time. The way I love her so much it's eating me up inside. I want her to love me the way she loved Nigel the Geek.*

Just thinking the name made him want to rip something apart. Instead he went back to shuffling papers. "If Maddy sent you down here to act as a go between, tell her there's no reason for her to leave. I'm perfectly capable of respecting the boundaries she set."

"Are you saying she's the one freezing you out?"

"It's not that simple." He scrubbed a hand over his face. "Look, I appreciate your concern, but I'm really not comfortable discussing certain things with my mother."

"Ah." A knowing twinkle came into her eyes. "She cut you off."

"Mom." Heat crept up his neck. "Do you mind?"

She laughed. "No wonder you're so grouchy."

"I'm not grouchy."

"Moody, then. Lack of sex can do that to a man."

He glared at her. "You're determined to discuss this, aren't you?"

She settled back in the chair. "How about if I save you from talking by telling you a story?"

"Suit yourself." He went back to his paperwork.

"I remember when I met the Colonel."

He groaned aloud at those familiar words, even though he liked this story. He just hated that it had a different purpose each time she told it.

"It was at a USO dance during the war. Not too many people considered him to be a particularly handsome man, even back then. But he was . . ." She tipped her head as if picturing him in her mind, and a glow came over her face. "Compelling."

Joe narrowed his eyes. "Last time you told this story, he was 'frightening.'"

"That too." She laughed. "I can still picture him as he walked into the room, scowling at everyone. The other girls were all too scared to go over and greet him, even though that was what we were there for, to make the servicemen feel at home. To get their minds off the war for a bit. So I watched him for a long time. Long enough to see how he looked at the couples cutting a rug on the dance floor, with this odd blend of longing and fear. Then he'd look at us girls and scowl even harder. I finally realized he was even more afraid of us than we were of him." Her eyes twinkled with laughter.

"So I marched right over there, my knees shaking the whole way—because what if I was wrong? Maybe he was as mean as he looked. I had no guarantee he wouldn't plumb take my head off in one big bite. Things are like that between men and women, you know. Very scary, with no guarantees."

Joe frowned in confusion. "We're already at the moral of the story?"

"Heavens no. The moral comes at the end. Now where was I?"

"You asked the Colonel to dance, only he wasn't a colonel back then. He was Major Patrick Fraser."

"Right. I asked him if he wanted to dance. He looked down at me from way up there." She tipped her head back, looking up, then rolled her eyes sideways to look at Joe. "Even before my bones shrank, I wasn't too tall. And do you know what he said?"

Joe lowered his voice to a deep bass. " 'I'm not sure that's wise, miss, since my feet are bigger than all of you put together.' "

She nodded. "So I asked him if he'd like to sit and talk instead. We were the last two to leave the USO that evening, and then only because they kicked us out. Major Patrick Fraser walked me out to my car. We didn't say a word the whole way across the big empty parking lot. I thought maybe he was mad at me because I'd teased him a bit about his big feet as we were leaving. Later he confessed it was because he wanted to kiss me so bad his knees were shaking.

"Imagine that." She grinned. "The Colonel with shaky knees."

"It happens to the best of men." Joe scowled at her.

"Yes, it does." She smothered her amusement. "When we reached my car, he mustered the courage to ask if he could kiss me. I said yes, of course, very matter-of-factly, expecting a peck good night.

But when he kissed me . . ." She patted her heart as her eyes turned dreamy. "Oh, when he kissed me . . . I knew. I just knew he was the man for me, no matter what the future held. I was gonna love that man as long as God let me."

Her eyes focused again, right on Joe, and he knew it was coming: the moral of the story.

"Now just imagine if I hadn't gotten up the courage to ask him to dance, or if he hadn't gotten up the courage to kiss me good night. We may have found happiness elsewhere, but I'm convinced it wouldn't have been near as rich. Some things are just meant. That doesn't mean happiness will fall into your lap. You have to work past the scary stage to earn it, then nurture it daily once you have it."

"And you think Maddy and I are 'meant'?"

"What do you think?"

"I think things don't always work out the way we want. And loving someone isn't always enough. Look at Jimmy," he said, referring to one of the older foster boys who had left the Frasers' home long before Joe arrived. Last they'd heard, Jimmy was serving a second prison sentence. "You gave him the same love you gave all of us, but even that wasn't enough. You can't tell me he didn't hurt you."

She nodded thoughtfully. "I hurt when I think of Jimmy, but I hurt for him, not for me. I don't regret opening my home and my heart to him. The Colonel and I gave him everything we knew how to give. But we gave it freely. There was no price tag attached. No stipulation that Jimmy had to do something with that love to please us."

"But he *hurt* you."

"He's hurt himself far more than he's hurt me." Her pale blue gaze bored into him. "Joe, love can be both joyous and painful. It's like an amusement park. You can ride the carousel, and go 'round and 'round nice and slow, or you can take the plunge on the roller coaster with all its big highs and lows.

"Now, there's a lot to be said for that carousel. That's what the Colonel and I had. A sweet ride filled with contentment and few surprises. And thank goodness for it, because you boys were a roller coaster, to be sure. It wasn't always fun. I won't lie to you—more than once I wanted to scream my head off. But in the end, I'm glad I had the whole amusement park, not just the carousel, and not just the roller coaster."

"Personally, I'd rather have just the carousel."

"I know." Her face softened with understanding. Most people would show shock at such a statement coming from thrill-seeking Joe Fraser, Army Ranger, explosives expert, adrenaline junkie. But when it came to relationships, he'd ridden the roller coaster enough by the time he reached manhood to never want to climb on it again.

And that's where Maddy scared him. She was the biggest, brightest ride at the fairground, with flashing lights and clanging bells. She drew him to her with all the awe and fear, longing and dread that drew a kid to a roller coaster.

"The thing is"—his mother leaned forward to pat his hand—"you don't always get to choose. Besides, you don't know how wild the ride will be until you get on. Maddy may surprise you this time around."

"Or not." He leaned back in his desk chair. "Which is why I refuse to draw a bull's-eye on my chest and tell her to take her best shot. Kevlar vests were invented for a reason, you know."

"Joe." A scowl wrinkled her face. "If you tell Maddy you'll only let her into your heart if she agrees to some list of conditions, then you haven't learned as much as I'd hoped you would about what it means to love."

"God." He covered his face with both hands. "I hate it when you're right."

"I know. Now about the art show . . ."

He dropped his hands and gave her a warning scowl—which she completely ignored.

"I'm hoping I can get a ride with you, since I don't enjoy driving at night the way I used to."

That made his brows go up. "You're admitting you're a hazard on the road?"

"I am not." She straightened her birdlike frame. "I said I don't *enjoy* driving at night."

"Because you can't *see* at night."

"I see just fine," she insisted. "And if you don't want to take me, very well. I'll drive myself."

"Don't be ridiculous. Of course I'll drive you."

"Good." She beamed as she stood. "Now, if you don't mind, I think I'll go watch the girls play until it's time for evening prayer."

It wasn't until she'd left that he realized how seamlessly she'd manipulated him. Thirty-three years old, and Mama Fraser still knew how to push his buttons.

God love her.

Love. He frowned at the word. Did he have what it took to love the way she did? To give it freely, absolutely, unconditionally with no guarantee on whether it brought pleasure, pain, or a combination of both?

Picking up the invitation, he thought about Maddy, ached for her. Was he destined to love this one woman his whole life? Taking both the pleasure and the pain she brought? Why was there so little free choice involved in love? That really sucked. He didn't want to be in love with her.

Yeah, but you are.

The question was, what was he going to do about it?

Marry her, idiot.

The answer popped into his head, knocking the breath out of his lungs. He'd already failed on that objective once. At present they weren't even talking to each other, so proposing was out of the question without laying some groundwork. A lot of groundwork.

What he needed was a plan. Yeah, he nodded as it took shape in his mind. The final objective was making Maddy a permanent part of his life. He'd have to get there, though, in phases.

Phase One: Get back to where they had been.

Phase Two: Get her to stay in Santa Fe.

Phase Three: Get a ring on her finger.

His heart pounded with memories of his past failure to accomplish that, but he'd been given seemingly impossible tasks before. All he had to do was stay focused on the task at hand. And not project too far into the future.

The first step of Phase One was to dispel the awkwardness.

Maddy was sitting with Dana and a whole table of campers having lunch when she looked up and found Joe standing beside her, holding his lunch tray. The sight of him looking right at her jolted her so hard she nearly dropped her fork.

"Hey," he said casually, as if days hadn't passed without them exchanging a single word.

"Hey," she managed to respond.

He dropped his gaze briefly, then looked back at her. "I noticed the invitation requested an RSVP."

"Yes?"

"I just wanted to let you know, I phoned Sylvia and told her to expect both Mom and me."

"Oh." Hope—and relief—filled her in a rush, blossoming into a warm glow over her face. "I'm glad."

He nodded. "I just thought you'd want to know."

With that, he turned and walked away to find an empty seat at another table. She turned back to find Dana smiling at her.

"You go, girl."

She released a laughing sigh, for once not caring that so many people knew the details of her love life. She'd offered an olive branch—and Joe had taken it.

Chapter 15

While success takes hard work, there's something to be said for taking the path of least resistance.
                                    —*How to Have a Perfect Life*

The day of the show arrived with a flurry of activity that kept Maddy so busy she could almost ignore the butterflies in her stomach. Since Mama had agreed to take over at the Craft Shack, she had the whole day off to help the gallery staff get ready.

One of the back alcoves had been set aside to showcase her work. After stripping the walls bare, she and Juanita started rehanging the area, filling it with her vibrant landscapes, jewel-tone wildflowers, and dramatic cloudscapes.

"Wow," Juanita said, stepping back to admire the progress they were making. "This looks great. I've already told you how much I love the pieces you brought in, but now that they're on the wall, they really pop."

"Thanks. The guys in the frame shop did a fabulous job."

"It's more than that," the gallery manager insisted. "You weren't kidding when you said you were good at displays."

"That's why I offered to help." Tape measure in hand, Maddy stepped around the framed pieces they'd laid out on the floor in an intricate grouping. Sylvia and some of the framers were working in the other alcoves, going through the same process. Tipping her head, she read off the measurements for the next nail placement.

"This is something the other artists rarely do." Juanita wrote down the numbers on a scrap of mat board. "Not that we mind. Their job is to create the art. Ours is to show it and sell it. To be honest"—Juanita lowered her voice—"most of them would muck this up if we let them try."

"Hanging a gallery wall is an art form in and of itself." Maddy pulled a nail from the pocket of the shirt she'd tied at the waist over a pair of tattered jeans.

"You got that right." Juanita laughed.

As Maddy drove the nail in, she realized how much she'd missed this world—not just the art itself, but the showing and selling too. Leading customers through a gallery was so much more than quoting prices. It was a performance, with stories to tell about each artist, the history of each piece, its connections to other works; and designing the displays was all part of setting the stage.

"What next?" Juanita asked when they'd finished hanging all of Maddy's pieces.

Maddy looked about. "Let's get a few bronzes in here to add dimension."

Together they muscled tree-trunk pedestals into position and topped them with bronzes.

"Perfect," Maddy announced as she dusted off her hands. The area looked as good as any Canyon Road gallery. Unfortunately, three hours remained until the show started, which left too much time to obsess about the coming night and thoughts of Joe.

He'd been friendlier toward her the last two days, but they still needed to sit down and really talk. So she and Mama had formed a plan for her to get Joe alone tonight after the show.

Nerves fluttered in her belly, so she pressed them down with a hand. "Do you want me to help with the rest of the gallery?"

"No, we're pretty much down to the pricing and cleaning up. Angelina." Juanita called to Sylvia's seven-year-old granddaughter. "You can sweep in here now if you want."

"Okay." The eager child, who'd been getting in the way more than helping most of the day, hurried forward with a broom that was taller than she was.

Juanita checked her watch. "Why don't you go ahead and get dressed? Sylvia wants pictures of you standing in front of *Sunrise Canyon* for the catalog We should do that before the madness begins."

Seeing little choice, Maddy headed through the door from the gallery into the noisy frame shop and offices.

If Images of the West were a woman, the gallery would be her face, beautifully made up to show the world, but this would be her heart and soul: bright, loud, and pulsing with life. Today that heart beat at a hectic pace as the staff scrambled to finish a few last pieces for the show. Fluorescent lights glared down from the exposed metal rafters while scraps of mat board littered the floor like giant confetti. Hard rock blared from a boom box, competing with the hiss of an air compressor blasting dust away from glass, and the nerve-jarring *pop* of a brad gun.

Maddy smiled at the whole disjointed, wonderful symphony of it as she made her way to the sales offices and employee bathroom at the back of the building.

There she found the dress she planned to wear hanging in its dry cleaner's bag. Excitement and anxiety tangled in her belly as she took it down and thought about the evening to come.

Joe steered his mother's powder blue land barge into the line of vehicles waiting to turn into the parking lot for Images of the West. "Looks like they got a crowd."

"Sure as shootin'," his mother said gleefully.

Ducking his head, he took in the whole effect. Luminarias lined the roof, while tiny white lights circled the porch posts. Brighter light spilled from the big windows across the front. Inside, he saw the cream of the Santa Fe art world—collectors, gallery owners, and artists—milling about. "Sylvia was a genius to play up the mystery artist angle."

"Maddy must be thrilled with the turnout," his mother said. "And nervous as all get-out."

"No doubt." Although Maddy wasn't the only one who was nervous. He'd managed step one in the first phase of his plan. Tonight he hoped to take another step toward getting things back to where they had been.

Finally, the line of cars moved forward. He maneuvered into a handicapped space near the front door, then turned to his mother. "Now this time wait for me to open your door, okay?"

"Don't be silly." She wrestled with the handle, her frail hands shaking. "I can manage."

"I mean it," he ordered in exasperation. The

stubborn woman never let him do anything for her without a battle. A less secure man would be positively emasculated in her presence, without her even realizing she was insulting him.

True to form, she made a face, but folded her hands as a sign of resignation. Satisfied, he stepped out of the car into the cool evening air. The voices of other gallerygoers and the sound of car doors slamming contrasted sharply with the quiet of the desert evening. Overhead, the twilight gathered as he opened the passenger door.

"Now see," he said. "That didn't hurt at all."

"Not at all," she agreed, with a smile that didn't mean a thing. Next time would be no different. He accepted that with the same patience that let him watch her struggle out of the passenger seat on her own. Her cane tangled with her legs, but she made it without tripping.

"All right." She straightened the Oriental silk jacket she wore with black leisure slacks and orthopedic shoes. "Let's go hobnob."

Joe hid a smile as they made their way across the parking lot. His mother couldn't be an art snob if she tried. She liked it all—from finger paintings by the campers to the works in his collection. The moment he opened the door the noise from inside washed over him.

"Joe." Sylvia stood ready to greet guests. "So glad you came."

"I wouldn't have missed it." He scanned the crowd for Maddy, but didn't see her. "I don't believe you've met my mother."

"No, I haven't." Sylvia extended a hand laden with turquoise and silver rings. "Your son has excellent taste in art . . . and artists, since he brought us Madeline. What a treasure! Everyone loves her work.''

''Of course they do,'' Mama replied. ''Madeline has always been very special.''

''I won't argue with that.'' Sylvia motioned toward the framing table, which had been converted into a buffet. A good-size crowd gathered around it, filling plates with finger food and accepting glasses of wine from the server at the far end. ''Why don't you two grab some refreshments and have a look around?''

''Thanks.'' Joe motioned for his mother to precede him and started to follow just as Maddy came into view.

She was talking to an older couple as she moved across the back of the crowded gallery. His focus narrowed, dimming everything but her as he tracked her progress, seeing her in snatches through the crowd. Her bright hair was set off by a cropped jacket done in rich, earthy shades, handpainted with stylized Indian ponies and dripping with leather fringe.

The crowd parted, granting him a brief glimpse of the copper-colored dress beneath the jacket. It flowed from a scooped neckline with buttons down the front, past her nipped-in waist, over nicely flared hips, then down her legs nearly to her ankles. A pair of sexy sandals with three-inch heels completed the outfit.

The sound of her laughter brought his gaze back up the length of her.

His chest tightened.

This was Maddy as he'd always pictured her. The bright, shining center of the art world. Both pride and doubt stirred within him. Pride that she was fulfilling her destiny, and doubt over whether that destiny included him.

"There she goes again," someone sighed in exasperation.

"Hmm, what?" Joe turned to find Juanita standing beside him with her hands on her hips.

"Madeline." The gallery manager motioned in frustration. "She keeps steering customers away from her own work to introduce them to the other artists. I admit, I love the fact that she's closed deals on four originals this evening, but I wish they'd been *her* originals. She's supposed to be our new star, not fill-in help for the sales staff."

Joe's gaze swung back to Maddy, watching as she pointed to various pieces on the wall, motioning with her hands as she talked. She was doing exactly what Juanita said: selling a painting by another artist.

"She's good, though." Juanita nodded. "You gotta give her that. She's really good."

"And completely exasperating." He started forward, pausing briefly to check on his mother at the food table. Then he marched over to Maddy, who was expounding on the painting before her.

"Hello, Maddy."

Maddy whirled around to find Joe standing directly behind her. She'd known he'd arrived—she'd caught a glimpse of him and her heart had done several somersaults—but she hadn't expected him to come straight over to her. Things were better between them, but not that much better.

"Joe. I'm so glad you made it."

"Yeah, me too." He turned to the older couple. "Mr. and Mrs. Colton, how are you this evening?"

"Fine. Just fine," Mr. Colton replied. "How's that granddaughter of ours liking summer camp?"

"She's having a blast. Now, if you'll excuse us"—
Joe slipped his arms about her waist—"I need to
talk to Madeline."

He eased her away from the Coltons, drawing
her as skillfully as a dancer through the crowd. His
touch made her light-headed enough that she didn't
question what was happening.

As they moved, he scanned the exhibit until his
gaze landed on the alcove that held her work. He
headed that way with her tucked into the warmth
of his side, his hand on her rib cage beneath her
jacket. When they reached the area, he stopped
before *Sunrise Canyon,* maneuvered her right in
front of it with both hands on her hips, then
stepped back.

"There." He nodded. "Much better."

"What?" She frowned at the loss of his arm
around her. Then her mind cleared and she
plopped her hands on her hips. "What was that
about?"

He stepped closer and lowered his voice as several patrons passed by. "It's about you."

"Me?"

He turned to a young couple admiring one of
her pieces. "Fabulous work, isn't it? Have you met
the artist? This is Madeline."

She went instantly into sales mode, trying to remove herself from the fact that she was praising
her own work. The moment the couple seemed absorbed enough to need privacy, she stepped back,
drawing Joe with her. "What are you doing? I was
about to close a sale over there."

"You're supposed to be selling your own work.
Or at least talking it up to the local gallery own-

ers." He looked around. "Who have turned out in droves."

"Don't remind me." She pressed a hand to her belly.

He studied her closely, his expression unreadable. "Why don't I get you a glass of wine?"

"I thought that was against camp rules, even when we're off duty."

"Sometimes I have this overwhelming need to break a rule or two just to prove to myself I'm still me."

"Okay then." She let her breath out in an audible rush. "Wine does sound pretty good right now."

"Then you stay." He held a hand up, palm out. "Stay."

"I'm not a dog." She laughed.

"I mean it. Stay."

She smiled and patted her heart as she watched him go. *Oh my.* As if she didn't have enough going on to make her pulse jump, he looked insanely handsome tonight in black slacks, a dark purple shirt, and a silver bolo tie. The color of the shirt made his skin look darker, his hair blacker, his eyes a deeper brown.

He was every inch the modern-day equivalent of an Indian warrior. Heat rushed through her at the thought that he might be back in her bed soon. Where things went from there . . . Well, she'd just have to wait and see.

Chapter 16

With all the people milling around the catering table, getting drinks took longer than Joe expected. He exchanged a few words with art collectors he'd met at other shows, then bumped into another couple who had children at the camp. The latter presented a minor problem. He didn't know if they knew about the no-drinking rule, but he wasn't about to take any chances.

He waited until they'd moved on, located the Coltons talking to his mother with their backs to him, and slid two soft drink cups to the bartender.

At last, he had two cups of white wine in hand and was making his way back toward Maddy. If all went well this evening, they'd move from simply speaking to really talking.

His stomach tightened at the thought, though. Why did relationships require so much talking? Women were supposed to be intuitive. Couldn't they figure out what was going on inside a guy without him having to say it out loud?

Although some guys, like Derrick, didn't seem

to have a problem verbalizing, even when it came
to really personal stuff. Maybe he could start with
something impersonal, keeping it light and friendly.
Then later, before leaving, he'd ask if he could
come to the Craft Shack after the show so they
could talk, since the middle of a crowded gallery
was not the place for a serious conversation.

From several feet away, he saw Maddy listening
to a tall, willowy woman who seemed to be admiring one of her pieces. Good, he and Maddy would
have a buffer to get them through the next few
minutes. As he drew closer, though, he noticed two
things. The woman didn't look like a collector. She
looked like an artist dressed in kitschy Goth attire,
and Maddy's eyes were frantic.

He quickened his pace, coming up on them just
as the woman turned and walked away. He looked
from the retreating back to Maddy, who stood frozen and pale.

"Okay," he said, "mind telling me what that
was about?"

She closed her eyes for a full three seconds, then
opened them. "Nothing."

"Then why are you upset?"

"I'm not. Is that for me?" She took one of the
cups from him and smiled at an approaching couple. When the couple moved past, she downed half
her wine in two big gulps.

"Give me that." He snagged the cup.

"Hey!" She scowled at him as she wiped a drop
from her chin.

He held the cup away. "Tell me what upset you."

She scanned the crowded area and spoke through
stiff lips. "This isn't the place to discuss it."

He narrowed his eyes in irritation. No matter

how carefully he planned things out, Maddy always threw in a monkey wrench. "Fine." He set both cups down on a pedestal, at the feet of a bronze bear, took her hand, and started walking. The deal with plans, though, is they had to stay fluid.

"Joe." She gasped, but resisted for only a second.

He spotted the door to the back room and headed in that direction.

"Juanita," he said as they passed the showroom manager. "Can you cover Maddy's area for a while?"

"Uh, certainly." She frowned at him.

Without a qualm, he went right through the door marked EMPLOYEES ONLY and closed it behind him. A quick glance around revealed a dark, cavernous space filled with the scent of wood glue and sawdust. Faint light from outside spilled through barred windows, casting striped shadows onto worktables and equipment.

"Jo-oe." Maddy jerked her hand out of his grasp, drawing his attention back to her. Scowling up at him, she rubbed her hand. "You've got to stop hauling me around."

"Did I hurt you?" He frowned at the thought.

"No." She dropped her hand to her hips. "But that's twice tonight you've done it. Next time you want me to move from point A to point B, do you think you could ask?"

"I could. But since you'd probably argue, my way's quicker."

"Well, silly me for thinking the human race had progressed past the caveman stage." She tossed her head in indignation, her eyes shining in the dim light. "I guess I'm lucky you don't knock me over my head and haul me about by my hair."

A smile spread over his face. "God, you look good tonight."

"What?" That drew her up short for a second. "Oh. Thank you. But I repeat, next time ask."

"Check. Now"—he settled the small of his back against one of the tables—"tell me what the bitch in black said to upset you."

"She's not a bitch." Maddy sighed, suddenly deflated. "She's just . . . understandably irritated."

"About . . . ?"

"We've been over this. I've barely arrived in Santa Fe and I'm already in a big show, everybody's raving about my work, and I'm going to have prints in an art catalog."

"So, she's jealous." He nodded. "Got that. Now, what'd she say?"

"She has a right to be jealous. It doesn't seem fair that she's been here for two years, working hard to get a break. She has some pieces in a small gallery, but she'd clearly give her eyeteeth to be featured in a show of this magnitude. What right do I have to swoop into town and steal her dream?"

"You're not stealing anyone's dream." Going with impulse, he reached out and took her hand as a compromise to pulling her to him for a hug. Even that small contact felt good, though. A warm intertwining of fingers. "Just because one artist makes it big doesn't mean another one can't. Although maybe she doesn't have what it takes and you do. Have you stopped to consider that?"

"It still doesn't seem fair."

"God." He chuckled. "You're such a woman."

Fire snapped into her eyes. "What's that supposed to mean!"

"It wasn't an insult." He swallowed his amusement. "Women always want everyone to win so no one gets their feelings hurt. Well, sorry, life doesn't work that way. It's like Ranger school. My class started out with nearly four hundred guys, all of whom thought they wanted it—until they found out how tough it was going to be. About half of them washed out the first day, it's that hard. Less than one hundred made it all the way to the end, because desire alone isn't enough. You have to have ability *and* conviction. That's why making the Rangers was one of the biggest highs of my life."

"But that's my point. You had to work to earn it. What did I do to earn this?"

He studied her, realizing she was serious. "Those pieces of art out there didn't create themselves."

She shrugged. "Well, no, but—"

"No buts. You've spent years developing a God-given talent, and you've spent the last few weeks working your tail off to produce enough work for this show. So, it's not like life just handed this to you. You earned it."

"I guess. I still feel bad for her."

"The bitch?"

"She's not a bitch."

"Tell me what she said, and I'll decide."

"It's not important."

"Mad-dy . . ." He lifted an eyebrow in warning.

"Oh, all right. She said, 'Yes, well, you do have a very . . . *colorful* style. I can see why Sylvia wants to do prints. They should be very popular with *decorators*.' Can you believe that?" The indignation he'd been looking for broke free. "She called my work decorator art! An artist never says something like that to another artist. Well, unless the other artist is actually trying to produce decorator art—

which is okay. There's nothing wrong with mass production to make a living, but in a situation like this, it's the ultimate insult. She's saying my work doesn't belong in a gallery. It belongs hanging over hotel beds, chosen solely on the merit of the colors matching the draperies.".

"Yep." Joe nodded. "She's a bitch."

"She is not! She's just frustrated. But that doesn't make her a bitch."

"No, but she said something specifically designed to hurt you, and *that* makes her a bitch. Now admit it. Say 'she's a bitch.' "

Maddy hedged. "She could be a nice person."

"Say it. B-I-T-C-H. Bitch."

She clamped her mouth shut with her lips tucked between her teeth.

He straightened to his full height, towering over her. "Am I going to have to tickle it out of you?"

"Ah!" She jumped back with hands raised to ward him off. "Don't you dare!"

"Then say it." He took a threatening step forward. She dashed around to the far side of the table, where she stopped to face him. "I won't."

"Now this is interesting." Something primal sparked inside him at the thought of chasing her. "You do realize you can't possibly escape if I decide to catch you."

She raised her stubborn chin. "Wanna bet?"

"Is that a challenge?" He raised a brow as arousal stirred.

She looked left, then right. He waited for her to pick her direction. "Maddy"—he dropped his voice purely for effect—"I'm bigger than you. I'm faster than you. I promise, I will catch you."

An answering excitement lit her eyes an instant

before she feinted left, then took off to the right. He moved to block her path to the door. She whirled with a laugh and headed the other way. He followed, methodically letting her elude him while corralling her steadily toward the darker shadows in the back.

He soon had her trapped in a corner with another table between them. They stood facing each other, their hands on the table, her breathing labored. His heart pounded in response.

"Ready to give up?" he asked, knowing that would egg her on.

"You don't have me yet." Her eyes shifted back and forth, but he already knew her pattern. She feinted every time, alternating the direction. This time it would be right then left. He waited for her to break. The second she did, he vaulted over the table and landed behind her just as she turned and collided with his chest.

"Gotcha!" His arms closed about her as she shrieked. Another quick move, and he had her wrists pinned to the small of her back. "Give?"

"Never." Her chin came up, her face flushed and glowing. Amusement faded as awareness grew, awareness of her body trapped against his, her heart beating against his chest. Her breath fanned over his chin as her gaze dropped to his mouth, then lifted back to his eyes.

Unable to resist, he lowered his head and touched his lips to hers. Possessiveness filled him as he took her mouth, claiming her as his own. His catch. His mate. He tilted his head, telling her with a kiss the things he wanted to voice, *You're mine, Maddy, mine. Forever.*

With a moan, she arched into him until her soft

belly cupped his arousal. The thought of taking her there in the darkness, against the table, filled his head. He tried to shake it, knowing it was ludicrous—they had a gallery full of people a short distance away, and unresolved issues to settle—but the idea took hold and grew.

Maybe this was the way to blast through the barrier between them. He'd show her what he felt. What he wanted.

Maddy moaned as he turned her so her back was against the table. He released her wrists and wrapped his arms about her, holding her tightly against him.

Lifting her hands, she cradled his face. Her fingers stroked his cheeks, grazed their joined lips.

Everything inside her went soft with wanting. She'd missed this so much. Missed him. She returned the kiss with every ounce of pent-up longing trapped inside her. She needed to talk to him so badly, but when his body pressed into hers, rational thought evaporated, leaving only raw emptiness aching to be filled.

"Maddy? Joe?"

They both froze. Maddy's eyes snapped open to find Joe's startled eyes staring back at her. Reality returned in a dizzy rush. They broke apart with a gasp.

Juanita turned toward the sound, then whirled away. "Oops. Sorry."

Maddy checked her clothes and hair. Everything was still in place, thank God. "D-did you need me out front?"

"There's two men from Taos I want you to meet. They own a gallery and are interested in handling some of your originals."

"I'll be right there." As soon as her heart stopped pounding. Glancing sideways, she saw that Joe's breathing was as ragged as her own. What had they been thinking to get so carried away?

"Take your time. No rush." Juanita started to move away, then stopped. "Oh, Joe, Mama asked me to tell you she was too tired to stay."

He cleared his throat. "Does she want me to drive her home?"

"No, she already left. She said you could get a ride back to the camp with Maddy."

"My mother left?" he nearly shouted. "Without me?"

"Joe, it's all right." Maddy patted his arm, confused by his reaction. "I'll give you a lift back to camp."

"You're missing the point." He turned to her with something akin to anger in his eyes. "My mother is driving. By herself. On a dark road."

"So?"

"The woman can't drive. Especially not at night."

"But—" No, that wasn't anger she saw. That was fear. "If she can't drive, why does she own a car?"

"Because she refuses to admit she can't drive."

"Joe, surely you're overreacting." Maddy tried to rein in her own mounting concern. "She wouldn't have taken off if she didn't feel competent. She'll be all right. Don't you think?"

"I don't know." He pulled a mobile phone from his pants pocket. "Why don't you go on out front? I'll join you in a minute."

"Come on, Maddy," Juanita said. "I'll introduce you to Dale and Rick."

Maddy started to argue, but Joe was already dialing and Juanita was heading back to the gallery.

Chewing her lip, Maddy followed Juanita, but her thoughts stayed with Joe. If anything happened, it would be all her fault. She was the one who'd come up with this as the way of getting Joe alone. But Mama had agreed so readily, the thought that her driving might be a problem hadn't even come to mind. And why would it? Her own parents were still young, so age issues were new territory. Still, she should have thought of it.

She chastised herself for the next several minutes, as Juanita introduced her to two older gentlemen who were both striking but in entirely different ways. Dale, with his height and silver hair, had a cultured manner, while his partner, Rick, had a stocky build and ruddy complexion. Learning that Rick was also an artist made his brimming enthusiasm for her work even more welcome. Between his praise for her art and Dale's flattery for her personal charm, the two men soon had her laughing and glowing, even while part of her mind remained fixed on that back door.

"Rick does fabulous abstracts," Juanita explained.

"I'd love to see some," Maddy said with genuine interest. Rarely had she felt such an instant affinity for anyone.

"I know!" Rick said, lighting up. "We'll have a show for you. Then you can come to Taos and stay with us. We'll introduce you around."

"An excellent idea," Dale agreed. "We haven't closed the resort for a party in ages."

"Resort?" Maddy cocked her head.

"Rick and Dale own a wonderful resort and health spa in the mountains," Juanita put in.

"Well, the resort is more Dale's area," Rick added. "It keeps him from going crazy now that he's retired. So, you'll come, then? Spend a few days?"

"I—"

"She'd love to," Juanita answered for her. "As for the show, give me a call so we can discuss which originals to send."

"Fabulous." Rick shook Juanita's hand, then kissed both of Maddy's cheeks. "You, dear, are a doll. I can't wait for everyone to meet you."

"Thank you," Maddy said, feeling a bit dazed.

"A true pleasure." Dale kissed her hand, making her blush. "We'll be in touch."

When they were out of earshot, Juanita grabbed her arm. "Oh my God! Rick and Dale are throwing you a show *and* a party!"

Maddy frowned. "Who were those two?"

"You don't know?" Juanita laughed. "I forget you're new around here. Dale's a former movie executive. He and Rick have been together forever and know lots of people in Hollywood. Their parties are famous. Once or twice a year, they close the whole resort for a few days so that actors and artists and musicians can play in private. I can't believe you got invited."

"Me either." Maddy raised a brow.

As soon as Juanita moved away, she dismissed the whole interlude. She may have been instantly taken with both men, but people said things at art shows all the time that never happened, like, "Darling, we simply must do lunch. I'll·call you next week." Add Hollywood to the equation, and the party invitation definitely fell into the not-gonna-happen category.

Joe came through the door and headed toward her. "Okay," he said, "I couldn't get Mom to answer her phone, but that's not surprising. She's always forgetting to turn it on or charge the battery. Plus, she could be out of a service area. So I called Harold. He's going to call me back as soon as Mom gets there so I'll know she made it."

"Unless . . ." She bit her lip. "Would you like to leave now? Maybe we can catch her, and you can drive her the rest of the way."

He considered the idea, then shook his head. "No. You need to stay here, and she's probably fine. The one saving grace is she's such a bad driver, people see her coming and get out of the way."

"Are you sure?" She touched his arm.

"Sort of." He chuckled dryly and squeezed her hand. "I'll be better once Harold calls back, but I'm okay."

The next hour passed with Joe pacing the gallery, checking his watch every few minutes. When the show finally wound down to a few of the rowdier guests hanging around the food and wine table, Maddy joined him. He was standing by Juanita's desk, staring out the front windows. "Still no word?"

"None. And she definitely should be there by now."

"Maybe you should call Harold again."

He checked his watch. "You're right." He pulled his phone out and dialed. "Sarg, any sign of my mother?" He listened for a minute, then his eyes bugged out. "What do you mean she's been there fifteen minutes? Why didn't you call?" He listened some more. "No, I told you to call me when she got there. Not if she didn't." He rolled his eyes. "I'm not biting your head off." He pinched the bridge of his nose. "Okay, fine. Thank you for keeping an eye out. I appreciate it."

Signing off, he sat back against the desk and looked heavenward as if begging for strength. "What is it with old people these days? They're so sensitive about everything!"

"Mama's all right?"

"Oh, she's fine. My heart may not recover, but she's dandy. Am I asking too much, though, for a little consideration? Do she and Harold have no clue how much I worry? No. They accuse me of being overprotective, when a simple phone call would have given me peace of mind. Is a phone call too much to ask?"

Maddy burst out laughing.

"What?" His eyes sharpened.

"You." She grinned and patted his upper arm. "You sound like a parent with a teenager."

"Oh God, you're right." A comical look of shock came over his face. "I'm turning into my mother."

"Look at it this way—there are worse mothers to be like." *Like mine,* she thought.

"True."

"It's odd, though, isn't it? Being the one to worry?"

"Yeah." He checked his watch. "It's getting late. We need to get back to the camp ourselves."

"I'll tell Sylvia and Juanita we're leaving."

"Good. Curfew's in forty-five minutes, and Harold's in enough of a snit to lock the gate just so he can lecture me."

Chapter 17

Maddy had never considered her car to be small, but with Joe in the passenger seat the space shrank to minuscule. His silence, even more than his body, filled the space.

What was he thinking? He'd barely spoken two words since they left the gallery. Although neither had she. Here at last was the moment she'd planned for days, and all the well-rehearsed words vanished from her brain. Where did she begin?

"I, um . . . I'm glad you made it to the show, even if you didn't get to enjoy much of it."

"I'm glad I made it too." He glanced her way briefly, almost nervously, it seemed.

What next? She racked her brain.

"So, um . . ." He shifted in his seat, as if trying to get his big body comfortable. "How'd you do?"

"Very well. We sold three of my originals and had a lot of people ask to be notified when prints of *Sunrise Canyon* become available."

"Great." He nodded, and silence returned.

Come on, Maddy, she ordered herself. She

needed to get a conversation going. Then ease into telling him she was sorry for pushing for more than he was comfortable sharing, but that she'd like the relationship to move to the next level.

Next level. There, that sounded good. No scary words like "love" or "long-term commitment." Now she just needed to open her mouth and say it. As soon as she figured out how to build up to it.

She tightened her grip on the steering wheel, watching the dark silhouettes of trees slip by the car. The moon's glow turned everything to shades of blue—until a colorful mass appeared in her headlights on the side of the road.

"What was that?" she asked as she drove past it.

"I don't know." Joe turned in his seat to look over his shoulder. "A wad of clothes maybe."

"Wait, here comes more." She leaned forward, peering at the colorful mound in the middle of the road.

"Don't hit it."

"I won't." She swerved around the object. "Could you make out what it was?"

"It looked like a pile of trash."

"From what, a colored-paper factory?"

Red taillights became visible up ahead. As she closed the gap, the dark shape of a delivery truck took form. Something bounced off the back and exploded against the pavement. Her headlights caught a burst of candy flying into the air.

"Oh my God!" She laughed as the candy hit her windshield like brightly colored hail.

"Was that a piñata?" Joe sounded equally incredulous.

"I think so." As she slowed to the same speed as the truck, she saw that the rolling door at the back hadn't been latched. Each time the truck hit a bump, the door bounced up, then down, revealing a load of piñatas.

"Watch out!" Joe shouted as the truck hit another bump. This time several piñatas flew out.

She fishtailed in an effort to maneuver around them. When the car steadied, she sped up and honked her horn.

"What are you doing?" Joe asked. "Slow down."

"Someone needs to tell him his door isn't latched." She honked again, but the truck kept bouncing along, spilling a menagerie of donkeys, rabbits, and pigs.

"Try going around him," Joe suggested.

"On this road? Are you crazy?"

"There's a fairly straight stretch up ahead. Can you see anyone coming?"

She leaned to the side. "I don't think so. Roll down your window and wave the guy over as I go past."

"You worry about driving. Leave the truck to me."

"Okay, here goes." She hit the accelerator and pulled into the other lane. Headlights appeared up ahead, coming too fast for comfort. "Oh shoot!" She jerked back into her lane just as a giant pink elephant flew out of the truck and exploded against her windshield. She screamed in surprise as her car slid on the candy, then went into a spin, spiraling toward the right shoulder. They left the road and came to jarring stop.

When the noise settled, she blinked a few times, then glanced over at Joe.

"Are you okay?" he asked.

"I'm fine." Since he obviously was too, she burst

out laughing. "This is so my life! One dramatic wreck after another."

"Hey, we survived." He glanced around. "Although we seem to be slanting."

She peered into the darkness beyond the windows. "Looks like I slid into a ditch. Should I try to back up?"

"Let me check things out first. You wait here."

"Gladly," she said, not sure her shaky knees would support her at the moment.

He got out and went to the front of the car, checking out both tires, then came around to the driver's side and waited for her to roll the window down.

"One of the tires dropped into a hole. I want you to back up gently while I push."

"Okay." She waited while he got into position, then put the car into reverse. When she depressed the accelerator, the tires spun in place.

"Turn it off," he called over the whine of the engine, then came back to her window. "You're really stuck."

"Do we need to call a tow truck?"

"We'll never get a signal in this valley."

"What are we going to do?"

"Do you have a jack?"

"It's in the trunk." She climbed out of the car to get it.

"I'll need a flashlight too, if you have one."

"Somewhere." They spent the next half hour with her holding the light while he wedged rocks and other debris under the tire. "Are you sure this will work?"

"We'll find out." He removed the jack. "All right, get back in and hit the gas on my signal."

She climbed behind the wheel as Joe braced his hands on the hood.

"Are you ready?" he called.

"Whenever you are."

"Okay, *go!*"

She pressed on the gas. The engine whined and the tires spun. Just when she thought it wasn't going to work, the car sprang free. She hit the brake to keep from shooting all the way across the road into the opposite ditch. "Woo-hoo! We did it!"

After putting the jack away, Joe came around to her side and opened the door. "Scoot over. I'm driving."

"What, I have one little accident, and now you don't trust me to drive?" Even as she complained, she moved over to the passenger seat.

"It's not that." He climbed in and put the car in gear. "We've busted curfew, so Harold's already locked the gate."

"Don't you have a key?"

"Of course. But he sleeps right there in the guardhouse. Trust me, the man's itching to dress me down."

"Joe, that's silly. He works for you."

The dashboard lights cast his face into sharp relief as he looked at her. "You clearly don't know Harold. He's a retired drill sergeant with a bruised ego about growing old. This is just the sort of thing he likes to jump on to prove the lion still has his roar."

"So, explain what happened."

He shook his head, chuckling. "There is absolutely no way I'm going to drive through that gate past curfew with a woman sitting beside me and claim we're late because we had a wreck with a pink elephant. That's even lamer than saying we ran out of gas."

"Well, it's true."

"Care to guess how fast this story will spread to the other coordinators? Then on to the counselors, who have to answer to me when they bust curfew? I'll have an insurrection on my hands. Total rebellion."

"And a lot of teasing."

"That too." His teeth flashed in the darkness.

"So what are we going to do?"

"You'll see." The eager note in his voice had her brows arching in curiosity. And concern.

They continued on toward the camp, following the colorful, candy-strewn trail. Joe slowed as they neared the last curve in the road before the gate would come into view. Turning off the headlights, he steered onto a private drive to a stable. A bridge took them over the river, where he pulled the car behind a bank of scruffy cedar. Quiet descended when he killed the engine.

"I need something to write on." He flipped on the dome light.

She rummaged through her purse until she unearthed an ancient grocery list and a pen. "What's the plan?"

"First, I write Bart, the stable owner, a note so he doesn't have your car towed before we can retrieve it."

"We're leaving it here all night?"

He nodded. "Tomorrow when I relieve Harold for his lunch break, I'll claim we returned before curfew, then say surely he heard us, unless he was sleeping on the job again." A grin split his face.

"Followed by my favorite question, 'So, Sarge, when's the last time you got those hearing aids checked?'"

"Oh, that'll win points."

"While he's at lunch, I'll jog over here and move your car to the Craft Shack."

"That still doesn't tell me how we'll get inside the camp, since it's surrounded by a twelve-foot security fence."

"You'll see as we go along." He got out of the car and slipped the note under the windshield wiper, then motioned for her to follow him. She wobbled along on her high heels, until they reached the fence. "I don't suppose you're much of a climber?"

She looked at the twelve-foot wrought-iron fence, then down at her dress and strappy sandals. "Dressed like this? Uh, no."

"I didn't think so." He studied the obstacle, then her. "If I had the right gear, I'd strap you to me and carry you over, but I guess we'll have to go with Plan B."

"What's Plan B?"

"You wait here. I'll be back."

"But—" She watched him pull his way up the metal posts hand over hand, using sheer upper-body strength. The sight made her heart flutter. "How long will you be gone?"

"Not long." He dropped to the ground and winced as his left leg buckled. After rubbing his knee, he straightened. "Just stay here."

With that he headed off at a jog, limping slightly as he vanished into the shadows. She shook her head, thinking old lions weren't the only ones who needed to prove they still had their roar.

The sound of a car approaching jolted her. What if it was Harold? Or someone who knew him and would mention seeing her? She ducked behind some bushes, squatting down where she couldn't be seen—and instantly felt ridiculous. Although beneath that was a little thrill of excitement. She hadn't done anything like this since the nights when she was grounded and Joe would help her climb out of her bedroom window.

Several long minutes passed with her straining to hear any sign of Joe's return. All she could hear was the lapping of the water against the riverbank, night bugs, the hoot of an owl.

"Maddy?"

With a screech, she landed on her backside and looked up to find Joe leaning over the bush. "You scared the tar out of me!"

"Why are you hiding?"

"I heard a car. And . . . I don't know. I thought it might be Harold out looking for us."

"Not a chance. He's sitting in the guardhouse clear on the other side of camp, lying in wait."

Seeing his grin, she narrowed her eyes. "You're enjoying this, aren't you?"

"Absolutely." He held out his hand. "You ready?"

Accepting his hand, she let him pull her to her feet, then gasped when he swept an arm behind her legs and lifted her off her feet. "Are you hauling me around again?"

"Just trying to keep your shoes dry." He carried her toward the river.

Turning her head, she saw a canoe pulled to the bank, barely visible in the moonlight. "Ah, I see." She circled his neck with her arms and smiled at him. "My brave Indian warrior, come to row me away in the moonlight."

"So, I've moved up from caveman?"

"A little." She tipped her head flirtatiously. "Although maybe I like strong he-men."

He glanced down, his face all sharp angles and strong planes in the darkness. "I know you do."

When they reached the water's edge, she realized he'd left his cowboy boots in the canoe and rolled up his pants legs. He waded into the water and settled her on one of two seats. With hardly a sound, he pushed the canoe away from the bank and leapt nimbly inside to settle on the seat facing her.

She watched him row as they slipped in and out of moonlight. His arms and shoulders moved with easy strength and fluid grace. Water dripped off the paddle like silver pearls that dropped back into the black river. Her mind conjured a fantasy of him bare-chested with glossy black braids that hung past his shoulders while a loincloth and buckskin chaps hugged his lower body. The image made desire throb deep in her belly. Savoring the mild discomfort of it, she tipped her head back and studied the star-strewn sky as wispy clouds drifted by the moon. "It's beautiful out tonight."

He glanced up as well. "It really is. One of the things I like about being away from city lights is all the stars."

She listened to the dip of the paddle as they glided along. "You always did like the out-of-doors."

"It sharpens the senses. Especially at night."

He guided the boat to shore in the shelter of a weeping willow, then stepped silently into the ankle-deep water. After pulling the boat onto the shore, he lifted her into his arms.

"Thank you," she said as he released her legs and let her slide to the bank.

"My pleasure." He stared down at her a long time, his face hidden in shadow. The throb in her belly built to an insistent ache. Just when she thought he would kiss her, he stepped away.

She looked around, trying to gather her scattered thoughts. "Are you going to leave the canoe here?"

"No. That would raise too many questions." He pulled it higher onto land and retrieved his boots. Leaning against the tree trunk, he dusted off his feet before putting the boots on. "I'll walk you home, then come back and put it away."

"Oh." Nerves fluttered as she debated what to do when they reached the Craft Shack. Should she invite him in so they could talk? Or maybe the progress they'd made tonight was enough for now—which raised the temptation to invite him in and not talk. But no, she'd sworn she wouldn't do that. No sex until they settled a few things.

"Ready?" He held his hand out to her.

Taking his hand, she let him lead her up one of the trails, through the trees. The path grew steeper, the ground rougher. With her mind distracted, she stepped wrong and nearly fell.

"I've got you." His arm went about her. "You okay?"

"I'm fine." She started to straighten and winced as pain stabbed her ankle. "I think."

"Did you twist your ankle?"

"Maybe."

"Hang on." He lifted her again, that effortless move that had her cradled in his arms, snug against his chest. Her arms went about his neck as he moved up the trail. In spite of her earlier complaint, she decided a woman could get really used to this.

They stopped in the Serenity Garden, an area at the side of the trail where Leah and the campers had planted wildflowers and berry bushes to attract butterflies and songbirds. He lowered her to a bench and knelt before her. Sitting back on his heels, he removed her sandal and placed her foot on his thigh.

"Does this hurt?" His fingers probed the ankle, sending little shivers of delight up her leg.

"Not too much." She suppressed a moan of pleasure when his hand continued its exploration. "I think it will be fine in . . . mmm, a minute or two."

He looked up, still cradling her ankle in his hand, his skin warm against hers. "Do you need me to carry you all the way home?"

Oh, wouldn't that be sexy? Especially if he carried her inside and laid her on the bed. Staring into his eyes, she decided they really needed to get past the talking portion of the evening, so they could get to the not-talking part. "No. Just give me a minute."

He nodded, but made no move to rise and join her on the bench.

She gathered her courage. "Joe—"

"Maddy—" he said at the same time, then laughed. "Sorry. You go ahead."

"No, that's okay. You first."

He took a long while to gather his thoughts, his fingers absently caressing her lower calf. "About your offer to design brochures for the boot camp. If, um, if you're still willing, I'd, uh . . ." His eyes lifted and looked deep into hers. "I'd like to take you up on that."

"You'd—" Her heart skipped. "You'd let me be part of it? Starting your business?"

"I would." He nodded stoically. "In fact, I'd like it very much. If the offer still stands."

Joy poured in as she realized what he was really saying. He was willing to open himself up to her again, maybe not all the way, but it was a step in the right direction. "Yes, the offer still stands."

"Are you sure?" He cupped her jaw with his free hand, searching her eyes.

She nodded as tears filled her eyes.

"Then why are you crying?"

"Because I'm scared I'll let you down."

He stroked her lips with his thumb. "I thought you said you were a good graphic artist."

"I am." She meant she feared hurting him again because she still hadn't figured out everything she wanted. She just knew she wanted more than casual sex. "I promise I'll try very hard not to disappoint you."

"Oh, Maddy." He came up on his knees and pressed his forehead to hers. His hands moved over her back in soothing circles. "You don't have to promise me anything. We'll just . . . take it as it comes, okay?"

"Okay." She wrapped her arms about him and held him tight. So many emotions filled her—fear, relief, happiness, love. And desire. "Make love to me, Joe. Right here."

"What?" His hands went still. "Here?"

"Please." She lifted her head to look at him. "Here in the moonlight, beneath the stars. Make love to me."

He looked at her, and she saw all her own emotions burning in his eyes as he cupped her face in both his hands.

"Here," he agreed on a sigh. Slowly he lowered his head and kissed her with a thoroughness that left her breathless. Wind sang through the trees as his hands ran over her, arousing all her senses.

Leaning into his touch, her head fell back as she gloried in the feeling of Joe touching her, caressing her. He slipped the jacket off and ran his palms up her bare arms. Needing more, she started to unbutton her dress, but his hands stopped her.

"Let me," he whispered, his voice hoarse with desire.

Dropping her hands back to the bench, she watched as he unbuttoned her dress and slowly parted it. Night air brushed her heated skin. Somewhere in the distance, an owl hooted as Joe lowered his head. She closed her eyes, listening to the night sounds as she absorbed the feel of his warm lips on the upper curve of each breast. A quiver went through her as he pulled the lace down and his mouth closed wetly over one nipple.

If she couldn't give him promises about the future, she'd give him now and the fullness of her response, letting him know he aroused more than her body. His gentle intensity went all the way to her heart.

Arching her back, she moaned as his tongue worked its magic over her tingling skin. His hands swept beneath her skirt, taking hold of her panties.

"I want to touch you," he said, tugging at the scrap of silk. "All of you."

"Yes," she breathed, lifting her hips so he could remove the barrier. His hands returned quickly,

pulling her forward so she sat on the front edge of
the bench. With the dress bunched up to her waist
and gaping at her breasts, she was completely open
to him, an offering for the taking.

Her eyes met his as he eased her thighs apart,
and a winsome smile curved her lips.

Oh, Maddy, he thought, aching to have and to
keep this time. Forever. He accepted that that
might never happen. Love had to be given freely.
No conditions.

The knowledge made him tremble as he ran his
hand purposefully up her thigh, toward the center
of her heat. Her gaze remained fixed on his and
she opened her thighs a fraction more.

He might not be able to hold her forever, but
for tonight, this moment, she was his.

Be mine, he told her with his eyes as he slipped
a finger slowly inside her. *Stay mine.*

"Yes," she sighed as if she'd heard his words.
"Yes."

He chained his own hunger and concentrated on
pleasuring her, slowly, deliberately, driving her up
and over the edge, soaring with male satisfaction
as she slowly drifted back down.

Only then did he release his own need. He took
a second to protect them both, then poised at the
entrance to all that heat. Pressing into her was like
entering heaven. She engulfed him, drew him in,
and held him tight.

He closed his eyes, thrilling to the sensation of
being part of her, yet loving her so much that he
feared it.

With a moan deep in her throat, she lifted her
hips, taking him even deeper, and he couldn't hold
back. He thrust hard and strong, every muscle in

his body tensing as the pleasure built, and when it burst free, he thought for one heart-stopping moment that he would die from it.

He braced himself, still buried deep inside her, his head back as his heart thundered. As he drifted back to his senses, he realized Maddy had wrapped herself about him, her arms and legs holding him tight as she pressed her head against his chest.

He wrapped his arms about her as well and rested his cheek against her hair, wishing he could hold her like that all night.

Eventually, though, his spent body eased from hers, breaking the connection. With a sigh of disappointment, she tipped her face to smile up at him.

"You're right," she said. "The senses are keener outside."

He smiled as he caressed her cheek. "Do you think you can walk on that ankle now?"

"Ankle?" Wicked delight danced in her eyes. "What ankle?"

They straightened their clothes and he helped her rise. "Come on. I'll take you home."

Chapter 18

It's true what they say: Time flies when you're having fun.
—*How to Have a Perfect Life*

Stretching languidly, Maddy came slowly awake, then went still as she realized this was not her bed. And she was not alone. Looking over her shoulder, she saw Joe lying behind her, sound asleep. Even with his hair mussed, he looked as handsome as ever. Maybe even more so with the muscles in his face—normally so tense—relaxed in sleep.

Fascinated, she rolled carefully toward him and propped her head on her hand. A smile of pure contentment welled up from deep inside her as she watched him.

In the week since the art show, she'd spent quite a bit of time in Joe's bed, but this was the first time she'd stayed until morning. Actually, it was the first time in her entire life she'd stayed with him until sunrise.

What would it be like to wake up with him every morning for the rest of her life? She expected the question to scare her. Instead, a sense of rightness settled over her.

Love filled her. Warm and vibrant and glowing. And she had her answer.

I want to spend my life with you.

He woke suddenly, startling her with his abrupt switch from sound sleep to full alertness. After a quick glance about, he let his head drop back onto his pillow and his body relaxed. He smiled up at her, all sleepy and rumpled and sexy. "Good morning."

"Good morning." She grinned. "You certainly wake up fast."

"Must have been the noise." He gathered her against him, positioning her until she lay with her head on his shoulder and her legs tangled with his.

"What noise?" She listened for something besides the bird singing in the cactus outside his bedroom window. The first session of camp had ended yesterday, leaving the camp almost eerily empty. "I don't hear anything."

"Exactly." His lips curved against her forehead. "Silence. One whole week with no screaming."

She felt a little pang in her heart as she remembered the closing day ceremonies and the last campfire followed by a day of loading buses and emotional good-byes. After the buses cleared out, the coordinators and counselors left as well for their own week off. Other than Mama and Harold, Maddy and Joe had the place to themselves. "You know, I think I miss Kaylee and Amanda already."

"Yeah, me too." He yawned. "But they'll be back next year."

Yes, but will I? She bit her lip to hold back the words. By some silent agreement, they never talked about the future in personal terms.

"Besides," he added, "we have another crop of little monsters arriving next week."

"Well, there's a cheerful thought." She sat up and stretched her arms over her head. The covers fell to her waist and cool morning air brushed her skin. "How about some coffee?"

"I'd rather have you." He ran a finger down her spine.

She glanced over her shoulder. The covers had slipped to his waist as well, leaving his whole gorgeous torso bare. He tucked an arm behind his head as he lowered his eyelids with promises of sensual pleasure.

Unfortunately, her gaze moved to the clock on the nightstand and she remembered all she had to do that day.

"Tempting." She laughed. "But I need caffeine."

Climbing out of bed, she gathered the clothes she'd left lying on the floor and headed for the bathroom. Once there, she found a denim shirt hanging on the back of the door that would make a perfect bathrobe.

She ducked her head back into the bedroom. "Do you mind if I borrow this?"

"No. I put it there for you."

"Oh." That drew her up short. He was always doing stuff like that. Stocking his refrigerator with the kind of cola she liked. Buying flavored potato chips when he liked them plain. And now a shirt for her to use as a bathrobe, when they hadn't actually discussed her staying the whole night. She'd simply fallen asleep, and he hadn't woken her.

She pulled back into the bathroom, wondering if these were all giant hints about his feelings, or if she was reading more into them than he intended. The fact that she'd mentioned her favorite flavor of ice cream and a half gallon of caramel turtle fudge had magically appeared in his freezer was not a declaration of undying love. Was it?

The question nettled her even when she stood in the kitchenette measuring coffee grounds. She heard water running in the bathroom and knew Joe would join her shortly. For all she knew, caramel turtle fudge was his favorite flavor too and it didn't mean anything.

With the coffeepot gurgling, she stared out the window, more frustrated than ever by all the unanswered questions. Maybe she was coming to terms with what she wanted, but that didn't mean Joe had. Maybe he was still thinking short term. Somehow that made her want a future with him even more.

Since the night of the art show, they'd talked a lot about plans for the boot camp, which they were both having a ball working on. They sat in his office every evening using his computer to design brochures, business cards, and even a Web site, which was going to take a lot more work to finish. But they never talked about where their relationship was going. Or what would happen when summer camp ended.

A dozen times at least, she'd started to tell him she loved him, which had seemed huge enough. Now here she stood, thinking about marriage and children and a lifetime together—God willing. Her heart swelled with the knowledge that she wanted all the things she'd rejected from him once— wanted them with a passion that made her ache to say the words aloud.

Would he believe her, though? After what he'd told her, she feared that words alone would never do it, and might even cause a setback. So, somehow, before summer camp ended, she had to find a way to show him she loved him, to make him feel secure enough about that love that when she finally said the words he would believe her.

Six weeks. Surely that would be long enough.

She was still staring out the window when Joe emerged from the bedroom.

He stopped as the sight hit him square in the chest. Morning sunlight streamed over her. She was so . . . Maddy, standing there barefoot with his big shirt hanging to her knees.

If he could have one wish, he decided, it would be this right here, to wake every morning for the rest of his life to find Maddy in his kitchen, bathed in sunlight.

A part of him wanted to toss his carefully laid plans out the window, to walk over there, scoop her into his arms and say, "Marry me." But impulse had been his undoing last time. He refused to repeat that mistake.

Drawing on patience, he headed toward her. "Is that coffee ready?"

She glanced over her shoulder, smiling with approval as her gaze ran over his bare chest and the sweatpants that rode low on his hips. "It just finished."

Getting down two mugs, she poured him a cup black, then went to the fridge to poke inside. "Do you have any cream?"

"In the door." He congratulated himself on snagging some from the kitchen in the dining hall yesterday when he remembered she liked her coffee doctored to the max. Attention to detail had always been his strong suit.

"Great." She backed out with the unopened carton.

He leaned a hip against the counter and took a few grateful sips of caffeine. "So, what would you say to jogging with me this morning?"

She blinked. "You're joking, right?"

"Not at all. I'll take it easy on you, and afterward we can take a dip in the river."

She faced him with a hand on one hip, which hiked the shirt higher on her thigh. "There are two problems with that idea. First, in case you haven't noticed, this body is not meant to sweat."

"I don't know." He grinned at her over the rim of the mug. "We worked up a pretty good sweat last night, and I didn't hear you complaining."

"And second," she continued, "I don't have time. I'm supposed to meet with Sylvia at the gallery this morning."

"Oh? Are you taking her more art?" He frowned as he realized he hadn't seen her work on any art all week.

"No." She turned to put the cream away. "The prints of *Sunrise Canyon* arrived a couple days ago. They need me to sign them."

He lowered his mug. "You didn't tell me that."

"I didn't?" She straightened. "Oh. I thought I did."

"You must be excited to see them."

"I am." She let out a nervous gust of air. "Although it feels really weird too, dashing off to spend the day signing prints of my work."

"It's not pretentious, Maddy. It's just part of the business."

"I suppose."

Since the subject made her uneasy, something he would never understand, he decided to shift the topic.

The time had come to move into Phase Two of his campaign: get Maddy to move to Santa Fe. His stomach tensed. "You know, I've been thinking . . ." *There, that sounded good. Nice and casual. No big deal. Just knocking ideas around in my head.*

"About what?" She leaned against the counter as well, sipping from her own mug.

"Plans for the boot camp are coming along so great, we should be ready to open this winter."

"Oh, I definitely think you could do that. You just need to get the word out and start signing people up."

"Yeah." The tension moved up into his throat. "So." He took a swallow of coffee to burn the knot away. "What I was thinking is, you're so good with promotion . . ." *Just spit it out, coward.* He swallowed more coffee. "What would you think about staying on a bit after summer camp ends to help Derrick and me get things going?"

She coughed into her mug, then gasped for air.

"Are you okay?" Alarmed, he rubbed her back.

"I'm fine." She didn't look fine. She looked scared.

Oh, crap! She was going to say no. He'd miscalculated somewhere. Read the signals wrong.

"How—" She pressed a hand to her chest. "How long would you want me to stay?"

Forever! "It, um, depends. I know you have a life back in Austin that you probably want to get back to, so it wouldn't have to be too long. Just . . . a few weeks?"

Her eyes watered from her coughing fit. "I can manage a few weeks."

"Really?" Relief swamped him so fast his knees went weak. "That would be . . . great."

"So . . ." When she turned away to put her mug in the sink, he saw her hands shake. Was she crying? Why would she be crying? "I, um, I guess I better shower and get dressed if I'm going into town."

"Hang on." He slipped a hand around her arm as she started toward the bedroom.

Before he could ask her what was wrong, or even get a good look at her face, she slipped her arms around his neck, went up on her toes and was kissing him so deeply that tiny explosions went off in his head. Adjusting quickly, he wrapped his arms around her and tilted his head for a better angle. Her hands were in his hair as her tongue danced with his. He ran his own hands down her back, then up under the shirt—where he found her bottom bare.

Ho-yeah! Coming up for air, he stared down at her in wonder. "Wow."

She grinned back at him, her whole face glowing.

He cleared his throat and tried to form a coherent thought. "So, um, you need any help with that shower?"

"That depends." Her smile grew even broader. "Do I get to scrub your back?"

Absolutely ho-yeah! "Only if I get to scrub yours."

"You got a deal, soldier." She turned and sashayed ahead of him into the bedroom.

*   *   *

Maddy sang with the radio all the way to the gallery, then breezed in with a cheerful hello for Juanita. "Is Sylvia here?"

"She's in the back getting things ready for you. I'll let her know you're here."

While Juanita picked up the phone, Maddy wandered back into the alcove that held her work. Her heart skipped a beat when she saw all the blank spots. Three of them she'd expected, from the sales made the night of the show, but apparently they'd sold two more of her originals: a large piece titled *Rushing River* and a small close-up of a cactus blossom.

"Sylvia's on her way," Juanita said, coming up behind her. "Do you need help getting anything out of your car?"

"What?"

"I can't wait to see what you've done since the show. As you can see, we really need some new pieces."

"Yes, I . . . see." She stared at the blank spots, feeling off kilter since she hadn't brought any more work. Her whole week had been taken up helping Joe. "I'll bring more pieces in next time."

"Maddy!" Sylvia sailed toward her, smiling broadly. "My new favorite person! Juanita told me about the show in Taos. *And* a party at Dale's resort." She slapped a hand over her heart.

"Oh, well." Maddy shrugged the words off. "That wasn't serious."

"Of course it was," Sylvia insisted. "I've been on the phone with Rick all week. They're very excited to have you come stay with them before the show."

"They are?" Maddy nearly stuttered in surprise.

"They're going to close the resort for three days, invite all their friends. Then end the party with a show at Rick's gallery. You're going to have a ball."

"Sylvia . . ." The air left her lungs. "I can't dash off to Taos for a party that lasts three days."

Sylvia's face went blank. "Excuse me?"

"I'm working at Camp Enchantment."

"Oh, that." She waved a hand. "Not to worry. Dale's too much of a businessman to close his resort during the summer tourist season. He's looking at early fall, in the lull before ski season starts."

"Yes, but—" Maddy started to explain that she'd just promised Joe to help him with his boot camp, but Sylvia grabbed her arm.

"Now come in the back and have a look at your prints."

Ah yes, the prints!

Maddy's pulse picked up as the woman led her into the noisy frame shop. An easel had been set up next to one of the worktables. Her gaze moved past it, then zipped back as she recognized *Sun rise Canyon*.

"Ohmygod." She pressed both hands to her mouth as wonder blossomed inside her. The image was smaller and not as vibrant as the original, but it was hers. "I can't believe this! I have prints."

Several of the framers paused in their work to watch her reaction. She realized this must be fun for them too—working with artists, framing and selling prints, building careers. And now she was one of those artists. How had that happened?

"The printer did an amazing job." Sylvia beamed until she got a look at Maddy's face. "Are you going to cry?"

"I may." Her vision blurred for the second time that day. Why did happiness make her so weepy? "I know we've been talking about this for weeks, but it didn't seem real . . . until now."

"Here, have a seat." Sylvia guided her to a barstool next to the worktable.

They'd created a little island of clean amid the mess for her to sign the prints. Bottled water sat beside a plate of fruit and cheese. Three sharpened pencils lay in a neat row. All this had been done for her.

"You just sit here and admire your print for a few minutes," Sylvia insisted. "I need to fetch my calendar. Mark, Todd?" She motioned two of the framers over, then turned back to Maddy. "Don't let these guys work you too hard. Take as many breaks as you need."

"Of course." Maddy felt like a pampered princess as the men brought the first stack of prints to be signed. Mark, the frame shop manager, used a magnifying glass to inspect the first few.

"Now, don't freak," he said in warning, then promptly tore the top five prints in half and tossed them on the floor.

Maddy gasped in horror. "What are you doing?"

"Culling out the rejects." When he had a small stack of acceptable prints, he numbered them in pencil, then passed them to her for her signature.

Sylvia returned carrying an appointment book. She hopped onto a barstool across from Maddy and laid the book on the table. "Okay, let's talk dates."

"Dates?" Maddy signed another print and Todd whisked it away.

"Show dates." Slipping on her reading glasses, Sylvia flipped through the calendar pages. "Rick's show will come first, which will be a fun way to kick things off. Then we'll get down to real business with the Professional Picture Framers Association Trade Show in L.A. followed by Market in Dallas. We'll try to fill in the gaps with gallery shows, but those will be slow at first, until we build up your name recognition. Are there any weeks this fall you're not available to travel?"

"What?" The floor tilted suddenly, and Maddy prayed she wouldn't fall off the barstool. "You want me to travel? This fall?"

"Of course."

The whole conversation with Joe flashed through her mind. He'd said a few weeks, but she hoped to stretch that into more. "I-I can't travel."

"Don't worry." Sylvia waved her words away. "We pay all your expenses."

"But—" Her heart beat painfully fast. "Can't you simply send my work?"

"Once you're established, you can skip the trade shows and just do gallery appearances, but at this stage we want you out there meeting the gallery owners so they can see you're the total package."

"Total package?" Another stack of prints was placed in front of her. She stared at them blankly.

"Absolutely." Sylvia made a sweeping gesture that encompassed Maddy from head to toe. "Not only is your work brilliant, but you're attractive, well spoken, friendly. We want the gallery owners to fall in love with you, just like Rick and Dale did, and pass that enthusiasm on to their collectors. Trust me, dear, you're going to have a stellar career."

"But . . ." The panic she'd fought her whole life rose up in a rush, knocking the breath from her lungs. She frantically pushed it back down, like a child scrambling away from the edge of a deep ravine, refusing to look at what lived in that dark abyss. If she ever looked, she'd know what really frightened her, and she didn't want to know. Anything that scared her this much had to be ugly. "I don't want a stellar career."

"Y-you what?" Sylvia went still, then shook her head as if to clear it. Mark and Todd stared at her strangely. The whole frame shop seemed to go quiet.

"I just— I just—" The panic struggled to break free. "I can't do the shows, Sylvia. I'm sorry."

A heartbeat of silence passed, then Sylvia calmly folded her hands on top of the appointment book. "Do you mind if I ask why?"

Because I'm on the verge of having something special with Joe. I put myself and my art before him once. How will he feel if I run out on my promise to help him with the boot camp? There was something more behind all that. Some other fear she really didn't want to see. "I don't need a stellar career. I really don't. If I can do well, that's enough. Truly."

Sylvia looked at the two framers. "If you'll excuse us, I need to talk to Maddy in my office."

Battling nausea, she followed the older woman into the largest of the glass cubicles, feeling like a child on her way to the principal's office.

"Have a seat." Sylvia closed the door, which offered little privacy since the whole shop could see inside. Crossing to a mini refrigerator, Sylvia pulled out a bottle of green tea and handed it to her.

Maddy sat as ordered and accepted the tea with

shaky hands. After a few sips, her throat loosened enough for her to breathe more evenly.

"Better?" Sylvia sat back in the swivel armchair at her desk.

Maddy nodded, still queasy but no longer afraid she'd actually throw up. "I'm sorry. I don't know what's wrong with me."

The older woman studied her a moment. "You know, I've worked with artists most of my life, but I don't pretend to understand what makes you tick. Frankly, I have this constant fear that all the artists of the world will go into therapy, conquer their demons, and art as we know it will cease to exist."

Maddy laughed weakly.

"Here's the deal." The desk chair squeaked as Sylvia leaned forward. "I can sympathize with whatever has you worked up, but in the end I'm a businesswoman. As such, I'm going to lay things on the line so you understand exactly where I'm coming from. Maddy, I've invested a lot of money in you. Since we want to do two more print editions for our fall catalog, I plan to invest a great deal more. Do you know how long it will take me to simply break even?"

"No." Maddy stared at the bottle.

"Months if things go well. Possibly a year. And that's with you helping us promote your work. If you had come to us with a built-in following, I could afford for you to sit at home, create your art, and let us do all the rest. But that's not the case. You came to us a complete unknown. So if you're going to flake out on me, do me a favor and say so right now."

Maddy stared at the design on the pale green

bottle, branches forking off in different directions. Some of them crisscrossing and continuing. Others ending.

She had two paths from which to choose. One was a simple life with Joe, the two of them working together running both the summer camp and his boot camp. She'd still do her art, but on a quieter scale. Along the other path lay the kind of career most artists would sell their soul to have: nationwide fame, gallery shows, traveling. The pace would be grueling, but she'd never minded hard work. Punctuating that work would be moments of glamour, of being a star.

She traced one of the crisscrossed branches with her thumbnail. If she chose the path Sylvia offered, could she still have Joe? How would he feel, though, watching her from the sidelines as her fame grew? As excited as he was about his boot camp, she knew it wasn't what he really wanted to do. It would never match being in the Rangers.

He also enjoyed watching her sell her art, but his expectations couldn't possibly match this.

Everything in her yearned to accept what Sylvia offered, but it wasn't worth risking what she hoped to have with Joe. What she'd decided just that morning to go after.

She traced the design back down to the fork.

Career or love—those were her choices.

Closing her eyes, she chose love, and felt a little piece of her soul die. It was worth it, though. Love was worth any sacrifice.

"I'm sorry." She opened her eyes, and felt steadier now that the decision was made. "I can't do the shows."

Sylvia sat a long while, absorbing the news. "All

right," she said at last. "I think you're making a huge mistake, but it's yours to make. I'll cancel our plans to do the other prints and have them struck from the catalog. *Sunrise Canyon* will stay in, of course, but it won't do as well without the rest of our plan in place."

The words sent pricks of pain to Maddy's heart, but she held firm. "I understand."

"Can I ask you a favor, though?"

She nodded, feeling guilty enough to grant nearly anything.

"Will you at least go to the party in Taos and do Rick's show? It's close enough for you to drive up there and back. We should be able to sell enough originals to offset some of my investment."

Maddy hesitated. Even this seemed risky, but not nearly as frightening as the rest. "Do you think they'd mind if I brought someone with me?"

"Of course not," Sylvia assured her. "The place is big enough that you could probably bring three or four guests."

"Oh." That perked her up some. She'd meant only to invite Joe, so that maybe he wouldn't mind her going, but maybe she could talk Christine and Amy into going too, since Christine would finally be done with her residency. "Very well. I'll do it."

"Thank you." Sylvia visibly relaxed. "Now, if you're up to it, let's sign a few more prints."

Maddy rose, eager to escape the office before she changed her mind.

"And Maddy," Sylvia added as they walked back into the frame shop, "we do a spring catalog as well. When winter gets here, if you change your mind, let me know. I'd still like the chance to work with you."

Maddy didn't know whether to laugh or cry. "I'll think about it," she said automatically, then chastised herself. She should have said no, that she wouldn't change her mind. Why did Sylvia have to leave this door open a crack, just when she thought she'd closed it firmly?

If only there was a way to take both paths.

When Maddy returned to the camp, she sent a long e-mail to her friends that set off a rapid exchange for the next two days. She'd meant to simply invite them to the party in Taos but had ended up telling them everything about her meeting with Sylvia.

Christine's response was fast and heated: *Of course we'll come to the party. (Shut up, Amy, I'll take care of everything. So you ARE going.) But Maddy, are you NUTS???*

Amy: *I don't understand. Why do you think Sylvia's plans would upset Joe? From the way you've described him, I think he'd be thrilled. And if I go to Taos, does that fulfill my challenge?*

Christine: *NO! Amy, I'll make all the arrangements. I'll pick you up at your front door and be with you every step of the way. Consider this a test run for you going somewhere on your own. As for your question to Maddy: Yeah, Mad, why do you think Joe will be upset?*

Maddy: *I told y'all, I've decided for sure I want to marry this man.*

Christine: *So? Is he asking you to choose between him and your dream? Because if he is, dump the jerk.*

Maddy: *He's not asking me to do anything. Are*

you kidding? We don't have "Big Conversations."
We keep everything very small and very safe.

Amy: *You mean you still haven't told him you*
love him?

Maddy: *I'll tell Joe I love him when the time is*
right. When I know he'll believe me.

The following day brought another blistering reply
from Christine, while Amy's response was disapprov-
ing but sympathetic. Before Maddy could answer, she
heard Joe coming up the stairs to her apartment, his
step light and happy. Her heart lifted.

Closing the laptop—which shut off her friends'
disapproval—she went to open the door. Christine
and Amy meant well, but they didn't understand.
How could they? They weren't the ones in love. In
fact, Amy had never had a serious boyfriend and
Christine was a loser magnet, so their advice was
suspect at best.

The minute Joe swept her into his arms and
kissed her crazy, doubts over her choice vanished.
Well, faded.

He lifted his head to smile at her. "Are you done
with your art for the day?"

"Actually, I was just— Never mind. Yes, I'm done."

"Great. I'm done with work as well." As he
stepped inside, she realized he wore a dark blue
dress shirt, black slacks, and cowboy boots. With
the bolo tie at his neck and silver ranger set on his
belt, he looked like he'd stepped out of an ad in
the *Santa Fean*.

"Wow," she said. "Don't you look nice."

"I just heard Bill Hearne is playing at the La
Fonda. So what do you say to dinner and dancing?"

"You're on!"

Chapter 19

Never underestimate gut instinct.
—How to Have a Perfect Life

Joe couldn't remember ever being happier. Which made him very nervous. Especially as the weeks flew by with increasing speed. Every day brought him closer to the end of summer and the time to relaunch Phase Two of his plan.

When the initial launch had nearly ended in disaster, he'd decided to retreat, regroup, and wait for better timing.

The month between the end of summer camp and when Derrick arrived seemed appropriate. This time, he would test the waters more carefully by mentioning the future casually in conversation so he didn't scare her off. No way would he blurt out a marriage proposal and ruin everything.

He did, however, have a ring picked out, and had even made a down payment. It was a custom design by one of the most talented jewelers in the area—much more Maddy-esque than the traditional solitaire he'd tried before. What a dumb choice that had been! Maddy needed something unique, like her, which made this ring perfect.

She was going to love it. He was sure.

At least he hoped.

First, though, he had to talk her into moving to Santa Fe permanently, since the last day of summer camp had somehow arrived. How had that happened? How had weeks vanished while he wasn't looking? Granted, between running his mother's camp, making plans for his own, and being with Maddy, he'd been having the time of his life. Plus, he accepted from his past experience that being in love made the brain malfunction, which was why he'd messed things up so badly before.

Not this time, though. This time, he was doing it right, moving in stages, so that when he popped the question, she'd say yes.

Even as he told himself that, he broke out in a nervous sweat. Or maybe that was the sun, he decided as he stood in the parking lot supervising the chaos of loading buses. All around him, little girls ran and screamed. Older girls cried and hugged.

Maddy stood with his mother, exchanging a few last words with the campers as they climbed onto the first bus. Looking at her never ceased to stir him up on every level. She excited, soothed, mesmerized, and . . . enchanted him. Yeah, he thought with an admittedly goofy smile, she flat out enchanted him.

Today she wore a cropped T-shirt covered with hand-painted flowers—the result of one of her craft projects—with a denim miniskirt she'd obviously made from an old pair of jeans. He'd long since accepted that uniforms and Maddy simply didn't go together. Since none of the other coordinators complained, he let it slide without comment. Besides, once she was his wife, not an employee, it wouldn't matter what she wore.

His smile got a bit goofier as she bent to accept a macaroni necklace from one of the little campers. She gushed with praise and thanks, which had the little girl beaming. What a great mom she'd make.

Finally the first bus was full. With a whoosh of brakes, it started down the hill toward the front gate. The chaos dimmed only momentarily, since they had several more buses to go, plus parents arriving in private cars.

Maddy turned and spotted him, then moved through the maze of campers lined up with their trunks, pillows, sleeping bags, and stuffed toys to join him.

"Is it always this hard to watch them go?" she asked.

"I'm afraid it might be." He offered her a sympathetic smile, barely resisting the urge to kiss the frown line away from her forehead. "All last summer, I thought I'd be relieved to have quiet and sanity return to my life. Then I remembered the screwed-up home life some of these kids are going back to, and I wanted to climb on the bus and go with them. Maybe knock some parents' heads together. I still do."

"I know what you mean." She shaded her eyes as the next bus pulled into position. "It's not so hard with the good kids. It's ones like Cory and her gang who get to me."

"Me too." He chuckled, since thirteen-year-old Cory had spent half her summer at Camp Enchantment on probation for smuggling in cigarettes—not once but three times. Carol blew her whistle and started calling roll. "We get them for five weeks every summer, though. I like to think it helps."

He tensed a bit at the Freudian slip. *We* get them every summer. Would she realize he'd meant the two of them, not the camp staff at large? He shifted his gaze sideways, but she showed no visible reaction. Although, the slip did fit the timetable for his plan, since camp was over. He was supposed to start dropping in references to the future to gauge her reaction. Only, she wasn't reacting. She was just standing there as still as stone.

Finally, she lowered her hand, but kept her gaze on the campers as she quoted the camp motto. " 'Building character and memories to last a lifetime.' "

"Yeah," he agreed, thinking of the two of them. He wanted more than a lifetime of remembering Maddy. He wanted a lifetime of making memories. He thought of the ring he'd picked out and fresh sweat broke out on his forehead

Somewhere over the den of noise, he heard the phone in the office ringing.

"I better get that," he said, leaping on the excuse to get away from this conversation before he said something stupid. He stepped gratefully into the cool, shady office and snapped up the handset. "Camp Enchantment."

"Yo, Scout."

He grinned at the sound of Derrick's voice. "What's up, Socrates?"

"Good news, my man. We have us our first victims."

"Campers. They're called campers."

"Ho-no, these guys definitely be victims." Derrick's deep chuckle came through full of good humor. "My sister told her boss about the boot camp. Apparently it's just the sort of team-building experience he's been wanting for his programmers. He wants to sign up for a corporate package."

"What?" The words wouldn't quite register in Joe's brain. "You sold a corporate package?"

"Yep. Looks like we're getting a whole slew of computer programmers to turn into super geeks."

"Wow, that's . . ." *Way ahead of schedule.* The main reason Maddy was staying was to help them sell the programs. "That's great, man."

"Do you think you could tone down the enthusiasm just a little?" Derrick asked in the same flat tone Joe had just used.

"Sorry." Joe shook his head, laughing at himself. "It is great. Really."

"So what's the problem?"

"You're messing with my plan."

"Uh-oh. You and the word 'plan' always scare me. So what are you planning to death this time? No, wait, let me guess. This has something to do with your lady, right?"

"I don't plan things to death." Joe scowled in offense. "I never heard you complain when we were on an op. I happen to excel at planning things out."

"In other words, you haven't followed Brother Derrick's advice for your love life, have you?"

Heat climbed up Joe's neck as he remembered how much he'd revealed to Derrick over the last several weeks. But if a man couldn't let down a few barriers with his Ranger buddy, who could he confide in? Besides, after working side by side in some extreme situations, they didn't need words to know what the other was thinking.

"So," Derrick persisted, "have you managed to articulate the big three words?"

"I told you," Joe said. "I have a plan."

"I'll take that as a big negatory."

"A plan that now I'll have to rework, since you just blew half of it out of the water."

"Joe, Joe, Joe." Derrick sighed. "You can't treat relationships like an op, working out every detail down to the last possible contingency."

"Well, why the hell not? That's what I'd like to know."

"Because . . ." Another sigh. "Terrorists are predictable. Women are not."

"I know. That's what worries me." He walked over to watch Maddy through the window. "Plus, I have this gut instinct telling me that something's wrong."

"Like what?"

"I don't know. I can't put my finger on it, but . . ." He remembered some of his conversations with Maddy lately, when he'd asked her how things were going with Sylvia and she'd changed the subject. "I have this nagging sense that she's keeping something from me. Something to do with her artwork."

"Isn't that what you said happened last time?"

"They say history repeats itself." Except this time she had no reason to keep things from him. Not that she had last time either.

"Have you considered the possibility that you're seeing ghosts from the past, inventing things to obsess over?"

"Maybe." He turned away from the window. "So, are you still coming next month?"

"Actually I thought I should come up sooner, for us to get rocking on the obstacle course for the super geeks."

"How much sooner?"

"I can be there week after next."

"Oh, man, you are shooting my schedule all to hell."

"Joe, get a grip," Derrick said dramatically. "Even on an op, sometimes your plan gets screwed and you have to go in with what you've got, guns blazing."

"Which, if you'll remember, is how I got shot."

"True. But have you considered this? If you hadn't taken that hit, you wouldn't be sitting in New Mexico right now. We'd both be sweating our asses off in some desert dodging car bombs. And your high school sweetheart would still be just a wistful memory."

"Are you saying I should be thankful I got shot?"

"Out of adversity comes opportunity. See ya in a couple of weeks, man. And, hey, good luck with your lady."

"Yeah. Thanks a lot."

The instant Joe hung up, he remembered a second reason he didn't want Derrick to come ahead of schedule. Maddy's show in Taos. He couldn't miss it. Her friends were going to be there, and he'd finally get to meet them.

Besides, it was the only show she had scheduled, which he found strange. Sylvia didn't seem to be doing much to promote Maddy's work. Was that why Maddy tensed up when he asked her how things were going?

Ill ease tickled the back of his neck, that sixth sense alerting him to danger. Something was definitely off kilter. Or maybe Derrick was right. Maybe he was seeing ghosts from the past. Maybe.

"I can't believe another session has come and gone." Sitting on the edge of the patio behind the office, Maddy stared up at the stars.

"Feels weird, doesn't it?" Joe dropped down beside her and held out a beer. "Here you go."

"Thanks." She popped the top with a satisfying spew, then drank quickly, before the foam spilled down the side. "Ah! I never knew beer could taste so good."

Joe took a long pull from his can and sighed loudly. "Abstinence makes the taste buds grow fonder."

They sat in easy silence watching fireflies blink off and on throughout the camp. Lights glowed from the various lodges where the counselors would spend one last night, then depart in the morning. A shriek of laughter drifted from the Chief's Lodge. Through the screen windows, she could make out the shapes of the coordinators moving about. A pillow flew, hitting the back of someone's head. More laughter followed.

Maddy smiled. "I just realized what this reminds me of."

"What's that?" He draped an arm over her shoulder.

"The last day of college." She leaned comfortably into him. "Classes are over, removing your reason for being there, yet you're still there, along with people who have been such a big part of your life. Then suddenly you realize you have no reason for seeing them every day. Everything inside you ping-pongs back and forth between excitement—because, yippee, you're finally out of school, ready to take on real life—and outbursts of tears because, oh my God, you're not going to see your friends every day anymore."

"Transitions are always tough," he said quietly.

"Yeah." She sighed, grateful that she wasn't leaving with the others tomorrow. She had one whole month to be with Joe before his friend Derrick arrived. Plenty of time for working up to the things she'd promised herself she'd tell him as soon as they had the camp back to themselves. Although there was no time like the present to start laying the groundwork. "It's very tough to say good-bye, but sometimes it's not necessary. If the bonds are strong enough, all those promises to stay close actually stick."

"Do they?" he asked.

"They did for Amy, Christine, and me. Three out of four's not bad."

"What happened to your fourth suitemate?"

"Ah, that would be Jane Redding."

"From the morning show?" He pulled back in surprise.

"Yep."

"You never told me that." He settled back against her, fitting her snugly to his side. "So what happened with her?"

"She went off to become rich and famous, and we fell out of touch." Oh man, she thought. This was not a good way to lead up to asking how he'd feel if she took Sylvia up on the offer to be in the spring catalog. "But it didn't have to be that way. We could have stayed close if Jane had been willing to put in the effort."

"Long-distance relationships are tough." He paused. "I'm, um, not sure I'd want to go through another one."

Why had he said that? she wondered. Oh yes, Janice. The woman he'd dated while still in the Army. The one he'd considered marrying until he realized she valued career over family.

And weren't those all the problems she and Joe would face if she moved her career up on her list of priorities, then had to travel to make it work?

From the Chief's Lodge, Carol's voice rose above the others, calling for quiet. Maddy glanced over at the sound. The screens obscured the figures inside, but she could see that they were making a toast. Cheap wine, paper cups, and promises.

Which of those promises would hold?

"I've always wondered, is it the same for men when you have to move on?"

He chuckled. "We have our own way of doing it. Generally without the emotional outbursts."

"Really?" She tipped her head to see his face. "What about the last day of Ranger school? I imagine that was pretty emotional."

A smile moved over his face. She loved the way he smiled, his muscles moving in such a masculine way. "It was . . . intense."

Laughing, she planted a quick kiss on his cheek. "I'm sure it was."

"Speaking of . . ." He stared at his beer can. "I heard from Derrick today."

"Oh?" She frowned at his flat tone. "Is something wrong?"

"No. Not at all. Actually, things couldn't be better. He, um, sold a corporate package."

"Really?" Twin jolts of elation and concern hit her at once. How fabulous for Joe—but where did this leave her? "Wow, that's . . . great."

He chuckled, which made her frown deepen.

"What's so funny?"

"Nothing." He took a sip of beer. "I don't have all the details yet, but he's coming earlier than expected so we can start building the obstacle course."

"How much earlier?" She shifted to face him.

"He'll be here in two weeks."

"But—"

"I know." When his arm dropped off her shoulder, he took her hand. "Your art show in Taos. This won't affect that. I promise. I'll just tell Derrick to entertain himself while we're gone."

"Is that what you want to do? We were just talking about the importance of friends, and I know you haven't seen Derrick in nearly two years. I don't want to interfere with that."

"Maddy . . ." He chuckled. "I'm not going to miss your art show."

"Good." She squeezed his hand. "I really do want you there."

"You know . . ." he said cautiously, gathering his thoughts and his courage. "I'm a little surprised that you don't have more shows coming up."

"Oh?" Her hand jerked.

"Yeah." An alarm went off in his head. Something was definitely wrong here. "You were such a big hit the night of Sylvia's show, I expected things to take off faster."

"Ah. Well, you know." She shrugged as if that should explain things.

He frowned at her. "What's that supposed to mean?"

"Nothing." Irritation edged into her voice.

"Everything is going okay, though, right?"

"Of course." She scowled at her beer.

"It's just that I've noticed you haven't been spending much time on your artwork, so I wondered—"

"Everything's fine. Really." Her eyes pleaded with him in the dark. "Can we please talk about something else?"

Shit! It was worse than he'd thought. Although fortunately the only thing she'd been hiding was her disappointment. He rubbed his thumb over her knuckles. "It's okay, Maddy. Sometimes the things we want take longer than we thought they would. That doesn't mean they won't happen."

"I'm not so sure. Joe, I want—" She hesitated, then gripped his hand tightly. "I've been wanting to tell you for weeks that . . . I want very much to make this work."

"This?" His mind whirled. What "this" did she mean?

"I want to stay here and . . . give this time. I don't have to have a huge art career, just something quiet and satisfying. That's enough for me, I swear. I just want . . . the chance to make this work."

"It will work for you, baby. I'm sure of it." Disappointment swamped him as he realized she was talking about her art, not what was growing between them. An ache of sympathy quickly followed. "And of course you can stay here as long as you need to while you're waiting for things to take off."

He kissed her forehead, his mind racing ahead. "In fact, something just occurred to me. Since Derrick and I got our first account, we're going to need to step up all our plans. You know, set up a bank account, office records, all that stuff. Which means we'll need some staff." He leaned back, beaming at the brilliant simplicity of the idea. "What do you say? Would you be interested in the position of office manager for our boot camp?"

"You mean"—her eyes went wide—"like what Carol does for the summer camp?"

"Exactly! Then you can live here as long as you like—which certainly appeals to me—while you wait for things with Sylvia to work out. And it will happen." He lifted her hand and kissed it. "Never lose faith, Maddy. Promise me that."

She blinked, as if overcome. "I'll try not to."

"Then you'll take the job?"

"I—I . . ." She smiled up at him. "I'd love to."

Chapter 20

One woman's dream is another woman's nightmare, so be careful what you wish for.
                              —*How to Have a Perfect Life*

"What have I gotten myself into?" Maddy wondered aloud as she sat at the desk in the camp office. She could be signing prints for Sylvia's catalog, getting ready for trade shows and gallery appearances, working on new originals. Instead, she was sitting before a computer, creating a spreadsheet that was turning into a disaster.

Why had she taken this job?

Not that she had any grounds to complain. She'd made sacrifices to help Nigel with his business. How could she do less for Joe? Joe might not be sick, but if she loved him, she owed him the same level of commitment.

If only she could get this stupid spreadsheet to work!

She dropped her head to the desk in despair, only to have her forehead crack against the keyboard.

Ouch! She raised up, rubbing her brow. Then her eyes widened at her computer screen, which

seemed to have gone haywire. All the numbers in
all the little boxes were ticking down like the timer
on a bomb about to go off. "No! Stop! What'd I
hit? Undo, undo!"

She frantically punched keys, until suddenly the
numbers reversed, going up now, faster than the
national debt. She froze in shock, watching it with
horrified fascination.

Up until now, she'd always thought she was good
with computers. She'd quickly learned that having an
innate ability with graphic design software did not
mean she had the same ability with bookkeeping software. Truth was, she made a much better business
owner's wife than she did an office manager.

She'd done well helping Nigel run his business
all those years because they'd had Betty manning
the front desk. All Maddy had to do was carry files
back and forth, boost morale, and keep tabs on
how things were going. After the past two weeks,
she was convinced Betty was the eighth wonder of
the world for being able to run an office so
smoothly.

Just then she heard Joe's pickup pull into the
parking lot. He was back from meeting Derrick at
the airport. Panic shot through her. She hit the
monitor casing a few times in a desperate effort to
stop the wildly growing numbers, then tried punch-
ing keys. ESCAPE! DELETE! UNDO!

Two truck doors slammed. Boot heels crunched
on gravel.

She jumped out of the chair and onto the desk
to block the computer screen with her body just as
Joe stepped into the office. A tall, leanly muscled
black man came in behind him.

"Hey, baby," Joe said, then frowned in curiosity at where she was sitting. "Is something wrong?"

"No. Not a thing."

Looking skeptical, he gestured to the other man. "Meet Corporal Derrick Harrelson."

"Hello, Derrick." She started to extend a hand in welcome but caught Joe trying to look behind her. She quickly shifted, reclining sideways. "We meet at last."

Derrick's eyebrows shot up, making her realize she was sprawled on the desktop like a lounge singer on a piano. "So you're, um, Maddy." He flashed a smile full of white teeth. "It's good to finally meet you." He sent Joe a look of approval.

Joe frowned at her. "You're sure everything's all right here?"

"Fine." She grinned. "Completely, one hundred percent under control."

"Because if you need help, I can ask Mom to come down and—"

"No!" She plastered her back against the computer screen. "I've got it. Seriously."

"Okay then." He hesitated. "I guess I'll leave you to it while I show Socrates to the Chief's Lodge."

"All right." She wiggled her fingers as they headed out the back door. "Good to meet you, Derrick."

The moment they were out of sight, she jumped back into the chair and looked at the screen.

The numbers had stopped going haywire. Which would have been a relief. Except that now all the little boxes were blank.

Heart racing, she pulled up the e-mail server and

shot a post off, praying that at least one of her friends was online.

Message: *Help! I'm making a mess and I don't know how to stop!*

Amy: *Calm down. I'm here. What's the newest bookkeeping disaster?*

Christine: *I'm here too. Lord, Maddy, when are you going to stop digging this hole deeper and start climbing out?*

Amy: *Ignore her. Just tell me what's wrong, and I'll try to walk you through it.*

Christine: *What's wrong is she won't TALK TO JOE!*

Maddy: *Is there an echo in here? That's all I hear anymore. Talk to Joe. Talk to Joe. Well, I'm sorry, it's not that easy! Especially when I'm messing up his business. I want out of this job so badly I could scream.*

Christine: *So tell him!*

Maddy: *What, say "Joe I love you and by the way I quit"? Yeah, that's a great start to becoming a husband/wife team running a business together. No, I have to fix this first. Help him get the camp going. And pray for the day he can afford an office assistant who understands bookkeeping. Maybe by then I'll be married and pregnant and I can quit to raise children.*

Christine: *I canNOT believe you said that! Another woman, yes, but not independent Maddy. Besides, if you can't say "I love you" you'll never get to say "I do."*

Maddy: *I told you, we're getting there in our own time and way. You don't have to make it sound like we've been dragging it out for years. I've only been here three and a half months.*

Amy: *Excuse me. Can we stick to the current problem, please?*

Maddy deleted all of Christine's posts before responding just to Amy: *I'm afraid I did something serious this time. See, I thought maybe if I opened Carol's files to see how she keeps the books for the summer camp, I could figure out how to do this. And I guess I sort of hit something I shouldn't have. Because, well, now all the numbers in all the little boxes are sort of . . . gone.*

Amy: *Oh dear.*

"What have I gotten myself into?" Joe asked the world at large as he and Derrick headed for the Chief's Lodge.

"Do you think you could be more specific?"

"Maddy!" Stopping, he flung a hand toward the office.

"Ah, that narrows it down some, but I'm afraid not enough."

"I can't believe I hired her as our office manager."

"I don't know." Derrick scratched his cheek, looking back toward the office. "She looks pretty good sitting on a desk to me. And she did a fantastic job with our promo material."

"Except she's completely incompetent at running an office." With his hands on his hips, he stared at his feet. After days of denial, the full magnitude of his blunder settled over him. "I'm going to have to fire her."

"Whoa, my man. I thought the plan was to marry her."

"It is!"

"Then might I suggest you propose before you fire her."

"Yeah." A dry laugh escaped. "Good plan."

"No, not 'plan.'" Derrick held up a finger. "Advice. I think you've done enough planning with this situation."

"No, I just need a new plan." He resumed walking, his mind racing. If only Maddy's art career would take off, he could encourage her to quit. Maybe he could do something there to help out. "Yeah, that's what I need. A new plan."

Groaning loudly, Derrick fell in step beside him.

Thank God for days off, Maddy thought as she packed for the party in Taos. If she had to spend one more minute reading software manuals that made no sense, her head would explode. Why couldn't she figure out how to make it all work? Although anytime she dealt with numbers, her brain turned to Teflon. The only reason she'd kept her math grades up in school was because of Joe and then Amy helping her.

No wonder he'd been shocked to learn she was such a good student in all her other courses.

As for the current situation, at least Joe never yelled at her the way her father yelled at her mother for every mistake, large or small. Joe just came quietly along behind her and fixed things.

Which made her feel awful. She was supposed to be helping him. Instead she was causing him more work.

Well, tomorrow they were heading for Taos, where she'd see her friends for the first time in months. Maybe if she sat down with Amy, they could figure out what she was doing wrong.

Comforted by the thought, she pulled two dresses from the closet to add to her growing pile of potential outfits for the night of the show. They were both simple, jersey knit, a flattering, forgiving fabric that could be dressed up or down. Stepping before the mirror that hung on the bathroom door, she held the hangers under her chin. The short red? Or the long black? Black was always great. Artsy. Sophisticated.

Funereal.

How appropriate.

Without warning she burst into tears. Loud, wet sobs shook her whole body.

Pressing the heel of her hand to her eyes, she wondered what was wrong with her lately. She always seemed on the verge of singing with joy or bawling her eyes out. If she hadn't just ended her period, she'd swear she was pregnant or PMSing.

She had no reason to be this way. Things were going great with Joe. Every day they were moving in the right direction, getting one step closer to the day when she would be able to say the words that felt like a living entity, trapped inside the center of her chest and struggling to get out. Christine was right; if she couldn't say "I love you," she'd never say "I do."

God, it hurt, physically hurt, not to voice those words. Once that happened, though, once she told him she loved him, maybe the rest would work out.

Who was she kidding? The rest would never work out. She was doomed to spend the rest of her life chained to the desk in the camp office, mucking up Joe's books and being miserable.

That thought drew her up short, had her sniffing back tears.

She wasn't miserable. She was happy! And she needed to stop all this stupid crying.

Moving to the sink, she splashed water on her face as her breathing steadied. She had a growing relationship with a man she adored. A new life helping him with his business. So of course she was happy.

As for her art, she hadn't given it up completely. Once the boot camp was up and running, she'd get back to it.

Lifting her head, she caught a look at her dripping face in the mirror. Good grief, she looked like hell. The curse of being a redhead was that her face turned blotchy at the first sign of tears. She ducked back down for a few more splashes of cold water, then reached for a hand towel and dared another look.

Okay, better, she decided. Not great, but not so noticeable.

She heard the slamming of a truck door and jolted. Was Joe already back from his trip into town? He and Derrick had gone to buy lumber for their obstacle course. A quick glance at the clock told her more time had passed than she'd realized. And here she was standing in nothing but her underwear so she could try on outfits as she packed.

She checked the mirror again, fluffed her hair, tried out a smile. Passable, she decided, then grabbed her robe and headed for the door. She opened it just as he reached the landing. "Hey, you're back. Great. You can help me decide what to pack."

He didn't take her into his arms for a kiss, as he normally did, or comment on her lack of attire. In fact, he didn't even return her smile.

"Do you mind if I come in?"

"What?" Since when did he ask to come in? "Of course not." Stepping back, she watched him stride to the middle of the room, wearing camouflage pants and an Army green T-shirt. His shoulders were set in a rigid line. "Is something wrong? You look upset."

He turned to face her. "I wanted to show off your artwork to Derrick, so we stopped by the gallery while we were in town."

Alarm snaked up her spine. "Oh?"

"Maddy—" He stared at her as if he'd never seen her before. "What the hell are you doing?"

"W-what do you mean?"

"Do not look at me like that!" Controlled anger vibrated in his voice. "Like you don't know what I'm talking about. Sylvia told me."

"Told you what?" Why was he so angry? What had Sylvia said?

"Everything!" He turned on his heels and paced. "I've spent the last several weeks thinking your career had somehow tanked before it even had a chance to take off, which made no sense to me. And now I learn it didn't tank. You threw it away! I can't begin to tell you—to explain what that means—how I feel— Christ! I can't even talk."

"Joe, I—" His fury had the blood draining from her face. "I told you, that's not the most important thing to me. Yes, I would have loved to accept her offer, but *this* is more important."

"This?" He shook his head, staring at her. "What 'this' are you talking about?"

"You and me." She took a step toward him. "I told you, I want a chance to make this work."

"Wait." He raised a hand to hold her off. "I

thought you were talking about your art career. Why didn't you tell me you were talking about us?"

"I did. I told you I wanted to stay here and make this work."

"You could have been a bit more clear about what you meant."

"Joe—" Frustration and fear had her heart racing. "You made me promise not to say it aloud unless I meant it, so I've been too scared to say it, scared you won't believe me. You didn't believe me before, even though it was true, and I don't know if you'll believe me now. I don't care, though." The pressure in her chest rose up to fill her throat. "I'm tired of not saying it. I love you! All right. There! I said it."

"And this is how you show it?" He gestured toward her. "By lying to me?"

"What?" She gaped at him. Why wasn't he saying he loved her too? "I didn't lie to you."

"Well, you sure as hell weren't being honest. Omission is a type of lie. What I can't figure out is why. Why didn't you tell me what was going on with Sylvia? And why in the world would you pass up such a great opportunity? That makes no sense. Are you insane?"

"Because . . . I had to make a choice. Last time, I chose my art, my independence, myself. This time, I chose you."

"Who's asking you to choose?" His hands went up in frustration. "Have I ever asked that of you?"

"No, but . . ." Why was he so upset? Didn't he understand? "It didn't seem fair for me to go off chasing all that. This is more important than that. You're more important than that."

"Fair? You're not making sense." He drew up short. Held a hand out. "Wait. No. Tell me I'm wrong. You think I'm settling for less than I want. Poor Joe got shot and had to leave the Rangers. He's not good enough for what he really wants. He has to settle for half a life. A less important life than being a successful artist."

"I didn't think of it that way. Exactly." But she had. Oh God, she had!

"Fuck! I'm right." He turned his back to her, visibly struggling to rein in his temper before he faced her again. "Damn it, Maddy, you've been working with me for weeks on this. How could you not see how much I want this? How could you think I was settling, when in fact I've found something I really want to do? I'll never make a lot of money, but what I do with those kids matters. And what I'm going to do with adults matters too."

"I do see that. And I want to be a part of it. That's why I chose to stay and help."

"Well, pardon me for pointing this out, but you're not that much help."

"I can't believe you said that." The words struck her square in the chest and had her earlier tears springing back to her eyes. "I'm not stupid. I can learn."

"I didn't say you were stupid, and don't you dare cry on me." He shook a finger at her face, making her cry harder. "I'm too furious right now to deal with tears."

"Then don't insult me, because it hurts." She swiped at the wet trails running down her cheeks. "And I cry when someone hurts me."

"What do you think I'm feeling?" He stared at

her with pain in his eyes. "Do you think what you did doesn't hurt? You've been pandering to me for two months!"

"I wasn't pandering to you."

"The hell you weren't! You thought I couldn't handle it if you became successful. Did you think I'd resent you?"

She bit her lips, which was answer enough.

"Jesus!"

"It's not like that. It's—" She couldn't seem to think straight. "It's about priorities. You're the one who broke up with Janice because she picked her career over family, and you're the one who said long-distance relationships were hard."

"What?" He pressed fingertips to his forehead. "Okay, first of all, Janice has nothing to do with us, especially since there are thousands of women who have careers and still manage to make family a top priority. And second, when I said long-distance relationships were hard, I was thinking about you moving back to Austin and how much I didn't want to fly back and forth constantly just to see you— even though I was fully prepared to do that."

"You were?"

"Yes, damn it! But instead, I offered you a job to keep you here. Frankly, I'm beginning to think flying back and forth would have been easier."

"Don't insult me!" She balled her fists, angry now too.

"You insulted me by thinking my male ego couldn't handle it if you became successful."

"I'm sorry, all right? I'm sorry!"

"Yeah, well, I am too." He shook his head with a look of disbelief. "I really thought we had a chance this time."

Fear hit her like a bolt of lightning. "What are you saying?"

"That I can't be with a woman who keeps things from me. Especially when she thinks so little of me that she thinks she has to be less in order to make me feel like I'm more."

"I didn't mean it that way. I was trying to put you first."

"I never asked you to. And you never gave me the chance to tell you to go for it. Or didn't it occur to you that we could have worked all this out?"

Her body started shaking. "Are you saying we can't now?"

"I don't know! I can't think straight. Jesus!" He turned away from her, as if he couldn't bear to look at her. "I think you should go to Taos alone. Maybe we can talk when you get back."

He strode toward the door.

"Joe, no! Don't go!"

He stopped with his hand on the doorknob.

Tears coursed down her cheeks. "I'm sorry I hurt you. I never meant to. Please don't leave me."

He turned back, came toward her with long strides and pulled her hard into his arms. "Goddamn it." His eyes blazed into hers. "I don't want to lose you. Not again. It nearly killed me the first time. I don't want to lose you all over again."

His mouth crushed down on hers, full of fear and fury. She kissed him back, weeping. His mouth left hers, kissing the tears from her cheeks.

"You don't have to lose me," she whispered hoarsely. "I won't let you. I love you."

Her head spun as he lifted her and laid her on the bed, coming down with her. *I won't let you lose me.* She caressed the hard lines of his face as he jerked at the belt of her robe. When his hands shook, she helped him untie it. *I love you!*

Desperate to touch him, she pulled his T-shirt free from his pants as he jerked the robe down her arms. She freed her arms and removed her bra, then gasped as his mouth moved to her breasts, hungry and demanding. She stroked his shoulders, feeling the hard muscles bunch as he jerked off her panties and tossed them to the floor.

Everything inside her clamored with need, but it was a need driven by fear rather than desire, a need of the heart, not the body.

When she was naked beneath him, he freed his erection and drove into her. She gasped at the shock of it, the hard invasion into dry flesh. Until that moment she hadn't even noticed her lack of response. Her eyes snapped wide in pain to find him frozen above her, his weight braced on straight arm.

Horror filled his eyes. "Oh my God. Maddy." He came down over her, cradling her. "I'm sorry. I'm sorry." He rained kisses over her face and tried to ease his body from hers.

"No, don't!" She clamped her legs about him, pulling him back. "Don't leave me."

"Okay, I won't move. Am I still hurting you?"

"Don't leave me." She lifted her hips, forcing him deeper, biting her lip against the increase in pain.

"Maddy, baby, hold still. I'm hurting you."

"I don't care." The physical pain began to ebb, while the pain in her heart grew. "Don't leave me." She kissed his jaw as her hips continued to move, back and forth. Slowly she warmed and softened around him. "Please."

"Maddy, you have to stop."

She felt his whole body strain with his effort to hold still against her. He straightened his arms again, gathering his strength and will to pull out of her.

"Stay." She looked up at his taut face, into his dark eyes as she lifted her hips into him, held him fully and deeply inside her.

"Maddy, I can't—" With a curse, he turned his head, his jaw clenched.

Stay with me. Love me. On one slow glide, she let her hips fall, slowly, slowly, till he almost slid from her body, then she lifted again. When she held him fully once more, squeezing tightly around him, his head fell back.

"Oh God." His restraint broke. He moved in her, with her, his whole body working like one big wave, riding toward fulfillment, release. Lowering over her, he held her, comforting her even as he pounded harder into her. She tightened her arms about him and welcomed every jarring thrust, needing him so much, tears came back to her eyes.

"I'm sorry," he whispered, kissing the tears away as his body gathered, focused, drove him toward its own selfish goal. Some small, functioning part of his brain knew her own release was a long way off, but his body didn't care.

The climax hit him with such a vicious punch that his body jerked from the force of it, then trembled as the pleasure kept on and on. When the storm ended, he collapsed against her, fearing his heart would thunder out of his chest.

His mind cleared by degrees, became aware of her arms wrapped tightly about him, her tear-stained face buried against his shoulder.

Mortified, he realized he was still hard from the adrenaline pumping through his body. Not as hard as before, but enough to cause her discomfort if she was raw. How could he have done this? Even though she'd encouraged him, there was no excuse for continuing once he realized she wasn't aroused.

Hating himself, he eased from her, wincing when she winced. He shifted to lie beside her, brushed the hair back from her face. Looking at her, meeting her eyes, was one of the hardest things he'd ever done. Her eyes were red from crying, filled with pain, but no accusation. "How badly did I hurt you?"

"You didn't really. Not the way you mean." She blinked against a fresh rise of tears. "Will you hold me?"

He felt as if a giant fist reached inside his chest and squeezed around his heart. "Of course."

She snuggled against his chest, burrowing into him as his arms went around her. Reaching past her, he gathered the bedspread and covered her, tucking it between their bodies. He rubbed her arms, struggling with what to say. Before he could decide, her breathing evened out and she fell asleep.

He lay a long time, holding her, listening to her shallow breaths, still aching with anger and confusion. Even in this, this mindless eruption of angry sex, she'd put herself aside for him. He wanted to shake her and comfort her and never hurt her again.

Most of all, he wanted to understand her. Which, of course, he never would.

Could he live with that, though? Live with a woman who had the power to rip out his guts without even realizing what she was doing? She would never intentionally hurt anyone, but God in heaven, she'd hurt him. She'd goddamn eviscerated him. And he wasn't sure she even got that.

He shifted to see her face, relaxed now in sleep but still ravaged by her tears. *What am I going to do with you, Maddy?*

Long minutes later, he rose, righted his clothes, and moved quietly toward the door.

"Joe?" She stirred behind him. "Don't go."

"Maddy—" He couldn't even turn to face her. "I can't talk right now. Go to Taos without me. We'll talk when you get back."

The following morning, Joe stood at the kitchen sink, his mind still numb with confusion. Renewed pain stabbed him when he looked out the window just as Maddy drove by. She glanced over long enough for their gazes to meet, and then the car carried her on, down the hill toward the gate.

A part of him was still so angry he wanted to throw his coffee mug into the sink and shatter it into a million pieces, while another part wanted to break down and cry as openly as she had.

Out of nowhere, the image of the Colonel sprang to mind, adding a ripping sense of grief to the pain already inside him. "I wish you were here, Dad. So you could tell me what to do."

Chapter 21

Truth hurts even when it sets you free.
—*How to Have a Perfect Life*

Maddy huddled in one of the big wooden chairs on the front porch of the resort's central lodge. Even though she wore the largest pair of sunglasses she owned, the light stabbed at her sensitive eyes. If only Christine and Amy would arrive, she could go to the suite they'd be sharing, close all the drapes, and hide out from the other guests until she got her emotions under control.

When she'd arrived an hour ago, she'd managed to put on a happy face long enough to get checked in, greet her hosts, and meet a few guests. The puffy eyes had been easily dismissed as allergies. She doubted that excuse would hold up if she joined the party going on in the bar and suddenly burst into tears for no apparent reason.

Sitting outside to "enjoy the mountain view" was a much safer bet.

Finally, she saw an SUV turn into the resort's long, twisting driveway. She tracked its progress past the horse stables, over the wooden bridge, then as it climbed past a scattering of guest lodges.

Rental vehicles had been arriving at a fairly steady pace, but she clung to the hope that this one would be carrying her friends.

It made the final turn into the long, narrow parking lot. After it slipped into an empty space, a tall blonde stepped out of the driver's side.

"Christine!" Maddy called, springing to her feet.

The woman turned, shading her eyes. A familiar smile broke over her face, the most welcome sight in the world.

"Maddy!" Christine waved as Maddy hurried off the porch and barreled toward her friends.

Amy emerged next, and Maddy soon found herself engulfed in a group hug. The comfort of it stirred all the emotions that had been too near the surface for the past twenty-four hours.

"I've missed you both so much. I'm so glad you made it!"

"Us, too," Christine said. "Although it was touch and go at the very last minute."

"What happened?" Maddy looked instinctively to Amy and noticed the lack of glasses. "Did you get contacts?"

"I did." She beamed, her green eyes sparkling. Her jumper also hung looser than normal.

"Hey, you look great!" Maddy stepped back for a better look.

Amy struck a diva pose. "Just forty more pounds to go."

"So what was the holdup?"

"Grandmother." Amy rolled her eyes, speaking volumes with that single word. "It's okay, though. Christine helped me handle it."

"Yeah." Christine snorted. "It's hell being a hypochondriac when there's a doctor in the room."

"But everything else went okay?" Maddy searched Amy's face for signs of strain, but realized her friend had never looked more excited. "You handled the plane all right?"

Amy laughed. "Christine's the one who hates flying. But since we had each other, the trip was really fun."

"It was," Christine agreed. "And now that she's had her first taste of travel, I suspect there'll be no stopping her."

"I don't know. Traveling solo still sounds pretty scary." Amy shaded her eyes as she looked about. "Goodness, what a place!"

"No kidding." Christine looked equally impressed, which was no mean feat for someone who had grown up with family money like hers. Then she turned back to Maddy. "So, where's Joe? We're dying to meet him."

"He's—" She managed to swallow down a rise of tears. "Not coming."

"Uh-oh." Christine narrowed her eyes, trying to see past the sunglasses.

"Why not?" Amy's smile turned into a worried frown.

"I'll tell you when we get inside." Though she said it calmly, nothing got past Christine. Her friend plucked the sunglasses right off her nose. After a two-day crying jag, she knew perfectly well how awful she looked.

Christine turned to Amy. "We need an emergency girlfriend crash cart. Stat. Did you bring the chocolate I put on your packing list?"

"I told you, it's not on my diet."

"Amy, calories don't count when you're out of town." Christine shook her head. "Never mind.

There's bound to be a restaurant or gift shop inside. See what you can scare up."

Amy bit her lip as she studied the central lodge. "Okay, I can do this."

"You don't need to." Maddy put the shades back on and realized her head was now pounding. "I'm okay."

"No, I can handle it," Amy insisted. "Where's the gift shop?"

"Right inside the door."

"And our room?"

"We're in Alta Vista." Maddy pointed to a three-story adobe building perched at the end of a footpath above the parking lot. "Bottom corner suite on the left."

"Got it." Amy hurried off, digging in her purse for her wallet.

Moving to the back of the SUV, Christine popped the hatch. Maddy followed to help her with the luggage and was shouldered away. "Patients aren't allowed to tote and carry. You just lead the way."

"Come on. Y'all are being silly," Maddy protested weakly as Christine herded her up the path with a suitcase in each hand.

With their suite on the bottom level, they had a patio rather than a balcony. The twin patio doors opened into two units that could be separated with double doors or opened into one big unit. Since Joe hadn't come, Maddy had opened the doors.

"I put you and Amy in here." Maddy led the way into the side with two double beds. She'd taken the one with the single king on the remote hope that Joe would show up.

"Nice digs." Christine looked around as she deposited the suitcases on the beds. "Western chic meets feng shui. Your new friends have good taste."

"I don't even want to think about what this room would cost if we were paying."

"Then don't. In fact, don't think about anything. Just sit." Christine pointed to the sofa before the kiva fireplace as she ducked into the bathroom.

Since obeying was easier than arguing, Maddy sat and rested her head against the back of the sofa. The draperies were open, so she left her sunglasses on and closed her eyes. A minute later she heard Christine return. The stinging red light behind her eyelids went wonderfully blue when the drapes closed with a swish of sound.

"Don't move," Christine told her, her voice coming closer. The sunglasses were removed—gently this time—and a damp washcloth settled over her eyes.

"Thank y-you—" Her voice broke, so she shut up.

"You just sit there and relax while I unpack a few things. We'll talk when Amy gets here."

Giving in to exhaustion, she stayed just as she was, struggling to regain control of her rioting emotions. She heard the zip of a suitcase being opened, rummaging, footsteps, the pop of a cork leaving a wine bottle.

Then the patio door opened with a tangible burst of happy energy and return of sunlight.

"Mission accomplished," Amy announced. "And I only took one wrong turn trying to find the kitchen."

"They didn't have chocolate bars in the gift shop?" Christine asked.

"They did. Really good ones, too. But I wanted to get this."

"You're that determined to stick to your diet?"

"No. It's for Maddy."

Christine burst out laughing.

Curious, Maddy lifted the corner of the washcloth. She found Amy standing just inside the patio door proudly holding a fistful of candy bars in one hand and an enormous cucumber in the other. She couldn't help it, she laughed as well.

"So"—Christine stifled her mirth—"is that supposed to console Maddy by replacing Joe?"

"What?" Amy frowned, then turned scarlet when understanding dawned. "You!" she scolded Christine as she closed the door, plunging the room back into semidarkness. "It's for her eyes. Cucumber slices take the swelling out."

"Ah." Christine grinned as she poured wine into hotel water glasses. "Well, bring it over and add it to the rest of our emergency supplies."

Maddy straightened, plucking at her hair where the cloth had dampened it. Christine had set a bottle of wine on the coffee table along with a manicure kit, her laptop, which was booting up, and a small stack of DVDs.

"You brought movies?" Maddy lifted a brow.

"I was hoping we could kick Joe out for one evening and have a girls' night ogling Orlando Bloom and Johnny Depp."

Maddy's throat went tight. "Looks like you got your wish."

"Oh, crap." Christine's shoulders slumped while Amy hurried over, sat on the sofa, and pulled Maddy into her arms.

"It's okay." Amy patted her back. Maddy gave in and slumped into her nurturing softness.

Big, humiliating, shoulder-shaking sobs wracked her body. "I'm sorry," she managed to say after several long minutes.

"Don't be." Amy soothed her by rubbing her palm on Maddy's back in circles. "Whatever happened, we're here. You can cry in front of us all you want."

"Thank you." Maddy sniffed as she straightened.

Christine sat on the coffee table facing her with a glass of red wine in her hand. "Here, drink this."

"Thanks." Maddy took a sip, hiccuping slightly.

"Now this." Christine held out a chocolate bar that was half unwrapped.

The chocolate was dark and rich and had a wonderful bite that made Maddy moan in unexpected ecstasy. Amy was right—they stocked the good stuff.

"Now," Christine said sternly. "Tell us what the bastard did, so we can decide whether or not he gets to live."

The chocolate turned to sawdust in Maddy's mouth. She managed to wash it down with a swallow of wine. "It wasn't him. It was me. Oh God, I've been so stupid!"

She bent forward in a rush, bracing her forearms against her thighs. The wineglass and chocolate bar magically disappeared, allowing her to hide her face in her hands. "Really, really *stupid*!"

Amy patted her back. "Can you tell us what happened?"

"Only if Christine promises not to say 'I told you so.' "

"I swear upon my Hippocratic oath."

"Well, you were right." She sat back and accepted the wine again. "I should have talked to Joe weeks ago. Not about telling him I loved him—we really were making progress there—but about Sylvia's offer."

"Ah." Christine raised a brow. "He found out."

"Oh yeah."

"And he didn't take it well."

"You could say that." She took a drink. "Actually, he pretty much lost it. At the time, I was stunned. I couldn't figure out why he was so angry. All the way up here, I kept trying to sort it out. Well, actually, I started out arguing with him in my head about how ridiculous he was being. This wasn't like last time, when I put my own dreams and independence before him. It was exactly the opposite. I was putting him first. Putting us first.

"But something he said kept ringing through my own tirade, until I finally got it. I finally understood what he was saying."

"What?" Amy asked.

"He said he couldn't be with a woman who thought so little of him that she thought she had to make herself less in order for him to feel like he's more. And suddenly I realized something in this blinding flash that's humiliating to admit."

"What?" Amy's eyes went round.

"I've turned into my mother!"

"Now, there's a frightening thought," Christine said.

"Maybe not for everyone, but it is for me." Maddy remembered when Joe had had the same revelation about him becoming more like his mother, but at least Mama Fraser was someone she would want to be like. "What's worse is I was treating Joe as if he was as big an insecure jerk as my Neanderthal father. No wonder he's insulted. I'm insulted for him." She covered her eyes. "And embarrassed and ashamed and really pissed at myself."

"Maddy"—Christine squeezed her knee—"this is hardly surprising. We all form our opinions about relationships based on the dynamics of our parents' relationship. It's what we grow up watching."

"Yes, but I grew up swearing I would never be like my mother."

"You love your mother," Christine said.

"Of course I do. That doesn't mean I always like her. And I sure don't respect her. She's an intelligent, talented, personable woman with incredible organizational skills. She ran our house so smoothly it was amazing. But it was all done behind my dad's back, with her dismissing everything she did as no big deal while praising anything Dad did, no matter how stupid. Like 'Oh wonder be, the man managed to lift his own butt out of his armchair and walk into the dining room all on his own power to eat this little ol' meal I fixed. Isn't he a miracle? Oh no, dear, don't get up to fetch another beer. You've been driving around in your squad car all day while all I did was grocery shopping, cleaning, mending, cooking, and running ten thousand errands for your five ungrateful kids. Let me wait on you.' Gag, gag, gag."

"You shouldn't be so hard on her," Amy said gently. "That's the way a lot of marriages from that generation work."

"Actually," Christine put in, "a lot of marriages are still that way. I guess it works for some people."

"I'm talking about an extreme case here," Maddy insisted. "One that's sickening to watch.

Mom sang in the church choir but laughed off any suggestion that she sing a solo. She worked in a department store for a while but turned down a promotion into management. She belonged to a garden club and refused to be president all three times she was asked. I grew up blaming all that on my dad and vowing that I would never, *never* let a man do that to me."

"Are you saying now it wasn't your dad's fault?"

"Yes and no. I'm getting to that. First, the part that's easier to understand. The reason I freaked when Joe asked me to marry him way back when is because I refused to get married right out of high school and spend my life subjugating myself to any man. I was going to work my tail off, go to college, be an independent woman. A successful artist. My own person. So in my head the two things became connected. Marrying Joe equaled having to become like my mother."

"So"—Christine held up a hand—"since you changed your mind about marrying Joe, you had to change your mind about the other."

"Yes!"

Amy frowned. "Then how come you weren't that way with Nigel?"

"I don't know." Maddy massaged her temple. "Maybe because he was so completely opposite from my father, while Joe is much more masculine, so not so opposite. Not that he's like my father, because he's not."

"Oo, I just had a thought." Christine pursed her lips. "One I don't think you'll like."

"What?" Maddy frowned when her friend hesitated. "You might as well tell me. I can't possibly lose any more respect for myself today."

"You did do it with Nigel." Christine shrugged apologetically. "It just wasn't as noticeable. He was very successful professionally, and he came from a reasonably well-off family. That gave you a pretty high ceiling to hit before your success topped his. Then he got sick, which jeopardized his professional status. Some women would have reacted to that by becoming more aggressive in their own careers to replace their husband's income. But you poured all your energy into guarding his success by running his business for him. That may be the real reason you stopped pursuing an art career. The ceiling got too low."

"Oh crap, you're right." Maddy hid her face behind her hand. "And this is where it all gets more complicated. I don't do it just with men. I do it with women too. Which is something Joe pointed out, but I didn't see just how bad I am about it until I was driving up here."

She lowered her hand. "So now, I feel like someone ripped a blindfold off my eyes and suddenly I'm looking at my mother and really seeing her for the first time. Maybe Mom can't let herself do all the things I know she's capable of for the same reasons I get all sick at my stomach when I do well. My success might hurt someone's feelings or make people not like me. Maybe that's the real reason she won't sing solo in the church choir. And that's why a marriage that looks completely unfair on the outside works for those two people. Dad gets a slave and a verbal whipping post to make him feel manly, and Mom gets a convenient excuse to hold herself back. How warped is that?"

"True," Christine agreed, "but like you said, it works for them."

"I hate that, though." Disgust sat sourly in Maddy's stomach. "And I don't want to be like that."

"You don't have to be." Christine unwrapped another candy bar. "The first step to breaking a pattern is recognizing it. Or, as Jane said in her book, face your inner fear."

"Except she was wrong. I'm not afraid of rejection."

"You're afraid of success." Christine held out the chocolate.

"What kind of a fear is that?" Maddy broke off a bite.

"A fairly common one, I think," Amy said.

"But why?" Maddy asked. "It's so stupid."

"Success changes things." Christine shrugged. "Sometimes in ways that aren't so comfortable. It requires responsibility and sacrifice and can open you up for undeserved criticism. It also changes how you see yourself and how others see you."

"Yeah." Maddy popped the bite of chocolate into her mouth. "It makes some people hate you."

"Only petty, selfish, insecure people. The trick is to realize that your success doesn't rob anyone of anything."

"But it can rob *you*," Maddy said. "Look at Jane. She was willing to sacrifice anything, which turned out to include us, to achieve her dream."

"She didn't have to," Amy said.

"You know"—Christine munched thoughtfully—"I've been thinking about her book a lot. Hidden among a lot of nonsense it has some pretty good gems of wisdom about how hard life can be. That makes me wonder if she's really as 'outrageously happy' as she would have the world believe."

"See?" Maddy gestured with her glass. "There

you go, right there. Success doesn't automatically equal happiness."

"Yet surely it doesn't automatically exclude it either," Amy argued. "I have to believe that happiness comes from finding the right balance. Maybe your balance is accepting that success can empower you without consuming you or diminishing others. Mostly, though, you don't have to sacrifice friendship to reach for your dream. The people who love you will be happy for you, and even get a vicarious thrill watching you."

"God, I love this woman," Christine said. "She's so damn wise. And she's right, Mad. Those of us who love you will be nothing but thrilled."

"Which I guess brings us back to Joe." Maddy stared at her nearly empty glass. "What am I going to do? I really insulted him."

Amy squeezed her hand. "Then apologize."

Christine shuddered. "Don't you just hate that?"

"Not when I've been this stupid." Maddy sighed. "I just hope we can work past this."

"If he loves you, you will." Christine swiveled on the coffee table to survey their supplies. "In the meantime, we have wine, chocolate, and Johnny Depp."

"Orlando Bloom," Amy countered. "He has the sweetest eyes."

"Okay, you get sweet, I get bad, and Maddy gets the cucumber."

"Christine!" Amy blushed.

"For her eyes." Christine blinked, the picture of pure innocence. "That is why you got it, right?"

Maddy smiled at both her friends, loving them so much she thought she might start crying again. Good thing Amy got that cucumber.

Chapter 22

The evening of the show, Maddy stood in the middle of the Taos gallery, feeling stunned. The crowd filled the place to overflowing, bodies bumping as people maneuvered from the food table to the bar. Voices bubbled as brightly as the champagne while the track lighting glinted off enough jewelry to stock Tiffany's.

They'd come because of Rick—the beautiful, the rich, and even the famous—not knowing or caring a thing about "Madeline." All that was changing right before her eyes.

"Looks like you sold another one." Christine nodded toward one of the sales staff as he slipped a SOLD tag in the corner of a frame. The couple standing next to him were practically glowing with pride. Glowing. At the thought of owning one of her originals.

She blinked in amazement. "I think I need to do more work."

"Ya think?" Christine smiled at her. "The new pieces really are incredible. The best work you've ever done. I guess if I'm going to buy *Sunrise Canyon* I'd better move quickly."

"Actually, it's not for sale." Maddy turned toward the piece, which hung in a place of prominence, the focal point of the room. "I've decided to give it to Joe, to hang over the fireplace in the dining hall. It's where it belongs."

It's where I belong.

Looking at the image, as the colors glimmered in the spotlight, she ached to be back at the camp.

Rick slipped up behind her, squeezed her shoulders. "We've sold fifty prints, my dear. Good for you."

After giving her cheek a smacking kiss, he moved on, calling out someone's name. His news left her staggered. Fifty prints in one show. "Wow!"

"Do you need to sit down?" Amy asked.

"No." She laughed, and felt light-headed. "I'm fine."

Christine tilted her head, studying her. "Good thing you decided to deal with that fear of success."

Maddy pressed a hand to her stomach. "Acknowledging it didn't instantly get rid of it."

"You'll get there. In the meantime . . ." Christine stopped a waiter passing through the crowd with a silver tray of champagne flutes. When they all had one she lifted hers. "Here's to my beautiful, talented, wonderful friend Madeline. I wish you success and joy."

"Me too," Amy said. A bright *ping* rang as the glasses touched.

"Thank you." Maddy's heart squeezed. "I'm glad both of you could be here for this. I don't think I could have handled the last few days as well without you."

"And that, right there"—Christine tipped her glass—"is what friends are all about."

"Lucky for me I picked two good ones." Maddy smiled at both of them.

"You know what this means, though," Christine said to Amy. "She's completed her challenge to get her work in a gallery."

"Most definitely." Amy looked around. "I guess that means we have to do ours now."

"Yep." Christine smiled flirtatiously as a cute guy walked by, then sighed in disappointment when he lit up and hugged another man. "This is getting depressing. Here we are, all three of us looking exceptionally hot, and every really good-looking guy in sight is gay."

"Well, you two certainly look hot," Amy countered, admiring Christine's ice blue cocktail dress that showed a mile of leg.

"Amy, if anyone looks hot tonight, it's you," Maddy insisted. She'd gone with the long black dress and added a small fortune's worth of silver jewelry on loan from the gallery. Then she'd pressed Amy into borrowing the little red number, and laughed at the wonder on her friend's face when she realized it fit—and looked spectacular on her.

"So"—Christine continued to scan the room over the rim of her champagne flute—"Amy, have you decided where you're going on your challenge?"

"That depends on what nanny jobs come in." Excitement danced into Amy's eyes, which Christine had accented with just the right amount of makeup. "But I've always wanted to go someplace tropical, like the Caribbean."

"Now there's a fabulous idea," Christine said.

"I'm thinking a cruise. As long as I stay on the ship, even I can't get lost."

Maddy narrowed her eyes. "I'm not sure, but I think that might be cheating. What do you say, Christine?"

"Oh my heavenly bodies!" Christine grabbed her arm, staring toward the door. "I swear to God, if this one's gay, I'm giving up on men."

Maddy turned. And felt her heart go still. The noise faded, the lights dimmed as she watched him scan the room. Then his gaze met hers. And he smiled.

"Joe," she whispered, relief and joy welling up inside her.

"Joe?" Christine repeated. Maddy didn't have to see her friend's face to picture the arched brow and look of approval. "Well, my, my. You definitely didn't exaggerate."

He came straight toward her, turning his broad shoulders this way and that to get through the crowd. Her pulse fluttered with hope.

Then he was standing right in front of her. "Hey."

"You came." She wanted desperately to hug him and feel his arm around her, to lay her head against his chest and feel his heart beat against her cheek.

His expression turned sheepish. "I remembered telling you I wouldn't miss it. The Colonel once told me to always be a man of my word."

The ache of missing him grew. "That's good advice for women too."

"So, you're Joe." Christine stepped closer.

"Oh. Sorry." Maddy shook herself. "Joe, these are my friends."

"Let me guess." He turned to the leggy blonde. "Christine Ashton?"

"I see Maddy's been talking about us." She shook his hand, her grip firm and straightforward.

"Nothing but praise, I assure you." He smiled at the pretty brunette, who managed to look both sexy and sweet. "And you must be Amy Baker."

"Yes." Amy took his hand in more of a finger cuddle than a shake. "It's good to meet you."

"Same here."

"You know, Amy"—Christine looped her arm through her friend's—"I'm really dying to take another stroll through the gallery, make sure we saw everything. How about you?"

"Hmm? Oh. Yes, I'd love to."

The two of them moved away, leaving Joe standing there with no buffer between him and Maddy. Nothing to lessen the punch of seeing her. She'd piled her hair up in some outrageously feminine way that accentuated the heart shape of her face.

Staring at her made him ache from the memory of the scene before she'd left and with longing to make things right again.

He glanced down, then back up. "All day I've been dying to talk to you, but . . . damn, Maddy, you always leave me speechless."

"Maybe that's good, since I have enough to say for both of us."

"Oh?" His heart clutched with fear.

"Would you go for a walk with me. Outside?" She looked so earnest. Panic squeezed his chest.

"Sure." He willed his mind to not race off, second-guessing what was going on inside her head. The time had come to ask her exactly what she meant, and keep asking until he felt certain he understood. Well, as certain as any man could be when trying to understand a woman. And then he'd tell her exactly what he meant, and what he wanted.

They stepped out of the bright, noisy gallery into the quiet night. The streets were deserted, everything closed but the gallery.

Maddy's heart pounded as she led the way across the street to the plaza, a little square in the middle of town. A large gazebo in the style of a bandstand stood in the middle. Wind whipped through the trees as they mounted the steps, and she wrapped her arms around herself.

"Are you cold?"

"No." *Scared,* she thought as they entered the gazebo. "Joe, I have so much to say, I don't know where to begin. And I'm afraid I'll bungle it by not getting it out right."

"Take your time." He leaned back against the handrail. "Then I get my turn."

Her stomach churned at his words, but she nodded. "First, I want you to know I have been sick with regret the past few days. On the way up here, I realized how much I insulted you. Without even thinking about it, without even stopping to question, I lumped you in with the kind of men who can't handle having a wife who makes more money than them. So I set about sabotaging my own success."

"Yeah, you did."

"I'm so sorry. In hindsight, I can see that that was an insult to both your self-confidence as a man and your camp. The latter because we don't know how well it will do." That thought gave her a hope she hadn't even considered. "For all we know, it could become hugely successful, and you'll make lots of money."

"Maddy." He fixed her with a look before she could carry that thought too far. "You're doing it again."

"I'm sorry." Her shoulders sagged. "This is very uncomfortable territory for me."

"Can I ask you something? Because I really need to know. Will you think less of me as a man if I make less money than you?"

"No! Good God, no."

"Then . . . why do you think I will?"

"I don't up here." She tapped her forehead, then placed her hand over her stomach. "But in here, that's how I was raised. That's hard to fight. You don't erase the teachings of a lifetime just by realizing that those teachings are faulty. I didn't even realize how much of that had sunk in or how deeply. So I can't promise some of this won't pop up again in the future. I can only promise to work on it. If you'll let me. Please, Joe, I'm sorry I insulted you, and I don't want to lose you."

"Oh, Maddy." He cupped her face. "Now, see, that look right there, that fear in your eyes, is why I need to apologize to you. I broke one of the biggest rules of loving someone. I didn't tell you."

She bit her lip, wondering if he was telling her now.

"I was so wrapped up with my conviction that actions mean more than words that I forgot the words are still important. And powerful. I had people say they cared for me on a whim. Say they'd be there for me, then vanish. Say they loved me when they didn't."

"I did—"

"Shh." His thumb moved over her lips. "I'm not accusing you of anything. I think maybe you did love me back then, but you weren't ready for it yet. That's not what I'm talking about, though. I'm talking about the words themselves. Do you know what a kick in the chest it was the very first time I actually believed Mama when she said 'I love you'? What a punch in the gut it was every single time the Colonel said it, and I believed it. God, there is nothing—*nothing*—in this world that beats that."

Maddy saw his eyes fill with tears, and her throat closed.

His hands tightened as he held her face, staring deep into her eyes. "I didn't give you that. And I'm sorry. To the very depth of me, I'm sorry."

"It's okay."

"No. It's not. If I learned nothing else from my warped childhood, it's the importance of security and assurance. I know what it's like to think if you take one wrong step you'll be sent packing.

"And I know how the opposite feels. To know you are loved absolutely, and nothing you do, no matter how brainless, will change that.

"Maddy, I love you absolutely. I have from the moment I first saw you, and I will with the last breath I take. Nothing you do will change that. I love your magic. I love your fire. I love you because you're a part of me and I'm a part of you. I want to spend my life watching you shine.

"I can't make you stay, though. Even if you love me back, that doesn't mean we're meant to be. But if you leave, I will still love you, always. I just want whatever is right for you. Although, I won't lie, I want you to stay. Really, really, want you to stay."

He pulled her to him and buried his face against her hair. "And I want you to love me back."

"You silly man." She hugged him so tight, her arms trembled. Her whole body trembled. "Of course I love you back. As for staying . . ." She pulled back to see his face. "I have one question."

"If it's about whether or not I can handle you becoming rich and famous" he managed a wobbly smile—"I promise you the answer is yes."

"No. It's something you asked me once. A really scary question that I don't think anyone should have to get up the courage to ask twice. So this time it's my turn." She took a deep breath. "Will you marry me?"

Rather than answer right away, he frowned. "That depends."

"What?" Her heart nearly stopped.

"Do I get a ring?"

"A ring?" Her mind raced. Was he serious? "I didn't even think about that."

He sighed loudly. "Which is why some things are still best left up to the man." Reaching into his pocket, he pulled out a small black box and opened it. Light flashed off a square-cut diamond framed by Native American stonework.

"Oh! My! That's a— That's a—"

"I was planning to pop the question again, but I guess this is my turn to give the answer—which, I must say, is a lot easier."

"D-diamond," she finally got out.

"Hmm? Oh, yes, it is." He looked down at it.

"A really big diamond!"

"It's not perfect."

"What?"

"The diamond. It has a couple of flaws." He

looked up at her, his expression slightly sheepish. "I just thought you should know. I'm not even sure it will fit."

Her heart melted. "Perhaps I should try it on."

He pulled it out of the box and slipped it on her finger. "Well?"

"It's a perfect fit." She flung her arms around his neck. "I take it this means your answer is yes?"

"Ho-yeah!"

"Even better."

He held her tight. "I love you."

Which were, she decided, the most perfect words in the world.

Epilogue

Maddy put the finishing touches on a new pastel, then grabbed a big sweater and stepped out onto the balcony for a breath of fresh air. Winter was in full swing, with snow covering the mountains. She wrapped her arms about herself to hold in the warmth and a glowing contentment.

On the hill near the front gate, she could see that the construction workers had made a lot of progress in putting up the framework for the new house. She and Joe had decided to build a two-story addition onto the owner's house. It would be twice as big as the original house and completely self-contained, but having it attached would allow them to be nearby for Mama in the coming years.

The sound of male voices ringing out like drill sergeants drew her attention to the center of camp, where Joe and Derrick were leading afternoon calisthenics. She still had trouble believing how many people would pay to be put through what looked to her like physical torture, but the list seemed endless. And Joe was like a big kid, having the time of his life.

A smile tugged at Maddy's lips as she remembered their discussion over breakfast. For the past several weeks, he'd been prodding her to set a date for the wedding. But with Sylvia running her ragged getting ready for the spring catalog, Maddy told him her mind couldn't handle making one more decision right now, much less the millions of decisions involved in planning a wedding.

Joe had looked right at her and announced she was fired as their wedding planner and he was taking over. Her jaw had dropped at the idea, but he'd reasoned that if a woman could propose, a man could plan the wedding. How he had the time with the boot camp taking off at surprising speed, she had no idea, but he assured her that he'd take care of everything.

"All right," she'd conceded with no small dose of amusement. "Just be sure and clear the date with Christine and Amy so they can be my bridesmaids."

"Not a problem," he'd insisted.

And with that, she'd gladly turned the whole thing over to him. Although she couldn't wait to share the news with her friends and see what they thought. If nothing else, a man's version of a wedding was bound to be interesting.

Thinking of Christine and Amy, she headed back inside to check her e-mail. The last few days had certainly held lots of developments for Christine. Maddy opened her laptop and found a new post from Christine who was currently in Colorado. Her eyes bulged as she read the latest installment in Christine's wild romance, then her fingers flew as she typed her response.

Subject: *What?*

Message: *Details, woman. We want details!*

Julie Ortolon's
recipe for
The Perfect Margarita

After years of drinking oversized, restaurant-style margaritas—which are frequently made with too much limeade from a sweet-'n-sour bar mix with a splash of tequila and triple sec—I set about developing The Perfect Margarita. First came some research. A little mystery and controversy surrounds the true origins of the drink. The stories date back to the mid nineteen hundreds to places like Acapulco, Tijuana, or Rosarita Beach, Mexico. Whichever tale you believe, an authentic margarita is a small drink that's strong enough to make breathing near an open flame a tiny bit dangerous. So I tinkered with the recipes a bit and came up with my own version, which can be adjusted to taste.

- 2 ounces of good tequila (most recipes call for 3 ounces)
- 1 ounce Cointreau (triple sec is a less expensive option)
- 1½ ounces of freshly squeezed lime juice (most recipes call for less)
- 1½ ounces of Rosie's sweetened lime juice (this ingredient isn't in any of the original recipes, but I find guests grimace a bit if I don't include it.)

Shake the above with ice.

For a Traditional Margarita: Swipe the rim of a margarita glass with a lime wedge and press the glass upside down into margarita salt. Fill it with crushed ice, and strain the drink into the glass. Garnish with a lime wedge. Then kick back and sip slowly.

For a Summer Drink to Quench Your Thirst: If the recipe is too tart or strong for your taste, add a splash of orange juice and just a hint of grenadine. Cointreau is an orange liqueur so this fits right in. Garnish with a slice of orange and a maraschino cherry.

For a Mexican Martini: This is my personal favorite. Double the recipe above. Be sure you have lots of ice in the shaker and leave the drink in the shaker with the ice. Salt the rims of two martini glasses. Spear some jalapeno-stuffed olives wih two toothpicks. Place the spears in the glasses and serve the drink a little at a time while you sit back, relax, and enjoy!

Fear is a funny thing: without it, no one is truly brave.
— *How to Have a Perfect Life*

Christine couldn't believe she'd let her friends talk her into this. Standing in the plaza at the base of Silver Mountain, she felt her heart palpitate just looking at the chairlift. It carried a steady stream of skiers up the mountain, all of them sitting calmly in the chairs—which were nothing more than narrow benches dangling a mile off the ground—chatting away as if gravity didn't even exist. As if the thought of slipping off that narrow seat and plummeting to the ground never entered any of their minds.

Growing up, she'd had a hard enough time riding the chairlift during her family's annual Christmas vacations to Colorado, but after doing her residency in a hospital emergency room, she had an all-too-vivid image in her head of exactly what the result of such a fall would look like.

How had she let Maddy and Amy talk her into this? Of course, sitting in a bookstore coffee shop with her friends last spring, the thought of facing her fear of heights hadn't seemed like that big a deal. Well, it had. Just not this big a deal.

She couldn't back down, though. The three of them had made a pact. Maddy had already fulfilled her challenge to face her fear of rejection and get her art in a gallery, but Amy had yet to face her fear of getting lost in order to travel on her own. If Christine backed down, Amy would be off the hook.

She had to do this.

For Amy, if not for herself.

And the best approach now was to get it over with as quickly as possible—like ripping off an adhesive strip.

The one problem being her ski instructor was nowhere in sight. They'd told her at the ski school to look for a tall blond guy wearing a green jacket who'd meet her at the trail map. Granted, she'd arrived a few minutes late, but not that late.

Please, Lord, let him be late too, not already come and gone.

Rubbing her gloved hands against the cold, she turned away from the slopes to scan the crowded plaza. People moved in and out of the shops and restaurants that had been festively decorated for the holiday. Miles of garland abounded, along with big red bows and colorful banners hanging from lampposts. Last night's snowfall dusted the roofs and windowsills of the tall lodge-style buildings.

But nowhere did she see a blond man in a green parka.

Growing desperate, she abandoned her post by the trail map and headed for the lift ticket window, walking awkwardly in her ski boots. Maybe someone there could help her.

"Excuse me," she said to the college-age girl behind one of the windows. "I'm looking for Alec Hunter. I don't know if you know him—"

"Crazy Alec?" The girl's face lit with a smile. "Of course, I do."

Crazy Alec? Christine frowned as the girl craned her neck to search the plaza. What did she mean *Crazy* Alec? No, no, no, she didn't want Crazy Alec. She wanted Very-Sane-Safety-Conscious Alec. The man at the ski school had said they were too shorthanded to spare one of their regular instructors for five days of private lessons, so he'd arranged for "a friend" to teach her. He hadn't mentioned anything about his friend being crazy. In fact, he'd made it sound like a great privilege that Alec Hunter had even agreed to work with her.

"There he is." The girl pointed. "That's him over there."

Christine turned but didn't see anyone who fit the description they'd given her. "I don't see him."

"Over there." The girl pointed again. "Talking to Lacy at the pub."

Christine looked again and finally spotted him. All this time, she'd been searching for a dark green parka, not an eye-popping fluorescent green. He stood at the edge of an outdoor eating area in front of St. Bernard's Pub, talking to a very pretty brunette holding a serving tray. The woman shook her head and laughed at something he said.

"Thanks," Christine told the ticket booth worker

and headed across the plaza to meet her instructor, her stomach somersaulting the whole way. Maybe she should cancel today's lesson and get a different instructor. But, no, she was here. He was here. And she wanted very much to get past the first trip up the mountain. Surely after that, it would get easier. *Please, God, let it get easier.*

Her instructor stood in profile, tall and lanky with short golden hair that had been streaked lighter by the sun.

The waitress started to move away, but he grabbed her hand and placed his free hand over his heart. She shook her head even while smiling into his eyes. He dropped to one knee, holding her hand in both of his now, pleading in earnest.

"Oh, all right!" The waitress relented as Christine drew close enough to hear. "But this is the last time."

"You're all heart, Lacy," he insisted. "And I'll pay you back tomorrow. I swear."

"You'll take a week to remember and you know it." The waitress laughed as she moved away.

"Alec Hunter?" Christine tipped her head to see his face.

Still down on one knee, he shifted toward her, revealing a boyishly handsome face with the bluest eyes she'd ever seen—brighter-than-the-sky blue—accented by long lashes a few shades darker than his hair. He didn't look crazy. He looked like a choirboy. A very mischievous choirboy, she amended as his eyes twinkled up at her. "That would be me."

"Oh, good." She hoped. "I'm Christine Ashton."

"Hey, you made it." A grin flashed across his face as he stood, showing off sparkling white, perfectly straight teeth. Goodness, this guy could make a killing doing toothpaste commercials. "I was about to give up on you."

"Sorry." She blinked at his height. Being five ten, she was eye level with most men, but he topped her by several inches. "I had an emergency phone call."

"Ah." His inflection dismissed the word "emergency" completely.

Not that it was any of his business, but the call had been a question about a repeat patient from the hospital back in Austin where she'd recently finished her residency. She couldn't very well tell them to please ask Mrs. Henderson to postpone any more myocardial infarctions until after her ski lesson.

Pushing the wry thought aside, she studied the man before her, judging him to be younger than her own age of thirty-three. Cute, but young. "I hope it won't offend you if I ask, but you are a qualified instructor, right?"

He flashed another killer grin. "If you're looking for someone to teach you how to ski, really ski, I'm your man."

Since that was indeed what she wanted, she refrained from questioning him further.

"Okay, Alec," Lacy returned. "Here you go."

Alec took the large to-go bag Lacy handed over. When the weight of it hit his hands, he knew he'd caught her in a generous mood. Good thing, since he was down to one power bar in his pocket and had forgotten his wallet. Again. "Thanks, darling. I owe you."

"Yes, you do. The receipt's inside. I expect a serious tip."

"Have I ever stiffed you?" He tried out a wounded puppy look, which she ignored with a snort and flounced off. Unfazed, he turned to the woman Bruce had begged him to instruct. "You ready?"

An odd look of apprehension passed over her face as she glanced toward the chairlift. Then she straightened her shoulders. "As I'll ever be."

"Great. Where are your skis?"

"I left them in a rack near the lift."

"Me, too." He headed across the plaza with her falling in step beside him, their boots clunking on the paving stones.

When they reached the racks to retrieve their gear, he couldn't help but raise a brow. Whoever this Christine Ashton was, she had money, no doubt about that. If the ice blue and white skiwear with the distinctive Spyder logo splashed everywhere hadn't tipped him off, her gear would have. Everything from her safety helmet to her skis were all brand-spanking-new and probably cost more than three months' rent on his apartment. Bruce had sworn up and down she was an intermediate skier looking to improve her skill, but her gear gave him doubts. Seasoned skiers rarely had all new equipment at once.

Darn it, he thought as he clicked into his well-used Salomen Hots. He'd actually been looking forward to this, once he'd resigned himself to playing ski instructor. The way he'd finally figured it, a week of private lessons with a decent student meant he'd get in some non-work-related ski time while burning up some of those vacation and sick days the county manager was hounding him to take. Cool deal—if it was true.

If not, his buddy Bruce was going to owe him big time for this.

His doubts grew as he watched her struggle with the bindings on her skis. There should be a law against people buying top-notch equipment they didn't know how to use just because they could afford it.

Although, even if she turned out to be a total novice, at least she offered some serious compensation in the eye candy department. His brows rose when she bent to adjust her boots and her pants tightened about her long, slender thighs. Legs always had been his weakness. The rest of her wasn't bad either—even if she had a little too much of that ice princess polish for his taste—but, man, those legs promised to have his libido whimpering before the day was over. He felt the first pitiful whine coming on as she bent even further forward. Her straight fall of white-blond hair slid over one shoulder in a slow, sexy glide. "You, um, need help with that?"

"No, I got it," she insisted, and finally managed to fasten the bindings.

"Great." He cleared his throat. "Let's get in line."

She skied to the lift line with enough ease to reassure him that she had at least been on skis before. The line was fairly long, so he opened the bag to see what Lacy had packed: ham and cheese sandwich, sour cream and onion potato chips, a can of cola to feed his sugar and caffeine addiction, and . . . he tilted the bag to see all the way to the bottom. Yes! A giant chocolate chunk cookie. "I *love* that woman."

"I take it that was your girlfriend."

"Who, Lacy?" He scowled at the idea. "Heck no. She's engaged to one of the guys. Here, hold these, will ya?" He handed his poles to her, then pulled out the sandwich and went to work appeasing his overactive metabolism. He'd long since given up hope that it would slow down someday. Small wonder, though, with his daily exertion level.

By the time they'd reached the lift house, he'd inhaled the entire sack lunch. He pocketed the receipt as a reminder to pay Lacy back, and shot the bag and empty soda can into the trash.

"Thanks," he said as he took the poles back, which was when he noticed his student was breathing a little too fast and had gone from pampered-princess pale to about-to-faint pale. "Hey, you didn't just arrive today, did you?"

"No, yesterday." She breathed in and out. "Why do you ask?"

"You look like you're having a little trouble with the altitude."

"I'm fine."

"You know, one of the dumbest mistakes people make every year is to step off a plane, hop on a ski lift, and faint at the top of a mountain. If we need to postpone your first lesson—"

"I told you, I'm fine." A hint of snootiness chilled her words. "I know how to handle the altitude."

Yeah, famous last words of low-landers everywhere.